PENGUIN BOOKS
Do Not Become Alarmed

Maile Meloy is the author of the novels *Liars and Saints* (which was shortlisted for the Orange Prize and chosen for the Richard and Judy book club) and *A Family Daughter*; the short-story collections *Half in Love* and *Both Ways Is the Only Way I Want It*; and the award-winning Apothecary trilogy for young readers. She has received the PEN/Malamud Award and a Guggenheim Fellowship, and was chosen as one of *Granta*'s Best Young American Novelists. She lives in Los Angeles.

DO NOT BECOME ALARMED

MAILE MELOY

PENGUIN BOOKS

PENGUIN BOOKS

UK | USA | Canada | Ireland | Australia
India | New Zealand | South Africa

Penguin Books is part of the Penguin Random House group of companies
whose addresses can be found at global.penguinrandomhouse.com.

First published in the United States of America by Riverhead Books 2017
First published in Great Britain by Penguin Books 2017

002

Printed in Great Britain by Clays Ltd, St Ives plc

A CIP catalogue record for this book is available from the British Library

ISBN: 978–0–241–30546–1

www.greenpenguin.co.uk

For my parents

Americans learn only from catastrophe and not from experience.

—THEODORE ROOSEVELT

It is a fact that it takes experience before one can realize what is a catastrophe and what is not.

—RICHARD HUGHES, *A High Wind in Jamaica*

1.

THE CRUISE SHIP towered over the dock in San Pedro like an enormous white layer cake, or a floating apartment building. The one thing it didn't look like was an oceangoing vessel. Liv and her family surrendered their bags to porters and carried their backpacks into the terminal building. Her husband, Benjamin, was fascinated by the quay, built to get thousands of people onto fifteen-deck ships.

As they checked in, Liv filled out a form attesting that neither she nor her children had been sick in the last two weeks. It was a lie. Sebastian and Penny were eight and eleven, and it was December— they were walking germ vectors.

"You're saying no illnesses, right?" her cousin Nora murmured beside her. Nora's son, Marcus, was eleven like Penny, and they'd both had the same cold. Nora's six-year-old, June, had a cough.

"Yes," Liv whispered back.

They turned in the forms. Surely everyone lied and no one was fooled. An agent with bright green glasses took their passports for safekeeping, in exchange for plastic IDs to serve as cabin keys and charge cards.

Penny gazed at her own ID. "So I can buy things with this?"

"If your mom authorizes it," the agent said.

"Authorize it!" Penny said, brandishing the card at Liv.

"What are you going to buy?" Liv asked.

"Things!"

Two pert young Australian women in white uniforms made them stop for a photograph in front of a life ring. Benjamin put his arm around Liv, with Penny and Sebastian in front of them. These were never satisfying pictures, the family photos. Liv was the same height as Benjamin and she felt herself slouch, even though it was ridiculous to care. The day was unseasonably warm, and she ran a hand up the damp back of her neck, feeling hot and flushed. She kept her hair cropped short so she could swim before work without losing time, but she was reminded by photos that her usually no-nonsense mother thought she should grow it out. Sebastian, blond like Liv, always looked a little wild-eyed in photos, the flash catching him by surprise. Penny had taken to striking poses, as if the world were her own red carpet.

They moved away and Raymond and Nora took their place in front of the life ring with Marcus and June. Liv watched. They were so handsome, Raymond with dark, smooth skin, Nora pale and brunette with a glossy ponytail, the kids tawny-limbed. They looked like an ad featuring a happy biracial family, one that would get horrible troll reactions online. Marcus was tall for eleven and had the beginnings of an Afro, and Junie wore tiny braids. Raymond had cut his hair close for a movie role as a cop.

"Is this the 'before' picture?" he asked, after the camera flashed.

"Something like that," one of the Australians said, smiling. "But you look like the 'after' picture."

Liv couldn't tell if they had recognized Raymond. She thought not. "He always looks like the 'after' picture," she said.

"I bet," the girl said.

"Oh my God," Nora said, as they moved on. "We're not even on *board* and they're flirting with him."

They made their way among milling passengers, across a central court with a patterned marble floor. A giant Christmas tree rose up through three decks.

"*Wow,*" Sebastian breathed.

"It's like *The Nutcracker*," Penny said. "But *real*."

They went up in a glass elevator, past the top of the tree, then down a blue-carpeted corridor. Liv and Nora had booked cabins next to each other, and Liv opened hers with the key card. There was a bottle of champagne and a bowl of fruit inside. The cabinets were pale wood, the bedcovers nautical navy and white. A couch in a little sitting area would pull out for the kids, so the cabin counted as a "suite." Mirrors made it all look bigger than it was, and the California sun glared bright through the balcony doors. Penny and Sebastian ran outside to look down.

"No going on the balcony unless an adult is here," Liv said. "Deal?"

"Deal," they sang in chorus. They ran back in to investigate the clever cupboards and the drawers that latched shut. Marcus and June arrived to compare notes.

"This is exactly backward from ours," Marcus pronounced.

"That's so *weird*," June said, flopping back on the bed, braids bouncing. "I feel like I'm in mirror land!"

A voice came over the loudspeaker, right into the cabin, announcing the lifeboat drill.

"What's *that*?" June asked.

Their stewardess put her head in the open door. Her name was Perla and she was tiny, her black hair parted in the middle. She showed them where to find the blocky orange foam life preservers in the closet, and pointed out their muster station on the ship's plan.

"Do we have to get *in* the lifeboats?" Sebastian asked.

"No," Perla said, laughing. "They only show you."

The two families headed down the carpeted stairs, past crew members on the landings. In the muster station in the Yacht Club bar, a graceful young man with a microphone—a dancer?—explained the emergency procedure. All the other passengers seemed to be eighty. There were no other children. Penny and Sebastian feigned agonized drowning, and Junie skipped across the carpet. The old people smiled warily at them. Marcus sat beside his parents.

"I'm hungry," Penny said. "This is taking too long."

Liv smoothed Penny's chestnut hair. Her child of appetite and opinion.

"I shouldn't be thinking about *Titanic*, right?" Raymond said, clicking the buckle over his chest.

"Yes, you should," Nora told him. "Think about how not to die if we sink."

Benjamin said, "You know the orange life jackets and the lights are just for finding bodies."

"I think that's on airplanes," Liv said.

"It's unlikely that we'll sink," Marcus said.

"I know, babe," Nora told her son. "We're joking."

The emergency signal sounded, and Marcus clapped his hands over his ears, digging his fingers into his curls.

"Sorry!" Nora said, pressing her hands over his. "It'll be over soon." Seven short blasts of the horn and one long one. Then they were released.

Liv checked the glucose monitor on Sebastian's waistband. "Let's go to the buffet."

"It's open?" Nora asked.

"It's *always* open, I think."

"I'll go unpack," Benjamin said, which meant he wanted a nap. Raymond wanted to check out the gym. The men carried everyone's life jackets away.

On the walk to the buffet, Nora linked her arm through Liv's and put her head on her shoulder, making Liv feel excessively tall. "I love you," Nora said. "This was a genius idea."

The children took trays and each got exactly what they wanted: Chinese noodles for Penny, chicken fingers for Sebastian, nori rolls for Marcus, taquitos for June. Watching them eat, Liv felt her mind relax, easing its calculation. Feeding children, even when you had all available resources, took so much planning and forethought. The low-grade anxiety about the next meal started when you were cleaning up the last. But for two weeks there would never be any question about what was for dinner, or lunch, or snack. That roving hunter-gatherer part of her brain, which sucked a lot of power and made the other lights dim—she could just turn it off.

The trip had been Liv's idea. Nora's mother died of pancreatic cancer in early summer: swift and painful. After the death, Nora had been flattened by waves of sadness, sobbing jags where she couldn't breathe or speak. Her mother had been problematic, borderline, sometimes absent. When they were eight, she'd sent Nora to live with Liv's family, because her new husband didn't want children around. The cousins had shared a bedroom for two years, until the new marriage failed and the prodigal mother came back. Nora had always been wry about her mother's flakiness, and trenchant about motherhood in general. No one had predicted that the loss would hit her so hard.

Nora had called Liv in October in despair about Christmas plans. She didn't want to go to Philadelphia to stay with Raymond's parents when she felt like such a mess. She didn't want to be with Liv's parents, the adoptive family of her abandoned childhood. And she didn't want to be home in LA, where the clear blue skies and the empty freeways would make her feel even more isolated and exposed. She wanted to be with family but *not* with family. She wanted to have Christmas but not have it *feel* like Christmas.

Liv was pragmatic, a problem-solver. She got it from her mother, a flinty Colorado litigator. She believed in finding a third way, when the options seemed intolerable, and she believed in throwing money at problems, when it was possible. She found a two-week cruise down the coast of Mexico and Central America, poking into the Panama Canal long enough to watch the locks work—bait for her engineer husband—and then heading north to LA again. It would be just the two families, Liv and Nora and their husbands and kids. They wouldn't have to fly, they could board in San Pedro. Raymond was between movies, and Liv's office was deserted over Christmas. Benjamin could make his own schedule as long as he kept pace on his projects. They could all take Nora away.

"You always said cruises were tacky," Benjamin said when Liv suggested it.

"They are," she said.

"And an environmental nightmare."

"That's why it's such a good idea," she said. "My parents won't want to go because of fossil fuels and norovirus. Your parents want to go to Cuba. So no hurt feelings. It will be just us, and it will be different. It's just what Nora wants."

"And the fossil fuels?"

She felt a little shudder of guilt. "The ship is going anyway?"

Benjamin said yes, and Liv called Nora, who started to cry again, and then they went online to look at cabins.

The kids would have each other to play with, their second cousins. When Nora had been crying on Liv's couch over the summer, she was also worrying about Marcus. At five he'd known every country and every capital in the world. (Penny, at the same age, had known Colorado, Disneyland, and Santa Monica, where her modern dance class was.) Certain things, like the emergency horn, were intolerable to Marcus, but he didn't meet all the parameters for a diagnosis. Nora had been looking for a school that would understand her son's strengths and his difficulties. Raymond wanted one where there might be other black kids. Liv had talked them into trying Penny and Sebastian's school. It was small, progressive, and at least working on diversity. Their late application was accepted, and Marcus seemed happy there. His teacher created a special geography project for him, and let him read what he wanted.

So now Penny and Marcus were in sixth grade at the same school, and they would grow up together almost as their mothers had. For most of history, the two sets of children would have been betrothed to each other from birth, and Liv would have been happy with that. Sebastian and June adored each other like two puppies, even though June was younger. Sebastian, sweet-tempered and pliable, could grow up and be drawn in by some damaged girl who would blame him for her pain. Liv would have loved to promise him to funny, curious June, and seal it now.

At the buffet table, Nora studied the ship's schedule. There was an evening movie in the Kids' Club, one of the *Madagascar* sequels. The ship started to move, and the children ran out on deck and leaned on the varnished honey-colored rail. The bow thrusters churned the blue water white against the dock. Liv hoped Benjamin was watching from the balcony. It was majestic, the stately movement out of San Pedro, the lacy trail of wake behind them, the tiny boats below.

When they were out to sea and had explored the ship—skirting the clanging casino and gaping at the terrible paintings for sale, of martinis and cars—the kids settled in to watch the movie. The chaperones seemed reasonably sane. A New Zealander named Deb promised to sit near Sebastian in case his monitor went off, and Liv and Nora went to change for a grown-up dinner.

When she got back to the cabin, Benjamin was stretched out on top of the bedcovers, waking up from his nap. "Wait, so we can just shunt them off to the Kids' Club?" he asked.

"Good, right?"

"And they're fine with it?"

"They're watching animated animals. They don't love us that much."

"Oh my God," Benjamin said, rubbing his hands in his hair. "This is amazing."

"Did you see the bow thrusters as we left?"

"Not if they weren't on the backs of my eyelids."

Liv showered and put on a cotton dress, and Benjamin took her place in the bathroom. The panoptic mirrors in the cabin left no secrets, and she wished she were thinner, and then wished she didn't wish that. Her hair was looking a little straw-like these days. She tucked the short strands behind her ears.

At dinner, Raymond ordered champagne from the Russian wine steward. "To Liv," he said, "for the best idea since Velcro kids' shoes."

Liv made a demurring noise but held her glass up anyway.

"*And* for generally running my life much better than I do," Nora said.

Liv smiled. "Not everyone will let me run theirs."

8

She had introduced Nora to Raymond. He'd played a marine lieutenant in the first movie Liv ever developed, and was nominated for an Image Award from the NAACP. Liv had invited Nora to the party and loaned her a dress. Nora wore her hair up in a dark sweep, and on her narrow shoulders the neckline of the dress hung fetchingly low. She had a heart-shaped, Quakerish face, and an adorable smallness that made Liv feel like a Norwegian giantess, especially in heels. As the three of them stood at a cocktail table eating passed appetizers, Raymond had turned to Nora with the full light of his dazzling actor handsomeness, and Liv had realized she was superfluous and gone off to get a drink.

The Russian wine steward brought them a bottle of rosé as soon as they finished the champagne. His name tag said YURI. "You were that astronaut in that movie," he said, pouring the first taste for Raymond.

"He was," Liv said. The astronaut movie had been hers, too.

"I knew it!" Yuri said. "I watch a lot of movies in my cabin."

"She made that film happen," Raymond said, indicating Liv, but the steward wasn't interested in development, only in stardom.

Caviar and toast arrived, with sour cream and egg and chopped onion in little silver dishes.

"A token of my admiration," Yuri said with a little bow. "Caviar from my country."

Liv took a bite, the salty beads bursting on her tongue. There was soup, and fish, and lemon tart. She got slightly, pleasantly drunk, as she and Benjamin never did at a restaurant in LA, where they'd have to drive home.

They collected the children at the Kids' Club and made their way back to their cabins, the surge of the ship making the carpeted corridor into an uphill walk, then a slightly downhill run. The kids raced down, laughing, then did an exaggerated mountaineering trudge when the corridor ran uphill again. There were congratulatory kisses all around as they said goodnight at the cabin doors, and there was a towel twisted into the shape of a swan on the foot of the bed.

In the morning, Benjamin took Penny and Sebastian off to the Kids' Club, leaving Liv to luxuriate in the empty cabin, in the wide, soft bed between the pressed, clean sheets. Ironed sheets always reminded her of her grandmother, looping the fabric at the ironing board to keep it off the floor. Pressed sheets seemed like the ultimate in both domestic comfort and domestic drudgery.

At lunch they met an Argentinian family, very glamorous, the father silver-haired, the mother with discreet and expensive-looking work done on her face. She'd left the forehead alone. They had two striking adolescent children, a boy and a girl, and they were all going ashore in Acapulco the next morning. After some private discussion, Liv and Nora decided not to join them. Why go ashore in a country of beheadings and food-borne pathogens? Everything they needed was here.

Marcus studied the chart on a wall near the bridge, where an officer updated the ship's position every hour. Nora stood with her son and talked through the itinerary, their turnaround in Panama and return back up the coast.

That night, the towel on the bed was shaped like an elephant. Liv and Benjamin got Penny and Sebastian into their pajamas, then crowded into Nora and Raymond's cabin for a bedtime book. Raymond read aloud from *Treasure Island*, doing all the pirate voices. The book was heavier going than Liv remembered, but it didn't matter with Raymond narrating. He was more than they deserved, as a bedtime reader. Most people's husbands just made you appreciate your own, but not Raymond. Marcus and June leaned against him in the big bed. Liv lay on the pullout beside Benjamin and fell asleep.

Sebastian had to prod her arm when it was time to go back to their own cabin.

The next morning, anchored in the blue sea off Acapulco, Liv went for a run on deck and came upon her husband with a notebook, sketching the davits that suspended the lifeboats. She loved Benjamin's capacity for total absorption in the structure of things, even though she sometimes felt she had to tug on his leg to get him back to earth.

Liv and Nora had an unserious game of paddle tennis after lunch, then sat in deck chairs reading novels and talking. Benjamin called it "estro-lock," the way the two women could talk for hours and lose track of time. They ended up in conversation across any table, screening out noise from kids and men. They could talk about shallow things without judgment and deep things without self-consciousness. They shared a childhood vocabulary, a set of references. Old ladies beamed at their handsome children in swimsuits—freckled Penny and towheaded Sebastian, tall Marcus with his long legs and tiny June in her many braids. Liv felt like a young mother in a Fitzgerald novel, glowing with life. If she'd had pearls she would have sunned them.

A few times during the day, Liv saw the ship's tenders ferrying people ashore and wondered if they should have gone. That was something she was trying to work on: not always second-guessing her decisions, wondering if she'd made the wrong one. But how could you know if you'd made the right decision, when you only saw one version play out?

The Argentinian family came aboard from their excursion, looking exhausted and hot. "We went snorkeling on a catamaran," the teenage daughter said. "I threw up four times."

So maybe that was all Liv needed—someone to check out the alternate path and report back.

At dinner, they debriefed on the day. Raymond said that the Brazilian trainer in the gym was trying to sell him one of the spa treatments.

Nora made a face. "She just wants to slather you in mud and roll you in cling wrap."

"Is that what the treatment is?" Liv asked. She hadn't been sure what the ads were selling. Pills? Colonics?

"I think they put electrodes on your—problem areas," Nora said.

"Wait," Benjamin said. "This woman thinks *Raymond* has problem areas?"

"Is it bad that I'm intrigued?" Raymond asked.

"Yes!" the rest of them said, all together.

After dinner, they gathered in the other cabin for Raymond to read aloud. The children stared wide-eyed in dread of the Black Spot, just as Liv had once.

"If I were in *Treasure Island*," Sebastian said, nestled under her arm, "there wouldn't be a book, because as soon as the first scary thing happened, I would just run home."

"*I* would go be a pirate," Junie whispered, into her father's shoulder.

"You would be a great pirate," Raymond told her. "And Sebastian could stay back and mind the fort. That's important, too."

Liv reminded herself to be grateful for Nora and Raymond, and never to take them for granted. They were her family, and they were also the family she had chosen, and she loved them and felt extraordinarily lucky. If hell was other people, you just had to find the people who weren't the inferno, and make space for them in your life.

CHRISTMAS DINNER WAS formal, and Benjamin pushed cuff links through the holes at his wrists. The kids were joining them in the dining room. As Benjamin knotted Sebastian's tie, the kid looked up at him with trusting eyes, and he felt an almost worrying pressure in his heart. But this wasn't a heart attack. It was that his son was so vulnerable, and such a miniature man, with his fine blond hair combed back, in his tiny jacket. Benjamin remembered his own father taking him to Brooks Brothers for his first blazer, the solemn instructions about buttons and shirt collars. And now Benjamin was the dad. It was so strange. He had some gray in his hair, more if he grew a beard. He considered it premature, but it wasn't: He was forty-one.

"Will Santa find us on the ship?" Sebastian asked.

"I think so. But the trip is the big present this year."

"I know," Sebastian said. "But he knows we're here?"

Benjamin looked for traces of disingenuousness in his son's eyes, but Sebastian seemed committed. And why not? What was the point of questioning Santa? Unless of course you were Penny, who had to look under every rock. At least she knew enough to keep her mouth shut around her little brother. They hadn't done Chanukah presents this year. Usually they tried to, but his parents, who cared the most, had gone to Cuba. And it was a lot to organize, amid the packing and getting out of town.

Penny wore a green velvet dress and had pestered Liv into curling her hair into ringlets. Marcus and June joined them, and the four kids ran down the corridor, June's silver skirt and her braids flying out behind her, Marcus tall in a blue blazer with a somber lope.

Almost no one else seemed to be in black tie, which made Benjamin self-conscious, but Raymond wore a white dinner jacket. The spectacular tree in the central court was lit up, and there was carol-singing led by the performers. They stayed for a couple of songs, and Benjamin heard Nora, beside him in a red silk dress, singing the unfamiliar second and third verses.

"Are you a Christmas elf?" he asked her.

"My mother really loved a carol service," she said, smiling. "Candleholders out of tinfoil, all that."

At dinner, the kids were excited by the grown-up dining room and the attention of the stewards. The table staff seemed to approve of their formal clothes, which made Benjamin feel less embarrassed. And they did look good, the kids with shining faces. Liv wore a low-backed blue dress that showed off her swimmer's shoulders, her short hair like a pale flame. Flat sandals for his sake, even though he'd told her he didn't care.

When the kids fell asleep that night, Benjamin and Liv arranged presents from Santa under the potted palm in their cabin: new swimsuits, small toys, a few books, green and gold flip-flops. In the morning, Penny and Sebastian ran next door to show their haul to their cousins, who had comparable loot, by previous agreement.

Hector, the Argentinian fifteen-year-old, had been given a guitar and he played a few American pop songs in a deck chair, singing softly, sending Penny into a swoon. She liked saying his name as the Argentinians did, "ECK-tor," rolling the *r* a little. She and Sebastian had a Guatemalan babysitter when they were younger, and a few weeks of Learn-in-Your-Car Spanish before the trip had uncovered a surprising facility, all these years later. She was a natural mimic.

Hector's sister, Isabel, had a new bottle of green nail polish, and she painted Penny's and June's toes. Then Sebastian wanted his done, too. The Argentinian girl was irresistible, with her long sun-streaked hair. She and her brother had a South American sophistication, jaded and worldly. Marcus hung back and watched as Isabel leaned over the small toes, wiping away extra polish where she'd messed up. Benjamin guessed that Marcus wanted her attention far too much to seek it. The teens didn't exactly court the adoration of the younger kids, but they seemed to enjoy it. There was no one their age on the ship.

Two unchanging sea days later, Benjamin lay on the made-up bed, enjoying the silence and reading the condensed *New York Times* on three sheets of printer paper. There was no cell service out here, and the expensive Wi-Fi was iffy. That was good for Liv—to be offline and away from the studio. Even when a movie got made, the path it took always sounded to him like a drug deal gone wrong. Lies, threats, incrimination, betrayal, last-minute bargaining, total lunacy. She needed a break. But Benjamin felt lost without his work. He turned on the cabin's TV, looking for news.

Flipping channels, he saw a young woman in a stewardess's uniform, with a black curtain behind her. She was olive-skinned, her hair pulled tightly back.

"It is very hard," she said. "The work is very hard. The hours are long, and you are all day on your feet. When I finish, I am tired. I go back to my cabin. It is very small, and I share it with another girl. It is okay."

An unseen interviewer asked her a question.

"My dream?" she asked. She looked startled and then thoughtful. "My dream is to find a job on land."

The next subject was a slim Indian man with salt-and-pepper hair. He sat in a booth beneath a big still life painting.

"I used to want to be Picasso," he said with a shy smile. "Or Matisse, you know? The *struggle*. When I was in art school, I wanted to be a great artist. And now—well." He looked at the painting of a bowl of fruit behind him. "I do the still life paintings that hang in the extra-tariff restaurants. But I make a living as an artist, which is not easy to do. I remind myself of that."

The door to the cabin opened and Liv walked in.

"Look at this," Benjamin said. "It's supposed to be a tour of the ship, and what everyone does, but they hate their jobs."

She sat at the end of the bed to watch. A pink New Zealander on the screen was talking with ambivalence about the Kids' Club.

"Why would they put this on the TV?" Liv asked.

"I don't know!" he said. "Couldn't they find *one* cheerful kid who wants to see the world? Or that Ukrainian girl who's just happy not to be in Crimea?"

Liv watched the screen, and Benjamin knew she was thinking about their stewardess, Perla, who had three kids in Manila. "Perla's on a nine-month contract," she said.

"I know."

"Imagine what she's missing, not seeing them grow up," Liv said. "Maybe the cruise line wants us to know that we should be hit by a bus, to even the score."

"*The* bus?" he said. "The bus that goes around hitting people?"

She looked over her shoulder at him and her face went from serious to laughing. He loved watching it change. He had made his own tribe with her, a tribe of two, and then of four. He had not known, in his unmoored youth, if it would happen.

"Yeah," she said. "The karmic bus."

He put on an interviewer's voice, and held the TV remote as a microphone. "We're talking to a passenger next," he said. "Tell me, madam, how does it feel to be the most desirable woman on the ship?"

"It's a low bar," she said. "Everyone else is eighty."

"So you admit that it's true."

"No," she said. "There's Nora."

He put down the remote. "Nora is a lovely person who doesn't do it for me."

"Also the dancers."

"There's a reason they don't have jobs on land."

"And the Argentinian girl."

"Let's reopen that discussion in ten years."

Liv laughed again. "Oh, I've seen the old dudes look at her."

"Hey, are Penny and Sebastian in the Kids' Club?"

"They are."

He turned off the TV. "How much time do you think we have?"

"An hour maybe? I'll need to check on Sebastian."

"Come up here."

"I have to shower."

"Don't."

She made a face, but she scooted up the bed. He lifted her shirt and kissed her stomach. Then she put her hand on top of his and said, "Did those interviews make you feel like your dreams are thwarted?"

"No," he said. "All my dreams have come true."

She crossed her legs. "Seriously?"

He sighed at the barrier of her thighs and lay back on the bed, and hoped they weren't going to have to talk about studio politics. "Yes."

"And that doesn't make you think we don't deserve our luck, that it'll all be taken away?"

"No."

She stared at the ceiling. "It does me."

"Do you think worrying helps?"

"Yes," she said. "Because the disaster will be the thing you don't expect. So you just have to expect *everything*."

He could feel the child-free time ticking away. "You know, at some point the kids will come back here."

"I know."

He reached for her. "So—can we table the disaster thoughts for now?"

3.

PENNY WAS ABOUT to win a game of Crazy Eights on the bright patterned carpet of the Kids' Club. Part of the game was luck, but Penny knew how to strategize. Her father had taught her to play the suit if she had more of it. If she didn't have more, she played the number. Marcus was better at geography and directions, but she was better at cards. She put down a two of diamonds.

Marcus drew a card and put down a seven.

Penny played the queen. "Last card."

Marcus drew and drew, and finally came up with an eight and laid it down, triumphant. "Clubs!"

Penny played the four of clubs and won. Marcus groaned.

"We can play again," Penny offered.

"No. You always win."

"Not always."

Marcus sat back and looked around. "Where's June?"

He was protective of his sister, who was only six. Penny's mother said Sebastian was sensitive and they had to be careful with him, too, but she didn't see it, really. Sebastian had almost died when he was little, and now he had an insulin pump in his back pocket with a line into a port in his skin. Her parents had to stick a new port in every couple of days, and it hurt. And he had to make his finger bleed all the time to check his blood. Penny thought it made him tougher than other kids, not more sensitive.

Marcus got up and checked the playhouse, which was empty. He asked Deb, the counselor from New Zealand, if she had seen his sister and Penny's brother. Deb said those two hadn't checked in after lunch.

"They were with us," Penny said.

"I don't think so," Deb said, and she got out her clipboard. "Look."

Penny saw check marks next to her name and Marcus's, but not next to Sebastian's and June's. "Can we be excused to go look for them?" she asked.

"I'd better call your parents."

"No!" Penny said. "I know where they are. It's okay."

Deb hesitated.

"We'll be right back, I promise."

Adults usually let Penny do what she wanted, because they thought she was responsible. They also expected more of her, but it was worth it.

Sebastian and June were not at the buffet. The lunch rush was over and only a few old people sat at the tables.

The elevators were slow, because old people in wheelchairs and on power scooters were always getting in and out. So they ran down the carpeted stairs to their own deck, dodging old people, and raced along the corridor. They didn't have their key cards, so they knocked at Marcus's door, out of breath, but no one answered. Then they knocked at Penny's door.

After a moment's pause, her father's muffled voice called, "Who is it?"

"It's me!"

There was another pause. Her mother opened the door a crack, in a bathrobe. Her hair was messier than usual. "Aren't you supposed to be at the Kids' Club?"

"Were you napping?"

"Yes," her mother said.

"Oh. Sorry."

"Is everything all right?" her mother asked.

"Is it just you and Dad in there?"

"Yes."

"Oh," Penny said. "Okay. We'll go back to the Kids' Club."

"Are you sure you're all right?"

"Yes."

"And the little ones?"

"Yes." It was probably true. As long as they didn't climb over the railings—which no one would anyway, because it made your stomach do crazy flips just to put your feet on the lowest rung—nothing was going to happen.

"Then we'll see you later," her mother said. "Go straight back to the Kids' Club." The door closed with a click.

"Why didn't you tell her?" Marcus whispered, as they headed back down the corridor.

"Because they're *napping*," Penny said. She knew there was something else going on, and she didn't. "Let's try the tennis court!"

They ran back up the staircase, to the very top of the ship. The court was smaller than for normal tennis, and had nets around it to keep the balls from flying into the sea. The racquets were flat and wooden, with little holes to let the air through. Penny and Marcus were both breathing hard by the time they got there.

The family from Argentina was playing doubles. The brother, Hector, was about to serve, his dark gold hair pushed back from his forehead. Penny watched his long, tan arm go up, and the swing of his racquet coming down. His sister whacked it back to him across the net. Their father's silver hair was damp with sweat. Their mother wore necklaces and bracelets with big colored stones in them. A jeweled family. Penny thought they looked like royalty. Hector and his mother won the point.

When the ball was dead, Penny asked, "Have you seen my little brother, and June?"

They hadn't. Hector walked over. "Did you try the basketball court?"

Penny felt a little dizzy, with his kind eyes looking down at her. Her stomach did one of those flips. "No."

They tried the basketball court, where the Filipino crewmen played at night. No one was there.

They checked all three swimming pools, even the one where kids weren't allowed. Penny experienced a thrill of fear, not entirely unpleasant, at the idea of seeing Sebastian's blond hair at the bottom of a pool, beneath the rippling water, like pale seaweed. She would have to dive in and swim to the bottom, through the blue silence. Then she would pull him up into the sunlight above. She was a good swimmer, with a strong kick. She longed to rescue someone. Would there be hope for Sebastian, underwater so long? She shivered, delighted and horrified. He would lie motionless on the deck, and then he would cough and start to breathe.

But Sebastian and June weren't in the pools or the hot tubs.

The Russian steward, Yuri, was working in the humid glassed-in spa café. "Ah, the little astronaut," he said to Marcus, and he patted his hair.

Marcus flinched. "We're looking for my sister," he said. "And Penny's brother."

Yuri frowned. "When did you see them?"

"At lunch," Penny said. "They didn't check back into the Kids' Club."

"I call security," Yuri said.

"No!" Penny said. "They'll tell our parents!"

Yuri raised his bushy black eyebrows. "Yes, of course."

A security officer in a white uniform and a white belt answered the call. He led Penny and Marcus to a huge cabin at the end of their own corridor. It was enormous, with a shiny black grand piano, and a bar with a green glass top. This must be where the rich people stayed. Sebastian and June were outside on the big balcony, on the other side of the sliding glass door. A kneeling man in coveralls was doing something with a screwdriver to the door's lower track.

Sebastian and June pounded on the glass with their flat palms.

"Tell them to stop that," the security officer said.

"Shh!" Penny said, making gestures and waving. "It's okay!"

The little ones calmed down and returned to watching the man work, through the glass.

The security officer said the children must have wandered into the suite, which had the door open. But the workman coming to fix the slider had been delayed, and the children had gone out through the balcony door. It had slid shut behind them and stuck.

"We're not supposed to be alone on our balcony," Penny reported. "My mother doesn't think it's safe."

"That's true," the security officer said. "She could keep better track of her children."

"It's not her fault," Penny said, feeling loyal. "They were supposed to be at the Kids' Club."

The man in coveralls got the sliding door open, and Sebastian and June tumbled into the cabin, talking over each other. They'd gone in to see the piano and then they wanted to see if there were dolphins, because someone said there were dolphins, and the door got stuck, and they had shouted and shouted for so long before anyone came. And now they were hungry. Could they go to the buffet?

"*First*, we go to see your parents," the security officer said.

"They're taking a nap," Penny said.

The officer raised his eyebrows. "Time to wake up."

So they all trooped off to the cabin. The officer rapped loudly on the door, and Penny's mother answered—dressed, to Penny's relief. Her hair was only a normal amount of messy. Sebastian charged into her arms. Nora and Raymond arrived next, in gym clothes. There were apologies, and a few belated tears.

"How did you get out of the Kids' Club?" her mother asked.

"We said we were looking for Sebastian and June," Penny said.

"But how did you not notice they weren't there?"

"We *did*!" Penny said. "And we went looking for them!"

Penny's dad said that if they only had a grand piano in *their* suite, none of this would have happened. The security officer laughed and everything was all right.

Her mother lifted Sebastian's shirt to check his glucose monitor. "Okay, guys," she said, "let's go get a snack."

4.

NOEMI WAS TEN, but she was small for her age. She lived with her grandmother in a house with a corrugated steel roof and three rooms: kitchen, living room, and the bedroom they shared. An outhouse across the backyard. She hadn't seen her parents in two years. They lived in Nueva York.

Her grandmother was old, and she was tired of taking care of Noemi. She said it was too hard. Noemi's parents sent money, but by the end of the month there was no food. Sometimes the neighbors helped, but sometimes they had no food, either. Her grandmother couldn't read, so she couldn't help Noemi with her schoolwork. Noemi tried to teach her to read, but her grandmother said it was too late. It was better that Noemi go to her parents. There she would go to an American school, and learn. Her parents could help, and feed her better. Noemi said her parents might stop sending money, if she went, but her grandmother said that didn't matter.

Still, her grandmother might have kept her, and life might have gone on as it was, except that a twelve-year-old girl on their street was having a baby. Noemi thought it was exciting news, but her grandmother did not. She made a potion on the kitchen stove, and made Noemi drink it to protect her from harm. It was bitter and dark. Noemi wanted to spit the liquid out, but she obeyed her grandmother and swallowed, and felt ill.

Then Ario, who lived next door and was only nine, was shot to death in their street. People said it was a warning to his father, or his uncle, or both. Noemi had seen him lying on the ground afterward, the blood dark and pooling around his head, and she sometimes saw him in her mind before she went to sleep. She and her friend Rosa walked around that part of the street when they came home from school.

Christmas was coming, and Noemi hoped for a dollhouse like the one Rosa's uncle had made for her. Her grandmother said nothing, but on Christmas Eve there were no presents. Her grandmother said Noemi had to go to her parents.

"That costs money," Noemi said. "Why can't we use the money so I can stay here?"

Her grandmother just shook her head.

A man came to the house, one Noemi had never seen before. He said his name was Chuy, but her grandmother called him Jesùs. He wore jeans and a shirt with buttons, the cuffs done up at the wrist, and a black leather jacket. He seemed older than her father, but it was hard to remember her father clearly now. She looked to her grandmother, who was stone-faced and determined.

So Noemi packed a small pink backpack with the things her grandmother told her to take: a change of clothes, a small hand towel, extra socks. Plus two comic books, her own idea. She shrugged the back-pack straps onto her shoulders and followed the man out of the house she had always lived in, looking back to see if her grandmother would cry. Her wrinkled face crumpled with pain, but Noemi saw no tears, so she would not cry, either.

The man had an orange car, and Noemi sat in the back seat, as her grandmother had told her to. She had rarely been in a car before, and she inspected the door handle, the seatbelt, the pocket in the seat in front of her. She and her grandmother always took the bus, or went on foot.

"Do you know my parents?" she asked.

There was a pause. "I know your father."

"How?"

The man didn't answer.

"Why are you taking me to them?"

"It's my job."

"Do you make a lot of money?"

He snorted. "Not enough."

"Do you have a family?"

He didn't answer.

Noemi watched the back of his head, the side of his square cheek, his short hair and broad forehead in the mirror. Then she got out a comic book and tried to read, but she felt sick to her stomach.

"You have to look out the window at one thing that isn't moving," the man said.

So she put the comic away and stared out the windshield at the distant mountains. She guessed they must be driving north. That was the way everyone went. She got to thinking about whether there were other directions to go.

"What's other from north?" she asked.

"What do you mean?"

She wasn't sure. "I mean, is there a different one?"

"There's south," he said. "And east and west."

She counted. "There are four?"

He looked at her in the rearview mirror. "What the hell do they teach you in school?"

She was silent, embarrassed. "My grandmother can't help me with my homework."

"There are four points of the compass," he said. "And also an infinite number. Because you can have southeast and northwest and every direction in between."

"Oh." That didn't make any sense at all.

"I got you a Christmas present," he said, and he handed something back to her. It was a plush toy pig, very pink, with tiny black eyes and a curly tail. She squeezed it and felt its softness.

"Thank you," she said.

Before they got to the Colombian border, Chuy told her to sit in the front seat. If the border patrol asked, she was his daughter. Did she understand?

She nodded.

When they stopped, he handed papers to the border guard and answered some questions.

The guard asked Noemi questions, and she leaned forward in her seat. Yes, this man was her papa. Yes, she was from Ecuador, and they were visiting her cousins in Cali. Yes, she liked her pig.

She must have done a good job, because afterward, Chuy seemed relieved. He put the papers on the seat and she saw that his last name was the same as hers.

They drove, and drove, and slept in the car, but then they stopped at a hotel. Noemi had never stayed in a hotel before. She pulled back the covers on her bed and saw a dark red smudge. She froze, thinking it was blood, but then she looked closer.

The red mark was really a scorpion, twitching its tail on the smooth white fitted sheet. Its back was crawling with something. "Chuy," she said.

He came to look. "It's a mama."

Now Noemi saw that the mother scorpion had babies all over her back, no bigger than grains of rice. Their tiny tails were waving. "Will they sting me?"

"Not if you don't scare her," he said.

"I'm scared."

He took a glass from the bathroom and trapped the scorpions beneath it. Then he borrowed her comic book and slid it under the upside-down glass, letting the mother scorpion step on. He carried them all outside. He and Noemi inspected the bedsheets together, shaking and smoothing them, to make sure there were no loose baby scorpions.

"She was looking for a warm, dry place for her babies, that's all," he said.

Noemi eyed the disordered sheets, uncertain.

"You want to trade?" he asked.

She nodded, and they checked the other bed for scorpions. Nothing was there, and Noemi climbed in. The sheets were cool and the mattress was soft. Chuy sat on the scorpion bed with his back to her and unbuttoned his shirt. He had tattoos on his back and arms. She was going to ask him about those, but decided not to, and she fell asleep.

At the border to Panama, she did a good job again. As a reward, they went to watch the ships go through the locks in the canal. Chuy explained how they worked, how the locks were like stairs, filling with water to float the ships so they could go up over the mountains, and then emptying so the ships could go down again on the other side. He told her thousands of people had died building the canal, because it was so dangerous, but also because they came from France and didn't know how to live in this country. He bought her an ice cream and they watched some more.

In Panama, they stayed in a room in someone's house, and the orange car was stolen in the night. Chuy swore and kicked the curb where it had been parked. But he said they weren't giving up, and they moved to a truck, and rode in the cargo space in the back, with some other people. Chuy was silent, or listened to a little radio, and Noemi spent her time in a made-up world of her own, whispering to the toy pig. She lived in the present now. Her past with her grandmother, her future with her parents, none of it was real.

She thought about the skinny girl on her street who was going to have a baby. She wondered what it would be like to have a baby of your own. Like a doll but real. Who would love you always.

"Crying and shitting all the time," her grandmother had said. "I promise you, mija, you don't want that."

When Chuy brought mangoes or tortas or coconut water in a plastic bag, Noemi ate and drank quickly. She never saved anything, or planned ahead. She didn't believe in the future anymore. It would come or it wouldn't. There were an infinite number of directions to go. She told all of this to the pig.

5

LIV STRETCHED OUT on the bed in the cabin and looked at the list of shore excursions. Benjamin had his feet up on the couch. They were all getting restless on the ship—the balcony episode had proven that. They needed an adventure.

"This is a good country for us to go ashore in," she said. "They call it the Switzerland of Latin America."

"Why?" Benjamin asked. "Self-righteousness and shady banking practices?"

"Ha," she said.

"Or good chocolate?"

"There's a hummingbird sanctuary," she said, "but it's up in the mountains."

"If hummingbirds were bugs, people would be grossed out by them," he said.

"You have officially become a spoiled Californian," she said. "Hummingbirds are magical."

"They're like giant flying cockroaches."

"Except they're not."

"I'm not sitting on a bus like a tourist."

"We *are* tourists."

"Still."

"We can't just take a random cab on the dock."

"Why not? They don't behead people here, right?"

"We'd need a minivan, at least, to fit all of us," she said. "And I want a driver the cruise ship has vetted."

"Like they vetted the people in that PR video?"

"Coffee plantation tour," she read.

"The kids would be bored. And why encourage caffeine? Is there a surfing lesson?"

"Everyone on the ship is too ancient for that. And there are sharks here. And riptides." Liv had once been caught in a riptide, at a beach with no lifeguard, on a Hawaiian vacation with her parents when she was fifteen. She had watched the beach getting farther away, and thought *This is how it ends*. When she finally made her way in, she'd collapsed exhausted on the sand. "There's an animal preserve," she said, "with howler monkeys and coatimundis."

"What's a coatimundi?"

"A small mammal with a stripy tail."

"We have skunks in LA."

"Wait, that's four hours in a bus."

"Just shoot me now."

"How about a zip-line tour of the rain forest canopy?" she asked. "Forty-five minutes by bus each way."

Benjamin perked up. "Seriously? I wonder what kind of rig they use."

She should have known it would be cables and carabiners that would lure him, not monkeys. She swung her legs off the bed and headed out of the cabin before he changed his mind. In the corridor, she ran into Perla, their stewardess.

"Will you go outside tomorrow, ma'am?" Perla asked.

Liv felt a guilty twinge. "Going outside" meant getting off the ship, which for Perla meant a chance to use a phone card to call her kids in Manila. Every time Liv saw a stewardess plumping pillows in an open cabin, she was stunned by the heartache of it. Never seeing her kids. Missing out on the tiny changes, the lost teeth, the dawning look of some small discovery on their faces. Making strangers' beds while your children learned to read. Perla didn't need praise for her towel-animal skills or questions about her kids' ages. She needed Liv to get out of the cabin so she could get her work done early and call home.

"Yes!" Liv said. "We're going outside."

Perla looked pleased, and Liv was embarrassed that they'd been such homebodies. Ship-bodies.

She knocked at Nora's door and Nora said yes to the zip-line tour. "I invited the Argentinians to join us for dinner," Nora said. "Gunther and Camila."

"Great!" Liv said. "See, we're sophisticated people of the world. We have international friends! We zip-line!"

At dinner, Camila sat between Benjamín and Raymond, wearing a black dress and a gold necklace as thick as Liv's little finger. Gunther sat on Liv's right, and leaned forward to say, "Did you see this video in the cabin? The crew interviews?"

"Yes!" Benjamin said. "Who signed off on that?"

"I think it must be a joke," Camila said. "Someone in the publicity department is taking revenge. And no one has noticed."

Gunther said, "If there is class war on this ship, I am telling you, we are outnumbered."

Yuri arrived with a bottle of Chilean red that Gunther had ordered, and they straightened in their chairs. Yuri poured the first taste for Gunther.

"It is fine," Gunther said, waving his hand over the glass. To Liv, he said, "All this sniffing, the wine is always fine."

With a barely perceptible frown, Yuri started to pour. Liv sensed that he didn't approve of Gunther invading their table. She looked to Raymond, who gave her an equally perceptible smile.

"Have you always lived in Argentina?" she asked Gunther, thinking of Nazis—she couldn't help thinking of Nazis.

"Of course," he said. "Since my grandfather's grandfather came from the Volga."

She didn't know exactly where the Volga was, but Marcus would know. She could quiz him later. An endive salad arrived. "Did a lot of Germans migrate there?" she asked.

"Also Italian and French," he said. "You know this joke? 'An Argentine is an Italian who speaks Spanish and thinks he is English.'"

She didn't know the joke. "What about the indigenous people?"

"They are there, too."

"But not in your family?"

"Are they in yours?" Gunther asked, with a meaningful smile at her pale hair.

"I don't think so," she said. "I mean, I haven't done a cheek swab. I'm Norwegian and Swedish and a little Irish."

"It is the same for us," Gunther said. "We are immigrants. There is a pride in my country in not being *mixed* with the indios, like our neighbor countries. It's not a nice thing, this pride."

"They say they are taking the zip-line tour tomorrow," Camila reported, across the table.

"Oh, this is terrible!" Gunther said, putting down his wine glass. "You will be thrown from tree to tree like a sack of potatoes!"

"Have you done it?" Nora asked.

"Never!"

"He hates all shore excursions," Camila said. "We went swimming with dolphins and he despised it."

"Animal abuse!" Gunther said. "These noble creatures do not want to see ugly tourists in bathing suits."

"Wait," Benjamin said. "Do you think dolphins have aesthetic taste in human beings?"

"Of course," Gunther said. "They must jump and clap and sing for us, and humiliate themselves. Prostitution. They are being pimped. Let them go."

"You think dolphins feel humiliated?" Benjamin asked.

"Dogs feel shame," Gunther said. "You see it in the body, when someone puts a hat on them, or a sweater. The hanging of the head. And dolphin brains are much bigger."

"But aren't we anthropomorphizing?" Benjamin persisted. "We don't actually know what they're thinking."

"I know what *my* dog is thinking," Gunther said.

"But you never know what *I* am thinking," Camila said, one eyebrow arched, and Liv thought again what good work she'd had done on her face.

Gunther turned to the men. "Listen to me," he said. "I have an English friend in this city. He invites me to the golf club tomorrow. Do you golf?"

Raymond turned to Nora, his face alight.

Nora leaned back in her chair. "I've just lost my husband."

Gunther clapped his hands together. "Excellent," he said. "*This* is gracious living. Benjamin?"

"Sure," he said. "If there's room for me."

"Of course!"

"So I guess we're on our own for the zip line," Liv said.

"A hen party," Gunther said, grinning. "I'm sure you girls will have a very pleasant time on your potato-sack trip." He turned to signal Yuri for more wine. Yuri poured, but didn't stay to talk.

In bed that night, after the children were asleep, Liv said, "You don't even like golf."

"Not enough to pay for a membership," Benjamin said. "But I like a ritualized stroll on a vast lawn."

"Maybe he's lying about his grandfather's grandfather, and he's descended from Nazis in hiding."

"Then they would've named him Antonio," Benjamin said.

"Or O'Hara."

"It could be interesting," he said. "Maybe I'll learn something about the country."

"You didn't even want to go ashore," she said. She knew she should let it go.

"Should I beg off?"

"No," she said. "Just don't come crying to me when you don't see any coatimundis at the golf course."

He smiled in the dark. "I promise."

"Yuri doesn't like Gunther."

"Operation Barbarossa," he said. "Old wounds."

In the morning she checked her work email on the annoyingly slow connection, then packed sunblock, hand sanitizer, bug repellent, water bottles. At the last minute she threw in the new Christmas swimsuits, just in case. They all ventured forth, blinking in the sunlight, from the cocoon of the giant ship. Gunther's friend pulled into the taxi area, in a boxy black military-looking Mercedes SUV. The husbands piled in and were off.

Marcus and Sebastian wandered away to look at the giant bollards the ship was tied to. Junie held Nora's hand. Penny, not fully awake, leaned against Liv. It was already too hot for clinging kids. Liv wasn't sure where to go.

"It's so *early*," Penny said. "Can't we just stay on the ship?"

A woman with a clipboard directed them to a smiling young man. He was slight, in his twenties, with a handsome, friendly face.

"I am Pedro," he said. "Welcome to my country. I will be your guide."

He gave Nora an extra-welcoming smile, which made Liv look at her cousin. Nora was wearing white shorts, a bright blue tank top, and aviator sunglasses, and she looked trim and sporty and young. Pedro led them all to a van with a toucan painted on the side. He offered his hand to Nora to help her in, and Nora gave him a funny look, then took it.

He offered the same help to Liv. "No thanks," she said.

Camila had signed up at the last minute, and boarded with her kids: Hector in madras shorts and a polo shirt, Isabel in a sundress with her hair loose. The teenagers looked like they'd come from a photo shoot, attractive and long-limbed, with sun-streaked hair and clear, tan skin. Liv wanted to ask Camila if they had some fancy European or Argentine acne product that could help Penny through the awkward years. The children clustered at the back of the van.

"Seatbelts!" Liv called.

"So, you work for a local company that contracts with the ship?" Nora asked Pedro, when they were under way, on a winding road.

"Exacto," Pedro said.

"Do you think we'll see monkeys?"

"*So* many monkeys!"

"Do they ever attack people?"

"No! They are very shy."

"You hear those stories about chimps," Nora said.

"Chimps live in Africa," Pedro said. "These are howler monkeys. Maybe a few capuchinos, if we're lucky."

"Cappuccino like the coffee?" Nora asked.

"Like the monk. They wear a little cap." He clasped his hands over his own head to demonstrate.

"Oh, of course," Nora said. "Capuchins."

Nora's cheeks had gone pink, and Liv looked again at Pedro. Was he that appealing? The idea of a twenty-five-year-old just made her kind of tired.

Just then there was a sharp blast, and the van jerked sideways. There were small screams from the back, and Liv looked to see her children's eyes wide on hers, seeking reassurance. The van hobbled down the road, tilting to the left.

"The tire," Pedro said. "It's okay."

"Car!" Nora said.

A green car was coming toward them, and there was a jarring crash, and the van was spinning, flying. The children were really screaming now. The world was full of noise. "Hang on," Liv heard herself saying into the din. "Just hang on."

When they came to a stop, there was a strange stillness. Liv's heart raced. She had to get her seatbelt off. If she could only reach her children, she could protect them. But her hands shook and she fumbled at the clasp.

"Is okay," Pedro was saying. "Is okay."

Leaves and branches pressed against the windows. Liv got herself free of the seatbelt and made her way to the back. Her legs trembled. She clutched her children to her. They were crying. Nora was there, too.

Marcus had his hands over his ears.

"It's all right," Nora told him. "It's all fine."

"Will the engine explode?" Marcus asked.

"No," Pedro said, without conviction.

"That's only in movies," Liv said.

"Everyone out!" Nora said. "Now!"

They trooped off the van and surveyed the damage. The front left tire had blown, leaving ragged edges of fibrous rubber around the wheel well. They must have veered into the oncoming lane, where the other car hit them. The van's right front corner was mangled and crushed. The other car, small and green and crumpled, had parked on the shoulder, and the two drivers were talking near it. Pedro climbed back into the van to use the radio.

Liv and Camila took out their phones, but neither of them could get a signal.

"I called my company," Pedro said when he emerged. "There is no other van now."

He had hit his head and was definitely bleeding. Nora fished a hand wipe out of her bag and gently cleaned the blood away.

"I asked for three taxis," he said. "It will take a long time, on a ship day. They are all busy. There is a bus at four o'clock."

"Four o'clock!" Liv heard the desperation in her own voice. "We can't stand here on the side of the road all day."

Pedro lifted his shoulders, then frowned across the road in thought. "Do you have your swimming clothes?"

"Yes," the women said.

"I think there is a beach," Pedro said.

"Are there sharks?" Liv asked.

"No," Pedro said. "There is a reef."

"Anything else that's dangerous?" Nora asked.

"You could trip and break your leg," he said. "Or the coatimundis could take your lunch."

"We were supposed to get lunch at the zip line," Nora said.

"I have snacks," Pedro said. He pronounced it "ess-nacks."

Camila asked him something in rapid Spanish that Liv didn't follow, and they had a short conversation. Then Camila pressed her lips together.

"I think we go to swim," she said. "It is boring to wait. The children will complain. And this road is very dangerous."

"You're *sure* this is a good place?" Liv asked Pedro. "No riptide?"

"It is very protected," he said. "Very calm and safe. A river comes out to the sea."

So Liv and Nora shouldered their bags. Pedro pulled a cooler and three inner tubes out of the back of the van. He passed one to Hector and one to Marcus. "We go to another river sometimes," he said.

There were ten of them: Liv, Penny, Sebastian, Nora and her children, Camila and the Argentinian teens, all following Pedro. Liv thought they must look absurd, trooping along on the shoulder, carrying inner tubes. But a trail soon veered off from the road, and Pedro led them into the trees. The undergrowth seemed ready to reclaim the trail the moment humans stopped trampling it.

Pedro stopped, and Nora bumped into him. Marcus, holding an inner tube, bumped into Nora, and Liv bumped into Marcus.

"Sorry," she said.

"Up there," Pedro whispered, pointing. A magnificent bird was perched on a branch above them, green with a blue head and a black mask. It had a long double tail with teardrop blue feathers at the end. It turned its head, revealing an orangey-brown throat.

"What is it?" Nora whispered.

"Blue-crowned motmot."

"See the bird?" Liv whispered to Penny and Sebastian, and they *oooh*ed appropriately. How had evolution made *that*? The bird flew off, trailing its ludicrous tail. Real nature! Her kids were too protected. This unexpected adventure would be good for them.

They trooped on. Nora and Pedro chatted about birds. Sebastian and June scampered ahead.

The trees opened and they walked out onto a pretty little beach at the mouth of a river, just as Pedro had promised. They could see the protective reef in the distance, and no surf made it inside. It was perfect. The children clamored for their bathing suits.

"Where do we change?" Penny asked.

"Right here," Liv said.

Penny looked doubtful, but she wasn't going to miss swimming for the sake of modesty. Hector peeled off his polo shirt. Isabel was already in a yellow bikini, her adolescent hips and small breasts resplendent in it. She must have had it on under her sundress. Liv averted her eyes and checked her phone again. Still no signal.

She held up a towel for the children to change, and smeared more sunscreen on their faces and shoulders while they squirmed and squinted. She removed Sebastian's insulin pump and sealed the port with its plastic cap. Then she looked to Pedro.

"You promise there's nothing dangerous in that water?"

"I go in first," Pedro said.

He had stripped down to nylon hiking shorts. He had an interesting scar on the side of his belly, like a deep thumbprint—appendix? And the pale sunburst of a smallpox vaccination above his brown tricep. Those were not first-world scars, Liv thought. He waded into the water and she was happy to see that it was shallow for a long way. He stepped carefully forward.

When he was chest deep, he screamed and was yanked under, leaving a small splash at the surface.

"Oh, shit!" Liv said, leaping to her feet.

Isabel screamed.

"Mommy!" June cried.

Pedro surfaced, smiling, then looked at their appalled faces and grew serious. "I am so sorry," he said. "This was not a good joke. Everything is fine, you see?" He stood, waist deep, and held up his hands. His shining hair and his smooth bare chest dripped with water. He looked cool as they sweltered. Liv wanted to strangle him.

"Oh my God," Nora said.

Camila said something angry, in fast Spanish. Pedro apologized again.

Liv's children looked to her, uncertain. There was no point in showing her rage. She breathed and smiled. *Be calm. Be reassuring.* "He was just teasing us for being afraid," she said. "It was a joke. There's nothing dangerous. Do you want to swim?"

They nodded. It was much too hot *not* to want to swim.

Liv was conscious of her pale thighs in her swimsuit, after feeling so attractive and young on the ship. Was it because Pedro was here? Was it because he clearly liked Nora? Why did she care about the idiot guide? She'd thought motherhood had cauterized her vanity. She tugged down the leg holes of the suit and tried to shake the feeling off. "Okay, you two," she said to Sebastian and Penny. "Race you in."

The water was warm, and the children played on the three inner tubes, their happy cries piercing the air. Liv swam alongside them for a while. She felt no current, and the water was barely salty, because of the fresh water from the river. When she was tired of swimming, she told Penny to keep an eye on her brother.

"I'm okay," Sebastian said.

"I know," she said lightly. "Just come in if you feel tired."

She knew Penny understood what she was asking, but she also knew her daughter would have rolled her eyes if she'd thought she could get away with it. She got out and toweled off. The kids kept swimming and shrieking.

Pedro produced some frozen rum drink from two thermos bottles and poured it into plastic cups. It was slushy and sweet in the heat, and felt decadent, but it was so deliciously *cold*. The drinks were supposed to be for after the zip line, he said. The taste reminded Liv of a spring break in her lost youth, sand on her sun-warmed body, a cute boy from Arizona she had hardly known, with a compact body like the guide's.

Pedro played some music on his phone, a man rapping and a woman singing. He leaned back on his elbows in the sand, singing to the girl's part. Liv didn't need a translation—it was all about sex—but Nora asked for one.

"The man says she's so beautiful," Pedro said. "She says, 'Don't try it. I know what you want.'"

"Got it," Nora said, smiling out at the water.

This flirtation was the kind of thing Liv might have shared a glance with Nora about, if it had been someone else flirting, but she couldn't because it was Nora. It was disorienting. She flipped through a *New Yorker* from her bag.

Nora's shadow came over her. "Will you keep an eye on the kids?" she asked. "Pedro heard some special bird call."

Liv squinted up at her, astonished. "Okay," she said.

Then Pedro and Nora walked into the trees. Liv put the magazine down and stared after them.

She wondered, not for the first time, if Nora felt physically eclipsed, being married to Raymond, a man so widely desired. His fans wrote to him online, and openly wished Nora didn't exist. Liv wondered if the eclipsed feeling was enough to push Nora to go make out with Pedro in the trees, just as proof of her own attractiveness.

She lay on her back on a towel and watched the children from under her sun hat. They were strong swimmers. Hector and Isabel were out there, old enough to babysit. And there was Camila, too, reading a mystery novel in Spanish. And Penny was watching Sebastian. The day was so sultry, the sun so warm, that Liv couldn't keep her eyes open. If she'd been driving, she would have pulled over. But she wasn't driving. She blinked, and struggled, and drifted deliciously into sleep.

6.

NORA HAD BEEN aware of Pedro's attention, and aware that Liv had noticed it. But still she'd followed the guide into the trees looking for a quetzal. She was pretty sure that they wouldn't see a quetzal, not here by the beach.

She knew what he was actually looking for. She was looking for it, too. Just a little no-strings attention, from someone who thought she was sexy and new. Someone who was handsome without looking better than she did, who smelled salty and warm and—different. She felt hypnotized by the way he smelled.

The trees were hung with parasitic vines that would eventually pull the trees down, to be food for the tiny shoots that would grow up and take their place. She thought of Werner Herzog's Bavarian voice, talking about the *overwhelming misery and fornication* of the jungle—something like that. If you stood here long enough you could watch the plants grow. Weird insects buzzed.

She'd never been unfaithful to Raymond, even now that it had started to feel like they had a business partnership, raising children, managing his career. She'd always understood that she was the lucky one. She was an ordinary person, and he was in movies. He could have had anyone. He used to pick her up at her terrible apartment in Los Feliz, or at the public school where she'd worked with kids with learning disabilities. The kids went nuts when they saw him. He was black *and* famous. He signed autographs and gave dap and they loved him.

She used to cut her own hair, back then, and wore jeans and sneakers to work. When she started seeing Raymond, she began to be photographed in public, and his fans had opinions about her hair and her body. She spent money on haircuts and got a stylist to help her buy clothes. She'd lost the weight instantly after both pregnancies, out of sheer terror of the judgment and nastiness.

She had come to think that actors, the best ones, were not like other people. They were vessels to be filled up with other lives, for the purpose of art. But to be a perfect vessel you had to be empty to begin with. When she saw a child actor at work, Nora thought of human sacrifice, the emptying out of one small soul for the purpose of entertainment. She hated it when agents and casting directors gave her children an appraising eye, admiring the shape of their faces, the warm color of their skin, the length of their limbs. She wanted to tell those vultures to back the fuck off.

She liked to think that Raymond was *not* a truly great actor, that he was handsome and photogenic and smart and skilled, so he would continue to work, but he would never be one of the uncanny, dissociated ones.

But still—the business did something to a person. There was so much attention, and so much pressure to be young and flawless. Raymond had joked about wanting the dumb reducing treatment in the spa, but she knew he really did want it. She thought she would've minded less if he'd been tempted by the Brazilian trainer, and not by the seaweed wrap and the electrodes. At least then the temptation would be about someone else. There was nothing sexy about incipient narcissism.

After June was born, Raymond had asked if she was having an affair, and Nora had realized that she was, in a way, because all of her emotional energy had gone to her children. She was infatuated with them, besotted. But that wasn't the real reason she wasn't that into sex anymore. Her therapist said that their situation was pretty normal, for a stable long-term couple in an equitable relationship. Power imbalances were erotically generative. So were fights. Her therapist said she should initiate sex more, maybe think of it like exercise. You didn't really want to do it beforehand, but it felt good afterward. It raised serotonin levels. It was supposed to be good for your skin.

But Nora always had about twelve other things she wanted or needed to do, at any given time.

She and Pedro were deep in the trees, talking about birds, and he was standing very close to her. She didn't move away. She felt like she was sixteen. Then he was kissing her against a tree, and she didn't pull away.

After a minute, he slipped a hand inside her white shorts, and she was embarrassed by the slide, by how wet she was already. There was no fumbling and hunting for the right spot. He made her come so quickly and expertly it took her breath away. It seemed to take about thirty seconds from the moment his hand pushed aside the silky nylon of her shorts. Her whole body was trembling, her legs weak, but he held her up with his other arm. With Raymond she had to really concentrate these days, and she had to be lying down. Was this hotter because it was all so strange and taboo? Or did Pedro have secret powers? He didn't seem surprised or disappointed by the speed of it. Everything seemed to be going according to his plan: He knew where the switch was, and he knew how to flip it. He did it again, and she found herself gasping, shaking as he held her upright.

She recovered, the world coming back into focus, with a hint of the remorse to come. "What about you?" she asked.

"No," he said. "No condom. No sexo."

"Oh." She realized she hadn't actually thought there would be *sexo*. In her teenage fog, she had reverted to the assumption that sexo itself was off the table. Actual intercourse was something grown-ups did.

"You have condom?" Pedro asked.

"No." She thought of her daypack full of cheese sticks and crackers. She thought of Raymond's vasectomy. Raymond out golfing. She shrank away from the guide a little. "No condom."

"So no sexo," Pedro said, shrugging. Then he brought himself off in the same quick, expert way he had worked on her, with no shame, convulsing at the end, in broad daylight, while she watched. She noted that his penis—what she could see of it, inside his shorts—was smaller than Raymond's, but he was smaller than Raymond in every way. He was built on a different scale. She noted it without judgment or even a sense of involvement.

Pedro wiped his hand off on a flat leaf and grinned at her. She'd had spa massages that were more emotionally compromising. It was as if she'd been to the car wash. *Just the basic, thanks. No wax.* "One more?" he asked.

"No, that's okay." She saw her own dazed expression in his mirrored sunglasses. Her legs were still weak. "Thanks. We should get back."

That was when they heard the first shout.

"Marcus!" she cried.

Later she would wonder why she'd said her son's name, and not June's, but in that moment she wasn't thinking at all. She went crashing back through the brush. They'd walked farther than she'd thought, and must have been gone for longer than she'd realized. Branches hit her face, but she didn't notice. Later she would see a red welt on her cheek, a scratch near her eyebrow.

Liv was standing alone on the beach in her swimsuit and hat, looking sunstruck, calling the children's names. The children were nowhere to be seen.

"Where are they?" Nora asked, breathless.

"I don't know!" Liv said. Camila had hiked back up the trail to the road, in case the children had gone to the van for something they'd left behind.

But Pedro stared at the flowing river. "Oh my God," he said.

"What?" Nora said.

"The tide," he said. "Took them up the river."

"Where are they?" she screamed. She would kill Pedro, if something had happened to her children. She would break his neck with her hands. Or she would hold him under the water until he drowned.

"That way." He pointed inland and she ran, blindly, but there was no trail along the river. There was only thick brush and she was fighting her way through it, unaware if the others were behind her. She sank into the mud on the bank, and couldn't move forward.

She was trying to make her way to clear water when she heard Camila's voice and turned. The Argentinian woman was standing with a police officer in uniform, who looked concerned and said something in Spanish.

Camila looked ashen. "The officer says there are crocodiles," she said.

"What?" Nora screamed.

Pedro waded in and put an arm around her waist.

She pulled free, almost losing her balance and falling in. "You said there was nothing dangerous!" She couldn't seem to speak normally anymore, she could only scream. She thought of the word *hysterical*, a word for which she had always had a feminist contempt.

"I didn't know," Pedro said.

"How could you not know?" she screamed. "How did this happen?"

"I'm sorry," he said. "I forget the tide. Come out of the water."

"Where the *fuck* are my children?" she screamed.

7.

THE KIDS WERE engrossed in a complicated game with the three inner tubes, making a kind of raft that they could stand on. It required a great deal of concentration. Hector was the master of the game, and he kept everyone involved. He didn't leave Sebastian and June out, or cut them any slack just because they were little. Penny admired that in him.

He tossed his wet hair off his face. If Hector had been in a band, Penny's friends would have fainted over him. And he *could* be in a band. He played guitar that well.

He was good at building a structure, too, like her father was. He gave directions, saying, "Hold there. Now, Penny, you sit there. Okay, now you can stand up there. Now Penny, too." He kept the whole three-ring raft stable. She loved hearing him say her name. His stomach was tan and slick above his pink-and-green checked shorts.

Every few minutes, someone would slip or step in the wrong place and everyone would go crashing into the water, screaming with delight, the inner tubes flying. Hector would make sure everyone was safe and afloat, and then they would start rebuilding.

They were so focused that they didn't notice when the tide changed. It must have paused when they were first in the water. Then it reversed, and began to flow inland. No one noticed that the water from the sea was pushing them upstream, slowly at first, and then with surprising force.

When they finally looked up, waterlogged, each with an arm slung over a tube and legs treading the silty water, they were in a different place. There was no beach. There were no mothers on towels. The river was starting to narrow. It was overhung with trees.

Penny squinted against the sun. She was hanging on to an inner tube with Isabel, and had one arm over the smaller tube June and Sebastian were on. Her fingertips were pruned. She felt her little brother's arm slide against hers. Hector and Marcus were on the third tube. Birds sang, and insects buzzed in the trees, but there were no human sounds.

"What do we do?" she asked.

They all looked to Hector, their leader. He frowned. Then he said, "We hold on and kick back." He rolled his long body over and started to kick.

They tried, all six of them, to propel themselves back toward the beach. But it was pointless, the tidal current was too strong. The little ones spluttered, water in their faces.

"Stop!" Hector commanded.

The song of insects and birds returned. On they floated, with the muscle of the river.

"Will they come find us?" Sebastian asked, in a small voice.

"Of course they will," Penny said. And really, what was keeping them? The jungle on the bank looked impenetrable, but their mothers would find a way.

"Should we shout?" Marcus asked.

Together they cried, *"Mom," "Mommy," "Mami,"* in one shrill, beseeching voice. Then they stopped, as if with the swipe of a conductor's wand, and waited in the silence. There was no response. The river swirled around them.

"I have to pee," June said.

"Just go in the water," her brother said.

"I can't."

"Why not?"

"I just can't. What about those fish that swim up the pee, inside you?"

"That's in the Amazon," Marcus said.

"Why couldn't they be here?" June asked.

"Because the Amazon doesn't connect to here," he said.

Penny already had peed, and hoped those fish really weren't in the water. On the left bank, there was a tiny sloping place. They all kicked to it and clambered out.

It felt good to be on solid ground. As soon as they stood up, it seemed clear that they should wait here, rather than traveling ever farther away from their mothers. It had been smart to get out.

Penny helped June find a place to peel down her wet bathing suit, behind a tree. The trees were like something out of fairy tales: thick, twisted, hung with vines. June peed into the damp ground, looking up.

"Are you scared, Penny?" she asked.

"No," Penny lied.

"Because they're going to find us?"

"Yes," Penny said. She helped June pull up her swimsuit straps and felt very grown-up. Isabel might be the oldest girl, but Penny was the one June knew and trusted. Her mother had told her to keep an eye on Sebastian and she had, but she hadn't known this would happen.

"I'm hungry," June said.

"We can go back to the buffet on the ship," Penny said. "When they find us."

They rejoined the group, and Hector announced, "I'm going to swim back."

"You can't swim against the river," Marcus said.

"I can," he said. "If I stay to the sides. Where the water goes the other direction."

Penny had been whitewater rafting with her grandparents. "You mean in the eddies," she said.

Isabel said something protesting.

"I'll come back for you," Hector said. He waded out, lowered his body in near the bank, and started swimming. He was very strong. His arms slashed through the water. They watched in silence as he disappeared around a bend. Then they were alone.

"We should be on the other side of the river," Marcus said.

"We can't get up that bank," Penny said.

They studied the other side of the river and the steep mud bank. And then the bank moved. At least it seemed to move. There were tangled roots, and a section of the mottled mud was sliding.

"Oh!" Penny said.

Isabel said something under her breath.

It was not mud sliding, but an enormous crocodile, sunning itself on the bank. It had moved its big sinister head, split by a row of teeth, but now it settled again, motionless.

Isabel put a hand over her mouth.

"Hector will be okay," Marcus said.

Sebastian and June weren't paying attention. They had started making a small mud castle in the soft ground. No one said anything more to alarm them. Penny imagined her mother picking her way through the trees on the opposite bank and coming across that monster. They had to get back before that happened. But there was no reason crocodiles wouldn't be on this side of the river, too. Penny stepped backward. She wanted to get away from the water, away from the muddy banks.

In the trees behind them, they heard an engine noise, and turned. "There's a road!" Penny said. She started toward it.

"We have to stay here," Isabel said. "And wait for Hector."

"We should find the road," Penny said.

They looked at each other. *A battle of wills.* Penny had read the phrase in books and knew that this was what it meant. Isabel was older. But Penny was smarter. She could not say in front of the little ones that they might be eaten by a crocodile if they stayed here, but she beamed the argument into Isabel's eyes.

"I'm hungry," Sebastian said.

"Me too," June said.

Penny thought of how her mother would panic when she saw they were gone. Sebastian needed food or his blood sugar would drop, but he also needed insulin or his blood sugar might go too high. And he didn't have his pump.

Marcus said they should hang the inner tubes on a branch, to show where they had left the river. Isabel clearly wasn't happy about the plan, but she didn't want to stay alone, so the five of them set off into the dense forest. The crocodile on the other bank hadn't moved again. Hector would be fine, Penny told herself.

There was no trail, and it was painful, climbing barefoot over roots and fallen trees. Beneath the undergrowth, things scuttled away. Penny saw ants marching in a column, carrying green pieces of leaves over their heads like sails. She took Sebastian's hand, a thing he would not usually tolerate.

They stumbled out into a clearing, where a Jeep was parked. Two men sat on the ground drinking bottles of Coke. They stared as if the children were fairies, materialized from the woods.

"Say something Spanish," Penny whispered to Isabel.

"No," Isabel whispered back.

"Hola!" Penny called.

The men just stared. There were two shovels on the ground and their clothes were dirty.

"Can I have a Coke?" Sebastian whispered to Penny.

The door of the Jeep opened, and a woman got out. She had strong brown arms, and she wore a beige tank top and cargo pants. Penny thought she looked like the girl action figure that goes with the toy Jeep. The woman asked them a question in too-fast Spanish.

Isabel didn't answer.

Penny said, "We're Americans." That seemed important to say.

"How long you stand here?" the woman asked in English.

"We just got here," Penny said. "We walked from the river."

"Why?"

"We were looking for a road."

"Is no road," the woman said.

"We heard an engine," Penny said, looking pointedly at the Jeep.

"Where are your parents?"

"At the big beach, down the river," Penny said. "We came from the ship, a big cruise ship, but then we had a car accident. We were swimming. Mi hermano es diabético." She'd been taught that sentence before they left, for emergencies.

Sebastian leaned into her. "Can I have a Coke?" he asked, louder than before.

The woman in the tank top frowned, then reached into the Jeep, brought out a bottle, and twisted off the top. Sebastian ran forward to grab it, then ran back to Penny's side and drank.

She wished her mother were here. If Sebastian was low, the Coke would be good, but if he was high, it could make him feel worse.

"Will you give us a ride?" Penny asked.

They were not supposed to get in cars with strangers, but there were five of them. And they were *asking* for a ride. That seemed to make it safer. And the driver was a woman. You were supposed to ask a woman for help, if you got in trouble. Preferably a mother, but this was who they had. And maybe she was a mother. Although Penny doubted it.

"Okay," the woman said, waving toward the Jeep.

Penny and Sebastian got in front together. The Jeep had an open top. Isabel looked toward the river and seemed like she might run, then got in the back seat with Marcus and June. The two men with the shovels crouched in the cargo area behind them. The woman reversed the Jeep.

Penny pulled the seatbelt over Sebastian's bare chest and buckled it over herself, too. "Are you okay?" she asked him.

"I'm a little sleepy."

"You should stay awake."

"Okay."

His blond hair was limp and damp on his forehead. Penny pushed it off his face.

"I have to poop," June said, in the back seat.

"Hold it," her brother said.

Penny looked back and saw June with her hands clamped on the crotch of her blue swimsuit, Marcus looking anxious beside her.

When she looked out the windshield again, they didn't seem to be going in the right direction. "We're going back to that beach, right?" Penny asked.

The woman nodded.

"I don't think this is the right way."

"We call them," the woman said.

"But their cell phones don't work here."

"We call the ship."

"But they aren't at the ship."

The Jeep was driving down a paved road among trees, just like the one where the tire had blown up. That seemed like a long time ago now. *Would* her mother have gone back to the ship?

"I really have to poop," June said.

"Keep holding it," her brother said.

"I am!"

The Jeep stopped at a place where another road crossed, and the two men hopped out of the back, leaving the shovels. The woman waved to them. Then the Jeep was climbing a mountain, and a few houses appeared on the side of the road. The road wound and twisted and then a man on a tall white horse was riding toward them. The Jeep slowed. Penny thought she might be imagining the horse, it was so white and bright. But then June whispered, "He's *beautiful*," and Penny knew that the others could see it, too.

The Jeep stopped, and the man on the horse looked down at them. He had dark, frowning eyebrows, and he spoke with the woman in Spanish. It was all too fast to understand. Penny looked to Isabel in the back seat for a translation, but Isabel ducked her chin toward her yellow bikini as if trying not to be seen.

The horse snorted. It had soft nostrils, gray and pink. The man on the horse smiled. His teeth were white and straight. "Welcome," he said.

"We need insulin," Penny told him. She felt blinded by embarrassment and confusion, the heat rising to her face. "Insulina. My brother is diabético. Also we need a bathroom."

"I have to poop!" June said.

"Pues, vámonos," the man said, turning the horse with the reins, and the Jeep started up the mountain again.

8

NORA'S HEAD THROBBED. All of her high school Spanish had vanished. She stammered and spoke English too loudly, as if that might make people understand and comply. What the fuck had she been thinking? She'd walked into the rain forest with Pedro in an erotic trance, and not like the mother of two children who needed to keep her act together.

Camila's policeman brought a boat, an inflatable with an outboard, and put it in the water. It took forever. The outboard took them up-river, and they found the inner tubes on the other bank. And the small footprints headed into the trees.

The inner tubes had been hung deliberately, and the policeman said the footprints didn't look like they were running, and there was no sign of blood, so it looked like they could rule out a crocodile.

Nora felt her lungs being squeezed; she could barely get a breath in and out.

They followed the footprints through the woods and found a clearing. There was a fresh rectangular disturbance in the ground. The cop tried to keep the women from trooping through his crime scene, but Nora fell to her knees at the edge of the freshly turned dirt, sure that her children were beneath it. She felt on the verge of insanity then, her world dissolving, her skin no longer containing her. Suicide had always seemed a mystery, but now she felt capable of killing herself to follow Marcus and June.

Shovels were brought. Men came, with stern voices. They cordoned everything off with tape. The grave was shallow, and soon they uncovered a body shrouded in a plastic tarp. It was too big to be a child. The police unwrapped it and found a man shot in the forehead.

Nora started shaking uncontrollably. "Who is that?" she cried. "What does that mean?"

Someone put a blanket around her shoulders. She finally got through to Raymond on a police officer's phone, the conversation confused and urgent. The husbands were on their way. That should have been reassuring. Instead it was terrifying.

News teams came, and she didn't want to talk to them, but Liv said that someone watching might know something, might have seen the children. Her cousin was stern with her, a little cold. She was keeping it together better than Nora was. So they talked to the cameras, pleading for the children's return. Afterward Nora had no idea what she'd said.

Then the police quietly separated the parents and started questioning them alone. Nora found herself alone in a squad car with a tall female officer. The car doors were closed. The woman said her name was Detective Rivera. She had short hair, spiked up in front, and good English.

"You do missing persons?" Nora asked her, trying to think what a person said in this situation.

"No," the detective said. "I usually do sex crimes."

"Oh, fuck."

"That's not why I'm here," the detective said quickly. "I was available. It's Christmas week. And I speak English. That's all."

"Where are my kids?"

"I don't know. That's what we're trying to find out."

As they talked, Nora realized she had not been ruled out as a suspect. The other mothers hadn't, either. Probably the fathers were suspects, too, even though they had been on the golf course all day. Did the detective think they had formed some Satanic cabal? The whole thing felt unreal.

"You think it's like *Murder on the Orient Express*?" Nora said. "Like, we all took turns killing them? You understand these are our *children*?"

"Did you go off alone with the guide?" the detective asked.

Nora froze. She'd forgotten her own actual guilt, for a minute. "Yes," she said. "We were looking for birds."

"What birds?"

"We saw a blue-crowned motmot on the trail. I wanted to see a quetzal."

"By the beach?"

"Yes."

"You are a bird-watcher?"

"Not really. We don't have birds in LA like you do here. I mean, there's a flock of feral parakeets, but that's not really the same. They're green and loud. And we have, like, crows, and seagulls. And hawks, and little birds like doves and robins. And pelicans. And there's an owl I hear at night." She was talking too fast.

"That sounds like a lot of birds."

"It's not," Nora said. "We don't have blue-crowned motmots. Or quetzals."

"What is your occupation?"

"I'm just—a mom. I used to be a teacher." She always hated that question. Her job was taking care of her family. And now the one time she had slipped, she had been punished like Job. God had sent a lightning bolt to destroy everything she cared about. She shivered.

"You had met Pedro before?" the detective asked.

"No," Nora said, and she realized that Pedro would be interrogated alone, too. He might be arrested. He had taken them to the beach. He had failed to warn them about the tide, or the crocodiles. They might give him a polygraph. And what would he say? That they'd been looking for blue-crowned motmots? That he had fingered her expertly in the trees but hadn't meant any harm? Were they recording these interviews? She looked around the car for a camera but didn't see one. Weren't interrogations supposed to have cameras?

"How did you meet Pedro?" the detective asked.

"Um—" she said, trying to remember. "We arranged for a shore excursion, on the ship. To go zip-lining. Pedro was the guide who came with the van to pick us up. It was arranged by the ship, through a local company. But then there was an accident. The tire blew out, and someone hit us when we swerved."

"Did you call the police?"

"I think he did," Nora said, but she found she couldn't remember. Pedro had radioed—someone. "It was going to take a long time to get another van, and the road wasn't safe, so we went to the beach."

"And you trusted this guide?"

"Well, yes," Nora said. "We thought all these people had been checked out by the ship. Should we not have trusted them?"

The detective shrugged. "Your children are missing."

"He should have told us about the tide. He definitely should have told us that. But I don't think he knew it would happen. And I was with him when it happened." She stopped.

"What were you doing?"

Nora felt her armpits dampen with sweat. "We were looking for birds."

The detective nodded and made a note.

"I'm not defending the decision to go to that particular beach," Nora said. "That was a terrible, terrible decision. But I just mean he didn't do anything to the kids."

She remembered Pedro wiping his hand on the soft flat leaf, and wondered if the forensics team would find that smear of evidence. Would Pedro admit to what they'd done, in order to explain his absence from the beach, the length of time? She thought of Raymond finding out. Her neck grew hot with shame.

Detective Rivera didn't seem to notice. "The other mothers," she said, "what were they doing?"

"They fell asleep," Nora said bitterly.

"Both of them?"

"I know," Nora said. "They woke up and the kids were gone. Liv said she would watch them."

"And you believe they fell asleep?"

"Of course."

"Why?"

"Because I know them. Liv is my cousin."

"And the woman from Argentina?"

"We just met on the ship. But she didn't do anything to the kids."

"So you have known her one week."

"Almost," Nora said. "Well, yes. A week."

"*Almost* one week," the detective said, making a note on the pad. "And were you drinking?"

Nora took a breath. "There was a slushy rum drink," she said. "Daiquiris. Not very strong, just a lot of sugar. We had one drink each."

"Who provided this drink?"

"Pedro," Nora said, with an odd chill, as if she were drinking the icy liquid now, as if it were sliding down her esophagus. "He said they usually serve it at the end of the day."

"Could it have been drugged?"

"No!" Nora said. She thought of date-rape drugs. Could that excuse her actions? But no, those knocked you out. And she had been fully conscious—more than conscious. Hyper-alert and vibrating. "I mean, sure, test the thermoses. But I had some, and I didn't fall asleep. And Liv wasn't asleep for that long. It was just hot out."

"I'm only asking questions," the detective said. "We are making no judgments at this time."

"This is *madness*," Nora said. "You could be looking for them right now! This country isn't even that big! They're out there!" She had a sudden image of Junie in the emergency room after dislocating her elbow on the monkey bars, being very brave but sobbing quietly, and she was plunged back into the pain. There was a physical ache in her chest.

"I promise you we are doing everything we can," the detective said.

"I need my kids," she moaned.

Detective Rivera watched her and made another note.

9.

AT THE TOP of the mountain, lost in the trees, Penny saw a house of bright, varnished wood, with a deck all the way around, looking over the forest. She remembered her parents talking about Switzerland, and this looked like Switzerland in books. Like Heidi lived here. The tank-top woman drove the Jeep through a security gate and up a road, and parked below the house. Sebastian had fallen asleep, his shirtless body sweaty against Penny's arm, and she jostled him awake. He moaned.

She unbuckled their seatbelt and helped him out. He had a red mark on his pale skin where the seatbelt had been. Marcus helped June. Isabel was trembling, hugging herself in her yellow bikini.

The man with the white horse swung off the saddle and unlocked a door in the lower level of the house. "Welcome," he said, standing back from the open door.

"I have to poop!" June said, and she ran inside.

Penny started to follow her, but Isabel reached for her arm. "Don't," she said.

"We *have* to," Penny said. "She can't go alone. She's six." Isabel was being so annoyingly chicken. Penny stepped into the house, and found herself in a large windowless room, a kind of entryway, with two doors off it to the left.

"June?" she called.

"I'm in here!"

Penny walked through one of the doors into a tidy bedroom, and then into a clean white-tiled bathroom. June had her swimsuit down and was folded in half on the toilet, legs dangling, with her chest on her thighs and an intense, staring look in her eye.

"You good?" Penny asked.

June nodded.

The woman from the Jeep led the rest of them—even reluctant Isabel—upstairs. The house was beautiful. Sunlight flooded in through enormous windows, and filtered through green trees. They could see a dappled valley far below. There were stables outside, and a big lawn.

The floors were polished wood, and a big sunken living room had low red couches, with a thick white rug between them. These people probably didn't have kids, if they had a white plush rug. Penny longed to stretch out on it and take a nap. But first she had to take care of Sebastian. And call their parents.

The kitchen was open and bright, with a big island in the middle. Penny's mother would like it. The man with the white horse spoke to a woman with a plump, nice face, who began to take food out of the refrigerator.

Then he said, in English, "I call the doctor for your brother."

"Can we call our parents?" Penny asked.

"After the doctor. It is important."

"My parents will be worried."

"Of course. So we take care of your brother."

"We're Americans," Penny said.

The man smiled his handsome smile. "Yes, I know this."

The woman was slicing papaya with her knife: *nick, nick, nick,* against the wooden cutting board.

"When will the doctor come?" Penny asked.

"Soon," the man said.

The woman set out a platter on the table: sliced papaya, mango, and banana, with white rectangles of cheese, like a fruit plate in a hotel.

"Please, eat," the man said.

"We have to wash our hands," Penny said.

He gestured to the sink.

Penny helped Sebastian wash his. Then she watched as he took fruit and cheese. Cheese was okay. Fruit was good if his blood sugar was low. But he'd already had the Coke. They needed to get back to his pump. The mango was soft and ripe and sweet. June came upstairs, her swimsuit straps twisted. Penny asked if she'd washed her hands.

"Of *course,*" June said, indignant, reaching for a piece of papaya, and sitting beside Marcus in the same kitchen chair. He moved over for her.

Only Isabel refused to eat, hugging herself in her swimsuit.

An older man came into the room. He was tall, with white hair and bushy eyebrows, in a button-down shirt.

"Hola, Papi," the man with the white horse said. Penny could tell he was trying to act casual.

The old man watched in silence as they ate, then shook his head and went upstairs to the third floor.

By the time the doctor came, Sebastian was like a rag doll, slumped on one of the low red couches in the big living room with all the windows. The doctor was a woman, and she seemed nervous. She had a bony face and her hair in a bun at the back of her neck. Penny answered her questions about the lost insulin pump.

"This thing, I don't have," the doctor said.

But she had a finger-stick monitor, and she helped Sebastian do a test. Then she read some instructions off her phone and asked Penny how much her brother weighed.

"Forty-five pounds?" Penny said.

"Forty-seven," Sebastian mumbled, without moving, still collapsed on the couch.

The doctor entered some numbers on the calculator on her phone. Then she peered at the finger-stick monitor.

"Do you know what you're doing?" Penny asked.

"I am not endocrinólogo," the doctor said. She filled a needle from a glass vial and tapped it, then gave Sebastian an injection. Penny kept her arm around her brother, but he didn't flinch with the pain.

The doctor took out Sebastian's port so it wouldn't get infected.

"But aren't we going back to our parents?" Penny asked. "They have the pump."

"This is more safe," the doctor said. She told Penny she was a good sister, very brave, and she produced a green lollipop from her bag.

Penny wondered if this counted as taking candy from a stranger. Was it okay if the stranger was a doctor? If you were trusting her to put needles in your brother's arm? She pulled off the clear wrapper and stuck the lollipop in her mouth. It tasted sugary and artificial, just like it was supposed to. "Can I call my parents from your phone?" she asked.

The doctor shook her head. "I am sorry."

"We're supposed to ask a woman for help, and you're a woman. And a doctor."

"I—can't."

The doctor's phone was still on the couch and Penny put her hand on it. The doctor caught her wrist and took the phone away, but seemed embarrassed. She looked anxious as she put the phone in her bag. Then she looked toward the kitchen.

A TV was on, the volume low with a steady stream of Spanish. A hush had fallen on the house as the adults gathered around. The Jeep woman watched with her arms crossed, and the white-haired man stood beside her. Penny moved toward the TV.

There was a shot of the ship tied up at the pier, huge and white. A reporter with big hair and heavy makeup spoke to the camera in Spanish. Then Penny was startled to see her frantic mother, her short blond hair damp and matted, her eyes red, begging anyone who had seen the children to call the police. Penny almost couldn't follow what she was saying, it was so disorienting to see her mother on the screen. A Spanish voice came in to translate after the first few words, and she could barely hear her mother's voice beneath the translation. Then Nora was talking on the screen, but she looked like she'd been hypnotized, like she was in a trance.

"That's my mom!" Junie said.

There were photos, all taken this week: Penny and Sebastian grinning with ice cream cones from the buffet. June and Marcus together in a deck chair. Isabel and Hector with their arms around each other on the tennis court. There was a video of the clearing in the woods where they had stumbled on the Jeep, except now the clearing was surrounded by police tape. A male reporter was talking over the image.

"What did he say?" Penny whispered to Isabel.

Isabel shook her head.

"Did it say they were coming to get us?" Penny asked.

Isabel shook her head again.

The white-haired man snapped off the TV. Penny could see that his breathing had changed beneath his soft shirt: He was angry and his eyebrows were terrifying. He glared at his son, and at the woman from the Jeep.

Penny stepped forward. "Take us back to the ship," she said. "Just drop us off, and you'll never have to see us again."

The old man frowned, his eyebrows coming together. "Where is the other boy?" he asked.

There was a pause, and then Isabel said in English, "He swam back."

The old man sized Isabel up, in her yellow bikini. "He is a strong swimmer?"

Isabel nodded.

"You are from Argentina," the old man said.

Isabel nodded again, and he asked her a few questions in Spanish. Penny thought they were talking about Hector. Hector hadn't been on the news. She remembered his arms striking through the water. And she remembered the crocodile.

"*Please* take us back to the ship," she said.

"Ah, but I can't," the old man said.

"Why not?"

None of the adults answered. "Because of the grave," Isabel said.

"What grave?"

"The police found a grave in the woods," Isabel said.

Penny remembered the shovels. "But we didn't see *anything*!"

The old man shrugged.

"We won't tell!" she cried. "Cross my heart and hope to die. *Please* take us back to the ship."

But the old man paid no attention to her. He began to argue in Spanish with his son, who argued back.

"What are they saying?" Penny asked Isabel.

"I *told* you we shouldn't come in here," Isabel said. "We should have waited for Hector."

"But Sebastian could've *died*," Penny said. "And June had to poop."

The man with the white horse lit a cigarette, a thing Penny had never seen anyone do inside a house. She coughed pointedly, waving her hand in front of her face. He ignored her and smoked.

The old man left the house, and then they were just waiting, but Penny didn't know what they were waiting for. There were wooden tic-tac-toe pieces in a tray on the coffee table between the red couches, smooth Xs and Os. She played some games with the others, caring less than usual if she won. The older woman's name was Maria and she gave them a deck of cards. They played some Crazy Eights.

"Where's Hector?" June asked, sitting on the white plush rug in her swimsuit.

"He swam back to our parents," Penny said.

"Is he with them now?"

"I think so."

"Why didn't we swim back?"

"Because we weren't strong enough," Penny said, thinking of the crocodile.

"I wish he'd come with us," Junie said.

"Me too."

Isabel said nothing, but sat on the couch with her knees pulled up and stared out the window at the trees.

Maria brought them sandwiches. Sebastian had slowly revived, like a wilting plant that had been watered. Penny wished her mother were here. What was she supposed to do about insulin? Was the doctor coming back? She let her brother have a sandwich.

It grew dark outside the enormous windows. Penny felt her energy leave her body. Being responsible was exhausting. She put her head on her arm on the back of the couch.

"I want my mom," Junie whimpered.

Marcus put his arm around her. "What should we do now?" he asked.

"I don't know," Penny said. She was already having a dream. "I don't think you should say that."

"Say what?"

But the thing she objected to was in the dream, and was lost.

Later—hours or minutes later, she didn't know—she felt herself being lifted from the couch and carried down the stairs. Still in her swimsuit, she was put into a bed with cool, tightly drawn sheets. She was just registering the impossible sweetness of the pillow beneath her head when Sebastian was put into the bed beside her. She could see his pale hair in the dark. She didn't want to share a bed with her brother, but she was too tired to protest.

"Don't kick," she murmured, and then she sank away.

10.

RAYMOND HAD GOTTEN the call from Nora on the golf course—a confused call from a strange number, the signal breaking up—and he'd told their host they had to leave. They hailed a golf cart to take them in. The club was outside the city in the wrong direction. Gunther's friend knew every shortcut, every alley to avoid the crush of cars, but still it took a long time to find the featureless clearing in the trees. A perfect, sunny day on an expanse of springy green lawn had turned into a confused nightmare of police cars and strange explanations.

When Raymond and Benjamin approached their wives, who had blankets around their shoulders, Gunther and Camila split off to talk in Spanish. Nora started crying and couldn't speak, like she had in the weeks after her mother's death. Raymond put his arms around her and looked to Liv.

"What happened?" he asked.

Liv's eyes were red and her hair was salt-dried. "We were at this quiet beach, and then the tide changed, and the river went inland. Sebastian doesn't have his pump."

"What happened to the zip line?" Benjamin asked.

"The van got a flat tire," Liv said. "Then a car hit us. We couldn't get a taxi, and the road seemed dangerous. I got no signal on my phone."

Nora sobbed against Raymond's chest.

"You could have borrowed a phone," Benjamin said.

"To tell you to come back and go to the beach with us?"

"To tell us you'd been in an accident," Raymond said. He'd made sure he had an international plan for his phone in case a work call came in, and he was impatient with Benjamin and Liv for thinking the world would take care of them. And was he impatient with Nora? Why hadn't he gotten a plan for Nora's phone?

"But no one was hurt, everyone was cheerful," Liv said. "We could walk to this little beach, we had swimsuits. We were just improvising."

"But you're afraid of riptide," Benjamin said.

"It was this very protected beach. The kids were playing in the water, there was no current. They were on these inner tubes. And the older kids were there. But I guess the tide changed. And I fell asleep. Camila did, too. I thought she was watching."

Raymond held Nora away from him, to see her face. "And you?"

Nora had gotten the sobbing under control, but she stared at the ground. "I was looking for birds."

"For *birds*?"

"I'm so sorry." A gasp, a half sob. "I thought they were watching. Liv said she would."

"I wish you'd gone with us," Liv moaned.

"Don't do that," Benjamin said.

"I don't mean I blame you," she said. "I just wish."

"You said you didn't care."

"I know," Liv said. "But I didn't know what would happen."

"So, the guide didn't know the tide would change?" Raymond asked.

Both women shook their heads.

"Where the fuck is he?"

"The police were interviewing him earlier," Liv said. "We just have to find the kids. Sebastian needs his insulin."

"You said something on the phone about a grave," Raymond said.

"They dug up this guy," Nora said. "They think maybe the kids saw the grave, and that's why someone took them."

He stared at her. This was really happening. "So who's in the grave?"

"We don't know."

A short-haired woman in a police windbreaker, as tall as Raymond, approached them. "May I talk to you, sir?"

Nora looked terrified.

"It's okay," Raymond told her. He followed the detective, thinking that of course they wanted to talk to the black man first.

The two of them sat in a cruiser, and the butch detective questioned him about his day. She asked for any information, any theories he might have about what had happened to the kids. After a minute he realized she was looking to him for *help*. He felt the briefest sensation of lightness, a weight lifting off his shoulders. Even with his minor celebrity, even with three solid white alibi witnesses,

LAPD would've found his actions suspicious. Golfing while black, that would've been the first red flag.

What had happened seemed obvious to him: The kids had stumbled on someone getting rid of a body. "Have you figured out who's in the grave?" he asked the detective.

"We're working on it."

"Do you think the guide's involved?"

"I don't know yet," she said. "I don't think so."

She asked him some questions about Gunther, about how long he'd known the others. Then she thanked him and gave him a card in case he learned anything. Her name was Angela Rivera. They were finished. That was it.

He hated that he'd been worrying that he might be a suspect, when his kids might be dead. He hated that there was no way for him *not* to worry about being a suspect. He went back to look for his wife. She was standing beside Liv and Benjamin, still wrapped in the gray blanket.

Raymond felt a shift, now that he was out of the cruiser. He went from feeling like a suspect to feeling like a cop, a role he'd played a lot. The corrupt cop, the noble cop, the jaded cop who saw what his white colleagues had missed.

"We have to find out who the guy in the grave is," he said, after Benjamin followed the detective away.

"I saw the body," Liv said.

"What did he look like?"

"He'd been dead a while. Dark hair. Not that old."

"And why were you at the beach, again?"

The women stared bleakly at him. "It seemed like a good idea at the time," Liv said, in a small voice. Nora was shivering, probably from exhaustion.

"We should get you inside," he said.

"I'm not leaving until we find them."

"Well, we're not going to find them here. This is the one place they won't be. We need to call the embassy, and we need a place to stay."

The women looked drained, ready to let him make decisions, and Raymond saw himself from a distance, dissociated from his own performance. Taking charge. But this wasn't a role. The director wasn't about to turn the cameras around and shoot the scene from the other side. His kids were really missing. He got on the phone and started making calls.

11.

NOEMI SAT AT a scratched table, waiting for Chuy to bring her rice with chicken. The restaurant was big and no one paid them any attention. The table was a little bit sticky and people had carved their initials into it. RN + JP. She was hungry and excited for the food. She never went to restaurants with her grandmother.

A television in a high corner was playing a telenovela. A man changed the channel, and Noemi hoped he would change it to cartoons. But he turned it to news, then stood back to watch. Noemi wondered if her parents had a television. Probably they did, and she could see cartoons. But she was not going to think about things like that. The future. Nueva York.

A reporter with big, wavy hair was talking into a microphone on the television. Then there were some pictures of children. Some were older, but there was a girl with lots of braids who might be Noemi's age. The reporter said they were Americans, and they had disappeared. The little blond boy needed medicine. They all wore swimsuits.

A red-eyed woman with blond hair, the boy's mother, came on the screen, crying, begging for anyone who knew where their children were to call a number. Noemi wondered if her parents ever cried like that about her. But she wasn't missing. She was with Chuy. Her parents knew she was on her way to them.

Chuy came with a tray and set it on the table. They watched the high television together for a little while, and then Chuy turned back to his food and shook hot sauce over the top.

"Those kids are missing," Noemi said.

"I know."

"Will their parents find them?"

"No."

"Why not?"

He shook his head.

Noemi watched Chuy fork chicken into his mouth. She thought of Ario, shot in the street. The pool of blood. "Are they dead?"

He shrugged. "Maybe not."

Noemi watched the TV. "Do their parents know they won't come back?"

"Their parents are American," he said. "They don't know anything."

"I'm going to be an American," she said.

He smiled, and took a drink of beer. "It's okay. You know enough already."

"Do you know where they are? Those kids?"

"No," he said. "But I know the kind of people who took them."

"How do you know?"

"Eat your food."

She took the paper off her straw and tasted her watermelon agua fresca. It was cold and sweet and thick. "Maybe those people will let them go," she said. "Maybe they'll see the mothers crying on TV and feel bad."

"I'm telling you," he said, "those people don't feel bad about anything."

She looked back up at the television. There was a picture of the oldest girl jumping into a pool, her hair flying out behind her. It could have been a picture in a magazine, the girl was so pretty. Then her mother was talking about her children in strange-sounding Spanish. Noemi's parents had been gone for two years, and she wondered if they missed her like this woman did. There was a picture of a black man in a white astronaut suit, which was confusing. Did they think the children were in space?

"Do my parents know we're coming?" Noemi asked.

"They do," Chuy said.

"Are they excited?"

"Of course." He shook more hot sauce on his food.

"We have the same name on the papers," she said. "You and me."

He said nothing, just scooped up a forkful of arroz con pollo.

"Is that just for the papers?" she asked. "Or is it real?"

Chuy picked up a paper napkin that looked very small in his hands. He wiped his mouth. "It's real."

"How is it real?"

"Your father is my little brother. Half brother."

It was the answer she'd been looking for, but still it surprised her. "Why didn't I know about you?"

"No one wanted you to know," Chuy said. "Eat up. We have to go."

12.

THE POLICE AND Gunther's friend drove the parents to a local hotel that had Wi-Fi. As soon as her phone was no longer an infuriating paperweight, Liv googled "How long Type 1 diabetes survive without insulin?" She read the results with her breath held, gripped by cold fear. The answer was two weeks, but the second week you'd spend in a coma. Sebastian probably had a couple of days before he would get really sick. She left a message at the doctor's office in Los Angeles, trying not to sound too panicked. But she *was* panicked, obsessed with the thought of Sebastian without his pump. Sebastian seizing, dying, ketone bodies poisoning his blood. She lay in the hotel bed, wide awake, with the memory of her son's body curled into her side, his warm back, his sweet smooth skin. It was like having a phantom limb. A phantom child.

Penny would look after her brother, but she couldn't do it alone. And what was happening to Penny? She remembered reading about an Amber alert, the police finding the DNA of the little girl's tears in the abductor's car. She squeezed her eyes closed to try to make the thought go away.

In her twenties, Liv had not been sure she wanted children. How could you know? It was a decision made at the brink of a widening abyss, based on rumors from the other side. Do you cross over? Do you leap? She hadn't been sure.

At twenty-two, she'd moved to Los Angeles and got a job at a production company, answering phones and ordering lunch. She didn't even have a cubicle, just a desk in a hallway. But she worked, and got promoted, and decided she would be vice president of a studio before she had children. When she met Benjamin, he was designing props for a sci-fi movie. In their first years together, they'd never even had a houseplant depending on them. She bought a cactus that shriveled and died. Benjamin had once owned a dog in New York, a Labrador mutt, but gave it to a cousin when he moved. The dog seemed happy in the suburbs, but still: It told.

"To have a child is to open an account at the heartbreak bank," Liv had said, one night in bed.

"I hear there are some benefits, too," he'd said.

She got a studio job, and made movies, and read a stack of screenplays on the weekends. Then, one sunny Sunday morning, she and Benjamin went to a brunch at a house where other people's children were building a fort out of lawn furniture in the backyard. Someone told the children that Benjamin was an engineer, and he was called in as a consultant.

"I don't do buildings," he'd said. But he followed the children onto the lawn.

Liv watched from the shaded patio, drinking coffee from an unfamiliar mug. She had no opinion about whether the game was safe, and only mild curiosity about whether the towering fort would stand. But then a chair fell, and Benjamin scooped up a toddler in a yellow sundress to get her out of the chair's tumbling path. He placed the child on his hip and directed the placement of the chair in a more stable spot.

It had been a golden morning, and the children were lit by sun. Benjamin had saved the little girl without having to think, and now she sat contented in his arms, surveying the progress of the fort from her queenly height. Liv was overcome with a feeling like ravenous hunger, so rooted was it, deep in her abdomen. She set down her mug in surprise. The sticky sweet rolls, the scrambled eggs, the fat red strawberries, they did nothing to curb it. Later she would connect the moment with the fact that Nora had just told her she was six weeks pregnant.

Benjamin drove them home on Sunset Boulevard, dodging the Sunday drivers. Liv watched the trees go by, a sharp-focused, saturated green against the blue sky. She said, "I think we should have a baby."

"Now?" Benjamin said.

"As soon as possible."

"I thought you wanted to be a vice president first."

"I don't care about that anymore." She'd never been so sure about anything.

"Okay," Benjamin had said, still looking at the road, his knuckles gripping the steering wheel. "Okay."

She was twenty-eight and it was easy. She went off the Pill and got instantly pregnant. They married in Colorado on her parents' back lawn. Benjamin's parents came from New York and made awkward conversation with her aunts and uncles. Nora, her only bridesmaid, was already showing, with that radiance that turned out to be a cliché that was also true. Nora and Raymond stayed up with them after the reception, the husbands sober in solidarity. They found the little cake someone had saved to freeze for their first anniversary, but it was the middle of the night and they were starving and ate it with their hands.

She went to prenatal yoga with Nora. Marcus was born first, quiet and watchful, and then Penny arrived screaming, demanding of attention. Sebastian, three years later, was mercifully mellow and cheerful.

But when he was sixteen months old, Sebastian went limp. At first it just seemed like tiredness, a flu. Then it got bad enough that they called a doctor friend at midnight for advice. She said, "Get the baby to the hospital. Not that one, they'll kill him. Have them test for Kawasaki."

At the hospital, Sebastian didn't have any pain response to the needle sticks for his blood. Meg, their doctor friend, sat with them and never left their side.

Those were bad days, the hospital days, and the last ambivalence Liv had felt about Benjamin, all her self-protective distance, burned away. By the time Sebastian was diagnosed and stabilized, the two of them were bound together by terror and love and anticipatory grief. She'd been right about the heartbreak bank. They had a joint account.

The idea that Liv might have forgone these two particular children and taken her chances with some unknown later zygotes sometimes made her catch her breath in the middle of an ordinary task. If she and Benjamin hadn't gone to that brunch, if the chair hadn't fallen and he hadn't swept the toddler onto his hip, then they wouldn't have started trying when they did, and there would be no Penny. And probably no Sebastian. Certainly no Sebastian with Penny as an older sister, which was part of who he was, and who he would be. Rationally, Liv knew that there would have been other children she would have loved just as much, but it didn't bear thinking about. Even the hypothetical loss made her dizzy with horror.

But now—how much worse to lose them *now*.

She remembered talking to the news cameras in that clearing in the trees. Babbling, crying, begging. If she had seen these parents on TV, these parents who had lost their children on a cruise, she would have thought how irresponsible they were, how careless. No one deserved such a fate, of course, but she would have judged them, and found them wanting.

She knew that Nora must be suffering the tortures of the damned for wandering off looking for quetzals with the flirty guide, but all she could think was that Nora, her best friend, her almost-sister, *should* suffer.

Some part of her brain still believed this was all a mistake, one of those panicky moments when the kids wander away to the candy aisle, or hide as a joke, and your heart races and your armpits sweat. And you search, and call their names, and imagine the worst. And then there they are! Safe and sound, asking for Twizzlers, or giggling at having tricked you. And you want to shake them, but you have to keep your voice under control, calm and in command, telling them, "You *have* to stay near me. You cannot walk away."

But this was not a mistake or a moment in the grocery store. She had seen a decaying dead body. She kept seeing the children in their swimsuits, playing in the water, and she kept trying in her mind to wade in after them, to pull them back to shore. Benjamin put his arms around her in the lumpy hotel bed. She tolerated it for a few minutes and then felt claustrophobic, suffocated.

"Sorry," she said. "I'm so sorry." And she rolled away, wrapped in the cheap comforter and her pain.

13.

IN THE MORNING, there were clothes folded at the end of Penny's bed: a too-big white T-shirt and a pair of red shorts. And a second set of matching clothes for Sebastian, who was still asleep. Penny leaned close to his face to see if he smelled sugary, a thing she had seen her mother do. He smelled like river water and cheese, and his breathing was deep and regular.

In the clean, white-tiled bathroom, she peeled off her swimsuit. There were grooves around her legs and over her shoulders, from the elastic seams. She peed and put the T-shirt on. It was as long as a dress, and she pulled the red shorts on under it. It felt weird not to have on underwear, but she didn't want to put the swimsuit back on, and the shorts fit. She went out into the entryway.

The door to the outside was locked with a deadbolt, with the key taken out. Penny pulled on the knob a few times, but the door just thumped against the solid lock.

Then she went upstairs, and found a new man eating cereal at the breakfast table. He wore a white polo shirt, long khaki shorts, and a baseball cap that said *Cal.* He gave her a friendly smile.

"Trying to get out?" he asked.

Penny felt her face get hot. She sat down at the table. "My dad went to Berkeley," she said.

"No way!" he said. "When?"

"I don't know. He's forty-one."

"He was ahead of me, then," the man said. "I'm George."

"Do you live here?"

"Sometimes. Until my brother drives me batshit. Then I leave."

"Is your brother the one with the white horse?"

George pointed his finger at her like a gun. "Smart kid."

"You don't have an accent."

"We all have accents," George said. "You, too, sweetheart."

"I mean like your brother's," Penny said. "You sound American."

"Raúl doesn't want to talk like a gabacho. I find it useful. You want cereal? Or Maria can make you eggs."

"Cereal," Penny said.

George pushed an unfamiliar box toward her, and a bottle of milk. "So you got a little bit lost, I hear."

"The river took us away from our parents."

"Bad luck. Why'd you go to that beach?"

"The guide said it was nice. We were supposed to go zip-lining."

"Huh," he said. "Some guide."

"I miss my parents," she said. She picked up the cereal and studied the picture of the golden flakes. George's hand dropped down on the top of the box. He had clean fingernails.

"Wait," he said. "Are you allergic to nuts?"

"No."

"I thought all American kids were."

"You're stereotyping," she said. He let go of the box and she poured the flakes, watching them slide into the bowl just like they did at home.

"How old are you?" he asked.

"Eleven."

"What about the others?"

"My brother, Sebastian, is eight. Marcus is eleven, too. June is six. Isabel is fourteen."

"Oh, man." George rubbed his eyes with his fingers and thumb.

"We didn't see anything," Penny said. "We just saw the Jeep."

He nodded, his eyes red where he had rubbed them. "So much trouble could've been avoided."

The glass bottle was heavy when she picked it up. "It's real milk?"

"Straight from the cow."

She sniffed it. It seemed fine. And it was cold, so it couldn't be *straight* from the cow. "Why was there a grave?"

"*Stop* being curious," he said. "That's how you ended up here."

"It's good to be curious."

"Tell that to the cat."

"What cat?"

"Never mind."

"Oh!" she said. "I get it now."

He drank his coffee, watching her. He had dark brown eyes and they looked amused.

"What's a gabacho?" she asked.

George put his feet up on one of the kitchen chairs. "It's an old word from Spain, for the people who lived in southern France. It means something like 'diseased people of the north.' It's like gringo, but fancier."

"So I'm a gabacho?"

"You're a gabacha," he said. "My mother was one, too."

"I'm not diseased."

"Of course not."

"But my brother has diabetes," she said. "He needs insulin."

"Yeah, I'm working on that."

"Like, he needs it so he can have breakfast. I don't think that doctor understood that."

"She does understand."

"Why is she so nervous?"

"Because she's a drug addict."

"Oh." Penny tried to make sense of this news, tried to square it with her understanding of doctors and her experience of the thin woman who had grabbed her wrist when she reached for her phone. "And the white-haired man is your father."

"He is."

"He doesn't think we should be here."

"He didn't," George admitted. "But he doesn't know what to do, so he left me to deal with it. As usual."

"Are you going to take us back to our parents?"

"I'm working on it."

"We won't say anything about the grave."

"Hm," George said.

Penny ate her cereal, then went downstairs. Sebastian wasn't in their room so she went to the other. He was sitting on Marcus and June's twin bed, at their feet. They were still under the white duvet. Isabel was in the other bed, her long hair messy. They all looked disoriented and sleepy. Isabel looked Penny up and down in the new clothes, as if she'd let them all down by putting them on. There were folded clothes at the end of their beds, too.

"I want to go see Mom and Dad," Junie said.

"There's a new man upstairs," Penny said. "He says he's working on it."

"Who is he?" Marcus asked.

"The brother of the man with the horse. His name is George and he talks like an American. He went to Berkeley."

Sebastian brightened. "He knows Dad?"

"No," Penny said. "He's younger. I told him we wouldn't say anything about the grave, so we can't. Okay?"

Isabel flopped sideways on her pillow. "But everyone already *knows* about the grave!" she said. "So it doesn't *matter* what we promise!"

"They could still take us back to the ship," Penny said, uncertainly.

"Don't be stupid," Isabel said, into the pillow.

Penny was stung. "Do you guys want breakfast?"

June and Marcus put on their new clothes in the bathroom. The clothes were all exactly the same, as if someone had gone to a store and picked up a stack of the first thing they saw, in different sizes. June ran upstairs first.

"Wait!" Isabel said. "Don't leave me alone!" She wrapped the white duvet around her bikini and dragged it after her.

Penny would have expected Isabel to be braver, with her green nail polish and her two languages. This was just like a sleepover in a new house, where you had to figure out all the rules.

Her heart sank a little when she saw June sitting on George's knees at the breakfast table. June had been upstairs for like *two* minutes! And George was really Penny's discovery. But no one was ever going to take Penny on their lap on first meeting her. She wasn't adorable like June. She knew that feminism was freedom—she had the T-shirt—but still the sight of June and George being such pals made her unhappy.

"Nice toes," George was saying. "They have medicine for that, you know."

"It's nail polish!" June said, laughing.

"Junie, get *down*," Marcus said.

"Why?"

"Just *do*."

June didn't.

"There's cereal," George said. "Or you can wait for Maria to make eggs."

No one moved forward.

"I had cereal," Penny said, in the awkward silence. "Sebastian, you should have eggs."

George lifted June to one shoulder, and she sat sidesaddle, clutching his head and laughing. George went to a cupboard, took out more bowls, and slid them onto the table with his free hand. Then he lowered June back down to his lap.

Penny's father carried Sebastian sometimes, but no one ever carried Penny anymore. She had once pretended to fall asleep in the car so her father would have to take her in, but he had known she was faking and left her in the garage, to come in when she was ready.

"I won't pour you cereal until you get down," Marcus said to his sister.

"Fine," June said, and she slid off George's knee.

Sebastian said he would wait for eggs.

"If you'll excuse me, I have some things to figure out," George said, raising an eyebrow at Penny, and he went up to the third floor they hadn't been to yet.

She felt a little better then. George had singled her out as the leader. It was better to be a leader than a lap-sitter.

Maria, the housekeeper, appeared with shopping bags and a small white bunny, which she lowered carefully into Sebastian's arms. June ran to Sebastian's side and they huddled together, cooing about the bunny's softness. Maria put a hand on June's head and then went to unpack the groceries. Penny wanted to pet the rabbit, but she didn't want to seem like a little kid, so she just stood watching. June wanted to call the bunny Baby Rabbit. Sebastian said it wouldn't be a baby forever, and they should call it Thumper or Puffball.

Maria broke eggs into a bowl.

Isabel leaned forward across the table. "Listen to me!" she whispered to Penny. "We have to *escape*."

"George will help us," Penny said.

"He won't," Isabel said. "You don't understand."

They heard voices below and a sharp bark, then toenails clicking on the stairs. A black dog came bounding up into the room where they sat. He ran to the table and greeted each of them in turn, panting. June shrieked and stood on a chair to protect the bunny. Marcus rubbed the dog's black ears and said, "Hello, hello, hello, hello." The dog's whole butt wagged back and forth, ecstatic.

The man with the white horse—Raúl—came upstairs. "Ah, you are already friends," he said. "His name is Sancho. He is very stupid."

"Hi, Sancho," Marcus said. "Hi, Sancho." The dog rolled its eyes with happiness, tongue out. "I *love* him," Marcus said passionately.

"He loves you, too, I think," Raúl said.

"Will he eat the bunny?" June asked, still standing on the chair.

"Maybe," Raúl said. "Maybe no."

Isabel was acting weird. With the duvet around her shoulders like a robe, still in her bikini, she sat with cold composure and began to eat her cereal, as if Raúl and the dog didn't exist. She wasn't trembling or cowering anymore.

George came back down from the third floor, and the two brothers talked quietly together in Spanish. They didn't look much alike. Raúl wore cowboy boots, his buttoned shirt tucked into tight jeans, his black hair swept back. George, in his khaki shorts and baseball cap, could have been one of her parents' friends.

Penny tried to follow what they said, but they spoke too fast. The only thing she could say that fast in Spanish was a song that her friend Sasha's nanny had taught them. It went with a hand-clapping game:

> Una vieja-ja
> mató un gato-to
> con la punta-ta
> del zapato-to
>
> Pobre vieja-ja
> pobre gato-to
> pobre punta-ta
> del zapato-to

It didn't really make any sense. *An old lady killed a cat with the point of her shoe. Poor old lady, poor cat, poor point of the shoe.* The cat was the one who was killed, so why feel sorry for the point of the old lady's shoe?

The conversation between the brothers had become an argument. Raúl smacked the wall with his open palm. Then he went downstairs, his boot heels striking hard. He shouted to the dog, who chased after him. The lock scraped and he went out. The lock scraped again.

"Fuck me," George said, leaning his head against the wall.

"He said the F-word," June whispered.

George went back up to the third floor.

Things got quiet again, with Raúl gone. The wind picked up outside the big windows, whipping the treetops. The living room had a high ceiling, and sometimes a big gust would shake the windows. The children all looked at the ceiling and waited.

The morning passed, and Penny taught June the clapping game and the song. Maria smiled at Penny and said, "No parece gringa." Then she taught them another clapping song, but it was more babyish: "Tortillitas para Mama, Tortillitas para Papa."

June dropped her hands to her lap. "I want my mom and dad."

Later, Maria brought them grass and carrot tops and sweet peas for the bunny, and more fruit and cheese. Marcus said the cubes of mango were like the Turkish delight the White Queen gives Edmund in Narnia: a trick to win them over. But Penny thought Maria really felt sorry for them, stuck here like this.

They played tic-tac-toe with the wooden pieces until that got boring. Marcus fixed June's braids that were coming undone. Penny offered to help.

"I can do it," Marcus said. He frowned with concentration over the tiny, wavy strands.

The TV in the kitchen had been turned off ever since they saw their parents on the news. Penny wished she'd brought a book. There weren't any in this whole house.

Sebastian whispered into the bunny's white fur.

"What are you saying?" she asked.

"I'm talking to the bunny," her brother said.

"About what?"

"None of your business."

In the afternoon, the drug-addict doctor returned. George let her in downstairs, and she sat on one of the red couches with Penny and

Sebastian, her bony knees sticking out from her skirt. She gave Penny a small box to open. The writing on the box was in Spanish, and inside was something that looked like a fat pen. The doctor showed them how to use it. It was electronic and had a cartridge of insulin inside, instead of ink.

There was also a little solar calculator, and the doctor showed Penny how to do the math based on Sebastian's blood sugar, his weight, and how many carbs he was eating.

"A piece of bread or fruit is fifteen grams," she said. "A glass of juice is thirty. A cup of rice is forty-five."

"This is too hard," Penny said.

"You need to learn," the doctor said.

Penny watched, miserable, as she gave Sebastian the finger-stick test. Then together they did the math on the calculator, and the doctor showed her how to use the pen to give Sebastian the injection. She'd brought another little box with extra insulin cartridges, in a paper bag.

Penny tried to concentrate on the math, so she could remember how to do it, but she felt scared and overwhelmed. "I don't know if we can do this," she said.

"I think you can," the doctor said.

Sebastian put the finger-stick monitor and the insulin pen in the pocket of his red shorts. "You keep the calculator," he said. "I don't know how to do the math."

"I don't either!" Penny grabbed the doctor's skinny hand. "You *have* to call our parents. I can give you their number."

The doctor looked embarrassed and shook her head.

"You're supposed to help people," Penny said. "You took an *oath*."

"I am sorry. It is a bad situation."

"Because you're a drug addict?"

The woman stared at her with hopeless eyes, then pulled her hand free.

"Are you even a real doctor?" Penny asked.

"I have to go." The woman gathered her bag.

"How can you say it's a bad situation? We're kids!"

The woman backed away. It was the stupidest thing Penny had ever heard. Her parents probably thought Sebastian was dead, and would be seriously freaking out by now. She slumped back into the couch. George let the doctor out and locked the door again.

14.

IN THE MORNING, at the terrible hotel, Nora got a text message asking her to pick up her family's passports at the port. Liv had the same message. The ship had sailed away on schedule, dumping their stuff unceremoniously onshore. Other people had a cruise to take. Nora was filled with rage at those people, eating their mediocre buffet food, playing the poker machines in the noisy casino, swimming in the pool. How could they just go on with their cruise when Marcus and June were missing? She craved her children, wanted to feel their bodies against her.

She found herself wanting a cigarette, a thing she hadn't had in years. She used to keep a pack in the freezer, when she was living alone and teaching, so she could smoke one on her apartment balcony when she'd had a hard day.

She'd listened to Raymond on the phone with the detective, asking about the best use of their time. Together they decided that the men would go to the capital to meet with someone at the embassy, and the women would go to the ship's agent. Because someone from each family had to go collect the passports. They would meet up in the capital, where there were more police resources.

The press was camped outside the little hotel, and the three couples walked out together into a barrage of news cameras, a chorus of people calling them by their names and asking for comment. One man got very close, and Gunther shouted at him in Spanish. Raymond was more practiced at evasion—he shielded her and steered her to a cab, asking the reporters please to give them some privacy. Nora was embarrassed at how she'd spilled her guts to those people last night. She'd been horrified by the sight of herself on the TV in the hotel room, and had to turn it off.

Then she found herself in the back seat of a moving taxi, sitting between Liv and Camila, trying to behave like a rational human being. A small part of her mind observed that she was probably in shock.

She imagined Perla, the stewardess, packing up their cabin, gathering the dirty laundry from the floor of the closet. She wondered if anyone had told Perla what had happened, why her passengers had never come back. Her kids might be far away in Manila, but at least she knew where they were.

Liv looked drawn and sleepless in the taxi, silent in her misery. Nora had such complicated feelings about her cousin now. She had not forgiven her for failing to watch the children when she'd said she would. But she was grateful to her for not saying anything to Raymond about her flirtation with the guide. Nora had told Liv nothing had happened, and she was ashamed of the lie, and ashamed of her gratitude to Liv for keeping a false secret, to protect her from being misunderstood. When the misunderstanding, of course, would be the truth.

Camila sat on Nora's right, a woman she was bound to only by tragedy.

"I am a piece of dirt, to Isabel, right now," Camila said to the cab window. "She treats me like you would not believe. It is just—she is fourteen, I know. Girls need to separate from their mother. But it is so painful, when this child who has depended on you wants *nothing* to do with you. She thinks you know nothing. You are in her way. So you tell yourself it is a necessary stage, it will pass. And it will pass." Her voice started to break. "Unless you never see her again. And then what you will remember is this time when she is awful. Simply awful. And you are sometimes awful back, because it is very hard not to respond. To be the adult. And that is the memory I will have, for the rest of my life. This is what I fear."

Nora closed her eyes and wished Camila wouldn't talk this way, as if the children might actually be *gone*. She thought of Marcus, her beautiful boy, nearly as tall as she was but just a child, not equipped to be on his own. He would be so anxious about taking care of June. They had spent one night alone now. Her hands started to shake and she held them tightly in her lap.

"And Hector," Camila went on. "My son. If I don't have my son, I do not know what I will do."

The taxi stopped at the address they'd been given, but they couldn't find the ship's agent at first. The driver peered at the address on Liv's phone screen. They tried two different buildings and walked a confusing hallway, and finally found the agent's glass-walled office.

The agent was a small, round man with wire-rimmed glasses and a blue suit that seemed too heavy for this weather. He acted as if nothing drastic had happened. He gave them each a form, to confirm that they'd received their passports and had left the ship voluntarily. When really the ship had jettisoned them. Nora signed her name to her own abandonment.

"There are many nice things to do in my country," the agent said.

"Yeah, like a zip-line tour," Liv said.

"Exactly!" the agent said. "Have you done this?"

Liv stared at him. "No."

"It's very good!" he said.

"You know our kids are missing?" she said. "From the zip-line tour."

Nora wished Liv wouldn't do this. Argue, bait people, be her sardonic self.

The man grew instantly solemn. "Of course. I am so sorry. I am sure they will appear."

"So we don't need tourism suggestions," Liv said. "Thank you."

The agent shrugged as if to say it really was a very nice country, but it was up to her.

"And by the way, we were with *your* guide," Liv said. "Who came recommended by the ship."

Nora felt dizzy, little spots appearing in her vision. "Let's just go," she said.

But Liv was warming up, getting ideas. "Are you the one who hires the guides for the shore excursions?"

The agent looked nervous. "I am."

"So you hired Pedro?"

"There are many Pedros."

"But this particular Pedro," she said. "Who took us halfway to the zip-line tour."

"I would have to check my records," he said.

"You do that," Liv said. "Because I think we might have a serious case of negligence on our hands."

"Liv, please," Nora said.

"There is a liability waiver," the agent said.

"Those aren't binding."

"I believe they are, señora."

"I want a copy."

"Of course, señora," the agent said, with a practiced, subservient bow, and he turned to a metal file cabinet and started rummaging through it.

"Can't you just print one out?" Liv asked.

"I will find it," he said, raising one hand.

"Please let's go," Nora said.

"Ah, here it is!" He flourished a piece of paper in the air. Nora recognized the waiver she had signed like so many in her life, acknowledging the inherent risks, skimming because you would never do anything if you read those things too carefully. Liv snatched it out of his hand.

They set off for the capital in the waiting cab, and Liv took the middle seat this time and read the waiver in silence.

Nora sat as close to the window and as far from her cousin as possible. She pressed her fingers to her temples, which just made the spotty vision worse. If there was a lawsuit, everything would come out. Pedro would have to testify. "I don't want a lawsuit," she said. "I just want my kids back. And it wasn't Pedro's fault."

"This thing isn't binding," Liv said. "Not if he was criminally negligent."

"That's not what matters now," Nora said.

"People have to be held responsible."

"We are not so litigious in my country," Camila said.

Nora waited for the choice things Liv would say about Argentina and its history of wrongs without redress, but instead her cousin pressed her lips together. Nora guessed she was trying to fight her own nature, to maintain peace.

"When we've found the kids, we'll revisit this question," Liv said. "And then we'll go after that fucking cruise line and make them pay."

15.

AFTER GETTING THE women into a taxi, past the clamoring reporters, Benjamin climbed with Raymond and Gunther into a black Suburban sent by the embassy to take them to the capital. He stared out the tinted window at the spreading canopy of trees, the fantastical lushness behind which his children were concealed somewhere. He had been awake all night, searching social media for any hint that someone knew something, hitting SEE TRANSLATION on any post that looked likely. He wished he knew more Spanish.

His mother had been worried, his whole childhood, about things going wrong. Pillows could suffocate you, acid rain was falling from the sky, going barefoot gave you pneumonia. She wouldn't go to the doctor because she might find out that something was wrong. She'd inherited fear from her own parents the way other people got piano lessons.

His father, on the other hand, was constitutionally unafraid, and could never take Benjamin's problems seriously. He was bullied at school? Ignore it. He was mugged on the way home? So he lost a couple of bucks, those kids who'd taken it must need it more. The scale was permanently zeroed out, for his father. Even as the Internet grew rabid with anti-Semitism, his father had the unanswerable test case: Are you escaping Nazis on foot, as Benjamin's grandfather had done at nine, hiding in a wagon with his brother? Are you living in a hole in the ground in Silesia? No? Then enjoy your phenomenal luck.

Benjamin had never really understood how his mother and father got along, but he guessed that they tempered each other, in both senses of the word. The baffling example of the other person hardened each of them in their convictions, but together they reached some kind of livable compromise.

Now he had a problem that even his father would recognize as a problem, and he had come to a new understanding of the paternal disaster scale of his childhood. If he tried to remember frustrations at work, or disagreements with Liv that had once absorbed his attention, he could not even fathom them. All minor regrets had been burned away. Those were the pain of touching a hot pan, this was a blowtorch.

His parents were in Cuba until after New Year's, and he hoped his life might be set right before his mother got back to the news. He wanted to protect her from the knowledge that the sky had actually fallen, this time. The thought of telling her put him in a cold sweat.

When they got to the capital, they stopped at the Argentinian embassy, which was a small office, closed for the Christmas week, but someone was coming in. The heat when they let Gunther out of the Suburban was intense. Then Benjamin and Raymond were sealed back in for the drive to their own embassy.

There was constraint between them now. Raymond had apologized for wanting to play golf, and Benjamin had told him that of course he didn't need to be sorry. Benjamin had wanted to go, too.

But in truth, he had agreed to let his family go off alone in a strange country because he would've felt unmanly turning down the golf. He hadn't wanted to say to Raymond, "No, I'll go on the zip-line tour with the ladies, and be strapped into a diaper harness and flung from tree to tree. You men go off in the luxury vehicle to the exclusive sporting club." He hadn't even been conscious of the implication, in the moment. He never thought, in his daily life, about being masculine or manly. But now he understood that on some primitive, atavistic level, he had gone to play golf to be a man among men, which in itself was ridiculous.

He kept returning to the idea that Liv would *never* have let him take the children by himself on an excursion in a foreign country. She didn't have his mother's fear, but she did think he was too spacey, he didn't pay enough attention, he lived too much in his mind. He would never have guessed that the kids would disappear on her watch.

"I wish you'd been here," she'd said in that clearing, wrapped in a blanket. She thought they'd still have their kids if he had gone along. And it was probably true. It was just a matter of numbers. If there'd been more eyeballs on them, they couldn't have drifted away.

Instead, he'd been out whacking that infuriating little white ball across the vast green lawn in the sunshine. And he'd enjoyed it. He'd taken an anthropological interest in Gunther's friend, who had the self-effacing manner of the British upper class in the aftermath of empire. A vague sadness about diminished expectations, although he'd made a fortune in ecotourism.

The conversation took a different tone in the absence of the women. Gunther didn't show off like he had at dinner on the ship; he'd stopped acting the South American swell. He seemed much more relaxed without any women around to charm. And Benjamin had enjoyed watching Raymond's absorption in the game. Usually Raymond had an actor's awareness of people looking at him. On the golf course, he furrowed his brow at the ball at his feet, oblivious to any eyes on him.

Benjamin had been absorbed, too, if less skilled. He'd thought about the arc of the ball's flight, and the obsessive quality of the desire to hit it correctly, with the correct tool. The different sounds it made: the resounding *thwock*, or the light tap. He had barely given a thought to Liv and the children until Nora's desperate call came in.

The truly manly move, of course, would have been to protect his family, guard his tribe, ensure his reproductive success. And now the bearer of his name, his treasure, the child who had, with total faith, watched Benjamin inexpertly tie his necktie for Christmas dinner, was out there in diabetic ketoacidosis, beginning to die. If he wasn't already dead.

The feeling of rage and impotence that welled up at this thought was overwhelming, and Benjamin tried to tamp it down. They rolled past enormous trees along the parkway, with huge spreading roots. It was true that Raymond's enthusiasm had given the golfing idea momentum. It was insane to hold that against him, but Benjamin secretly did.

"How long can Sebastian go without insulin?" Raymond asked.

"Two weeks max," Benjamin said, looking out the window. "But he'll be really sick after a couple of days."

It made him nauseated just to say it. His mouth felt dry. Even on the insulin pump, Sebastian had swings in the night. Benjamin would hear the alarm and walk down the hall half-asleep, do a test, adjust the pump, wait until the levels evened out. Sebastian could be having a seizure right now, with no one to help him. They'd taught Penny the basics, but all that meant was that she knew how to ask for help, in English and Spanish. And in French, for good measure. At home she had a brother "with diabetes" but in other languages they had cleared her to use the adjective. She knew to give him sugar in an emergency if she didn't know if he was high or low, and she knew how to use the pump, which was now useless in Liv's bag. Without insulin, Sebastian would eventually start to seize; he would go into a coma. Benjamin saw his son's small blond head lolling, hair flopping, the limp body getting dumped on a roadside. He tasted bile in the back of his throat.

They arrived at a brutalist concrete building, behind solid walls and black-barred gates. The small, high windows had slanting sills. The driver spoke to someone in a guard station and told them where to check in. The heat outside the air-conditioned car was oppressive. As Benjamin and Raymond walked toward the building, a young woman approached them, holding a little boy by the hand. She had dyed red hair with dark roots. The kid had a runny nose.

"Excuse me," she said, in accented English. "I have seen you on television."

Raymond gave her the vague smile he gave to crazy fans.

"My name is Consuelo Bolaños," the woman said. "My husband was in this grave. The one your children found."

"Oh," Raymond said, shifting gears. "I'm so sorry."

"I made an appointment," she said. "I was hoping to reach you."

"Walk inside with us," Benjamin said. "It's too hot out here."

Consuelo Bolaños glanced around, as if she expected security to throw her out. She pulled the kid beside her. He stuck a finger into his nose and then in his mouth.

"My husband disappeared, since three weeks," she said. "I could not find him. Everything seemed impossible."

Benjamin realized that in his mind, the tragic accident of the grave had been that his children had stumbled onto it. Not that a husband and father had been murdered. That had not been his concern. But here was Consuelo Bolaños, bereft and angry. He tried to imagine how it would feel to have your loved one pulled from the ground, wrapped in a tarp. His intestines seemed to liquefy and his head went light. He wasn't sure he could carry on this conversation.

"Why do you think he was killed?" Raymond asked.

"Drugs," Consuelo said. "Some fight."

"He sells drugs?" Raymond asked.

"He carries," she said. "Mostly."

"So who does he work for?"

"Different people. He is Colombian."

"Do you know the people's names?"

She shook her head.

"Had he received any threats?" Raymond asked. "Were there people who might've held grudges against him?"

Consuelo Bolaños made a defeated gesture that suggested that many people held a grudge against her husband. Benjamin was impressed that Raymond was able to formulate questions. He could barely think straight. They were inside the building now, in a lobby, where the air was cool, and they stopped.

"Have you spoken to Detective Rivera?" Raymond asked. "The woman?"

Consuelo glanced around the lobby and shook her head. "There was another detective, before," she said. "A man. He did nothing. The police are only looking now because they want your children. Because you are Americans."

"You should talk to Detective Rivera," Raymond said. "Tell her your story."

Consuelo seemed defeated by the idea of talking to the police. She nodded.

A lean young man in a lightweight linen suit came through a turnstile and strode across the lobby. "Kenji Kirby," he said, reaching out a hand to shake. "We spoke on the phone. I'm so sorry for what you've been through."

"This is Consuelo Bolaños," Benjamin said.

"Of course," Kenji said. Deeper sorrow took over his face, and he said a few swift words to her in beautiful Spanish. Benjamin was distracted from his confusion and pain by the young man's preternatural smoothness. Kenji had light brown hair, an epicanthic fold, and a delicately pointed chin.

Consuelo was speaking urgently back to him. Kenji reached into his jacket and produced a card for her, presenting it as a gift. She took it with an air of defeat.

"I assure you, we are doing everything we can," the young diplomat told her, and Benjamin understood that he had switched to English to include him and Raymond. Then Kenji steered them away, leaving Consuelo and her runny-nosed child near the door, without seeming to actually abandon them. It was a neat trick.

"She might have useful information," Raymond said, as they passed through the turnstile.

"I promise you we know everything she knows," Kenji said. His formality fell away as they drew out of earshot, and now he was pragmatic and confiding.

"Then why hasn't she talked to Detective Rivera?" Raymond asked.

"She *has* talked to Rivera. She's talked to everyone. Did she tell you she hadn't?"

"Why didn't you tell us about her?"

"I was going to, when we met." They were in an elevator lobby now.

"Is it true that no one was looking for her husband?" Benjamin asked.

Kenji hesitated, but it seemed to be for effect, and not because he was at a real loss for words. "It's true that the police look harder for a bunch of American children than for one drug mule," he said. "Yes. He's also not her husband, not legally. He has a real widow in Colombia."

"But they wouldn't have found the grave if not for our kids," Benjamin said.

"Maybe not," Kenji said. "But he'd just been buried, so who knows?"

Benjamin looked over his shoulder and saw Consuelo and her child still standing on the far side of the lobby, looking small and hopeless.

"Are you looking for his associates?" Raymond asked.

"Of course. We're doing everything we can think of." The elevator door opened, and Kenji held out an arm to usher them in.

MARCUS WOKE ALONE on the second morning in the house. At first he couldn't remember where he was. Morning light came through the windows. Then he remembered: the Jeep, the horse, the mango, the bunny. He climbed out of the bed he'd shared with his sister and pulled the covers straight. His mom said it was important to make your bed in the morning, because it made you feel better and more organized for the rest of the day. It was one of their strategies, to make him feel more in control. She would be able to think of some others for being in this house, if she were here. But if his mother were here, she would just take him away.

He knew that his parents were looking for him. Their most important job was to keep him and June safe, they always said that.

Now it was Marcus's job to keep June safe. And Isabel, too, because her brother wasn't here. She'd left the sheets on her bed in a tangled mess, so Marcus pulled them tight and straightened the duvet, which had dusty streaks from her dragging it through the house. He lifted the pillow to see if it smelled like her hair, but he couldn't tell. He fluffed it and put it back.

He had only known Isabel for a few days, but that didn't matter. He was eleven and she was fourteen, but that didn't matter either. When you were grown up, age difference was less important. When he was thirty and Isabel thirty-three, it wouldn't matter at all.

There had been a picture on the television of Isabel in her yellow bikini, jumping into the pool, with her arms thrown back and her hair streaming. It gave Marcus a tingling, aching feeling. He had once thought he was in love with Hannelore, a girl in his music class, but that was nothing like this. He knew that Isabel thought of him as a child and paired him with Penny, like the grown-ups did. But Penny always had to be right, and win games, and tell everyone what to do.

In the entryway, he studied the deadbolt lock on the door that led outside. If they could just get out of this place, then he could get them back to the port. He knew what directions they had come. But the ship would have moved on to Panama by now. So maybe he could get to a police station, walk to the main road and flag down a car. Although flagging down the Jeep hadn't worked so well.

And none of them had shoes. The main road was too long a walk without shoes.

He had just headed upstairs to find his sister when he heard someone come out of the other bedroom. Maria the housekeeper stood in the doorway with a cloth in her hand.

"Buenos días," she said.

"Hi."

"You okay?" she asked.

He nodded.

She peered past him, up the stairs. Then she leaned forward. "The girls okay?"

"I think so." He hadn't seen them yet this morning.

"Tell them have careful here," she whispered.

"Okay."

Maria looked at him unhappily. "Careful of Raúl," she said. "You understand?"

"Can't you just call our parents?"

She shook her head.

"Then can you open that door?"

But Maria was looking at something above him. Marcus turned to see Raúl standing at the top of the stairs.

"What are you doing?" Raúl called.

"Nothing," Marcus said.

Raúl came downstairs, boots thudding on each step, his body filling the stairwell. Marcus withdrew and crouched.

"You're talking to Maria?" Raúl said.

"Yes."

"About what?"

"Just saying good morning."

Raúl looked suspicious. "Go upstairs."

"Why?"

"They are playing with Sancho."

But the dog must have heard his name, because he came running down the stairs to his master's side, panting and smiling. He sat proudly at Raúl's feet.

"Ayii, tonto," Raúl said, rubbing the dog's head. "Okay, you come."

He unlocked the door with the key from his pocket, went outside with the dog, and locked the door again from the outside.

Marcus watched the deadbolt slide shut. "Where's he going?" he asked.

Maria shook her head.

Marcus ran up the stairs, noting June on the couch with the bunny, and found a window on the side of the house where the door was. He could see the security gate below. There was a police car parked outside the gate, and two uniformed policemen stood waiting. Marcus's heart leaped. The policemen would ask to come in and search the house. Maybe they would even force their way past Raúl.

But then Raúl came into view, walking down the driveway, all swagger, the dog prancing at his side. He reached the gate and leaned against it, and the three men talked for a while. The policemen weren't yelling. It looked like a friendly conversation. Raúl handed something to the policemen, through the gate. They both tucked whatever it was away, and talked a little longer, and shook Raúl's hand. Then they turned to go.

"No!" Marcus cried. He pounded his fists on the window.

The policemen glanced up at the house. So did Raúl.

Marcus couldn't tell if they could see him, but he kept pounding. "We're here!" he shouted, and he waved his arms.

The policemen turned and walked toward their car.

Marcus felt an arm come around his middle and pull him away from the window. "Cut it out," George said.

"You can't keep us here!" Marcus shouted, thrashing. "You can't, you can't, you can't!"

"Stop it," George said. He spun him around and held his shoulders hard. "Listen to me."

"Why did the policemen go away?" Marcus screamed, still struggling. "Why didn't they come inside?"

"Because we can't let them," George said.

"Because Raúl gave them money," Isabel said.

Marcus hadn't noticed Isabel, he'd been so focused on the scene outside. She stood by the window, in the white T-shirt and red shorts, her arms hanging at her sides and her hair stringy and long. She looked like a messenger of doom, like a girl in a horror movie poster that Marcus would have to look away from because it was too scary. But she was still so beautiful.

"I'm going to get you out of here, I promise," George said. "You just have to trust me and stay out of Raúl's way, okay?"

"I *don't* trust you!" Marcus said.

"I don't either," Isabel said. "Raúl's your brother."

"Just give me a little more time," George said. "Try to stay out of his way. And stay together, okay?"

They heard the door open downstairs, and George let Marcus go and stepped away from him. They heard Sancho's toenails clicking on the wood, then Raúl's booted heels climbing the stairs. He came into the room and held his arms out wide, grinning.

"Who wants to see Sancho do tricks?" he cried.

17.

LIV WAS HOARSE from pleading and crying, and her digestion was shot. Every time she ate something, it went right through her. Her body was on strike; it didn't want to keep functioning. But she needed it to, if she was going to get her children back. She had tried meditating, in desperation. If she could just clear her mind, focus on her breathing, even for five minutes, she might feel less crazy. But it turned out there were limits to meditation, or else she was just doing it wrong. When she closed her eyes and tried to think of nothing but breathing, she saw Sebastian in a coma, or Penny in her swimsuit with a man's hand around her arm.

She had thought it impossible that six kids could just disappear in a modern country, in the alleged Switzerland of Latin America. But now that she had seen the capital, with its heat and dust, the gaping holes in the streets and sidewalks, she had started to believe it could be true. A relentless, hot wind blew grit up from the streets. The press had found them in their new hotel in the capital and bayed at them when they left for the embassy in the morning.

There wasn't even a U.S. ambassador, and hadn't been one for over a year, because the Senate wouldn't approve the president's nominee. Liv hadn't known there was a backlog of nominees. Kenji Kirby, the young diplomat Benjamin and Raymond had met the day before, assured her he was there for them, for anything they needed. They were the first priority for the embassy.

Kenji also explained that there was still a kind of feudalism here. There were criminal families that controlled the activity in their own regions or neighborhoods. One of those families had probably killed the Colombian drug mule the police had found in the grave, and so knew something about the children.

"So we just need to know who Bolaños worked for," Liv said.

"Those guys don't keep records," Kenji said.

"But presumably it's whatever family controls that region," Benjamin said. "Where the kids disappeared."

Kenji said there were multiple possibilities not far from the site. "We've mobilized a team," he said. "We're short-staffed at Christmas, but I assure you we're working on it."

Liv leaned forward, over the desk. "I'm sorry about people's vacations," she said. "But this is the third day they've been missing. Every minute, something terrible might be happening to my children. Do you understand that? You understand how I can't think about anything else?"

"I do," he said.

"What about asking in the local towns? People must know something."

Kenji shook his head, regret on his face. He was so young. She pictured him out in the clubs at night, dancing and sweating, kissing—boys? Probably boys. "It's very hard to get people to talk," he said.

"About *children*?" she said. "There must be someone with a conscience who would talk to the police. A woman. A mother."

"Many of the police take bribes," Kenji said.

"So bribe them better!"

Benjamin said, "Liv. He's been very helpful."

She whirled on her husband. "*Don't* be the peacemaker. *Don't* act like I'm the crazy one."

"I'm not," he said, holding his hands up.

"I just don't understand," she said to Kenji. "I don't understand what your job is, if it isn't helping us. I want to talk to this team you've mobilized."

"They're in the field," he said.

"*What* field? Where? Let us talk to them! Is it just the lesbian detective? Is *she* the team?"

Kenji raised his eyebrows in reproach.

"We need to offer a reward," she said. "For information."

"You can do that," he said. "But you'll get flooded with tips."

"Good!" she said. "I *want* to be flooded with tips! Why hasn't there been a demand for ransom? Doesn't that happen all the time down here? Isn't it just ransom city here?"

"This is a different kind of kidnapping."

"How do you *know* that?"

He pressed his lips together. "I'm not supposed to tell you this, but the police do have leads. And a flood of tips can drown out useful information."

Her heart stopped, then started again. "What leads?"

"I can't jeopardize the investigation."

"Just tell me if the leads say they're okay," Liv said. "Just tell me that, please."

Kenji nodded imperceptibly.

"Oh my God," she said. "Tell me what the leads are!"

"I'm sorry, I can't."

"*Why* are we not in the loop on this? What the fuck? *Why* do you know when we don't?"

She felt the collected, competent person she had always been starting to dissolve. Why was she swearing at Kenji? The observing part of her brain wondered if this was a psychotic break. But if the observing part still functioned, *could* it be a psychotic break? She thought she might just collapse in his office, like those toy figures that buckled when you pressed the button at the base.

"Honey," Benjamin said. "Let's go."

"Don't fucking touch me!" He was still trying to play the reasonable, calm man, and she hated him for it.

"I'm sorry," Benjamin said to Kenji.

"Don't apologize to him! He is not our friend!"

"Liv. This isn't helping."

"Nothing is helping! No one is helping!"

"I know," he said. "I know."

Benjamin steered her out of the office as she started to hyperventilate. She caught Kenji's concerned gaze as Benjamin closed the door. His concerned, sad, compassionate face. She wanted to tear it off.

"Fuck fuck fuck fuck fuck fuck fuck fuck," she whispered, when she could breathe.

Benjamin put his arms around her. "We'll find them," he said. "I *promise* you, we'll find them."

18.

BENJAMIN LAY IN bed, unable to sleep, watching the video feed from the security cameras at their house in Los Angeles. The light from his phone gave the rumpled hotel blankets a cool digital glow. The cameras had been installed right before they left on the cruise. Their old security system had been a glass break alarm with a loud robotic voice, and it had started to malfunction, going off when no glass had broken, scaring the shit out of him in the middle of the night. He would leap out of bed and stumble downstairs in his underwear, his heart racing. After it happened twice, he bought a wooden baseball bat and kept it under his side of the bed.

"Are you really going to club someone with that?" Liv had asked.

"I just want to have something," he said. "I hate being empty-handed."

"Maybe we should get rid of the alarm."

Liv had grown up in a small Colorado town with unlocked doors. When the alarm went off, she rolled over and went back to sleep. Benjamin had grown up in Manhattan in the last days of getting mugged for your pocket money on the way home from school. It made your brain different. The next time the alarm went off he'd prowled the house with the bat and stayed awake until morning. Then he'd ordered a new alarm system with cameras.

The feed went straight to a server, so he could see their quiet house in real time from six angles on his phone. Nothing was happening. The street and the backyard and the covered pool were empty and quiet. His heart rate jumped once, when a skunk scurried past the lemon tree by the front door. And meanwhile his kids were missing, on the least adventurous vacation possible, in a supposedly safe country. He was convinced, now, that if he'd been the one at the beach, their kids would still be here. Liv's nervous system was not trained for real fear.

They'd tried having sex, which might have been reassuring, but it had gone horribly wrong. Liv had ended up crying, and Benjamin had felt guilty and weird. Now she'd taken an Ambien, and was comatose next to him. One of them needed to stay clearheaded, in case some news came in the night. But at 2:00 A.M. it was tempting to take something. He refreshed the video feed on his phone. The back door in Los Angeles, the empty street, the lemon tree, no skunk. He thought about jerking off.

"That light," Liv muttered. "It's so bright."

So she wasn't comatose. He turned off the screen and put the phone on his chest.

The clock radio on the bedside table glowed red—2:27—and a faint line seeped under the door from the hotel hallway. They were past the first forty-eight hours now, in which crimes were usually solved. They were almost at sixty-four hours. He had been obsessively googling kidnapping statistics and knew the chances were grim.

Liv's breathing was regular again, and Benjamin picked up his phone. He had heard the guide's full name on that first night, but he couldn't remember it now. He searched online, starting with the cruise line website, and then with the zip-line company. Pedro wasn't there, but Benjamin followed a link to another ecotourism website. There he found a photo of a grinning asshole in sunglasses, giving a double thumbs-up. Pedro Navares.

Next he searched Facebook and Twitter, and there were lots of accounts with that name, but none of the profile photos seemed to be the right one. He searched Instagram, and one unlocked account looked promising, the bio in Spanish, the tiny photo possibly of Pedro. The posts were of sunsets, beaches, pints of beer. A young man enjoying his life; nothing incriminating. But what had Benjamin expected to find? Photos of the children? Pedro didn't have the children. He was just the closest person to blame.

Benjamin had asked his wife about Nora wandering off with Pedro. She said they'd been looking for birds. Nora had told her so, and she believed it. But Liv seemed mildly evasive, and then changed the subject.

Finally he fell asleep, and had a dream. He was standing with his arms around Liv at a party, looking at Nora standing behind her. Nora was facing away from him, and her hair was put up in some complicated way, with twists at the nape of her neck. He realized that his mind must be creating each of those strands of hair, because he was in a dream. He was creating every person at the party. He took Liv by the hand and said, "Let's go find the kids." They left the house and went outside. They needed to get in a car and go, but there were no cars in the driveway. He knew he should be able to create a car in the driveway with his mind, because this was a dream, but no car appeared.

There was a knock at the door. Benjamin leaped out of bed. He experienced a stab of regret: He could have just *flown*, in the dream, to the children. But now he was awake, and the children were gone. He felt crushed. It was as if they'd been taken away all over again. Liv, beneath the covers, murmured a protest. The clock radio said 5:01. Benjamin went to the door and answered it in his T-shirt and boxers.

The tall detective was standing outside in the hall with a male cop a foot shorter than she was. Benjamin was afraid of what they were going to say.

"I'm Detective Rivera," she said. "We met before. This is Officer Arnal. Will you please come answer some more questions?"

"Did you find anything?" he asked.

"If you come with us, we can talk about it."

"Do you want my wife to come?"

"Just you," Arnal said. His tone was mildly threatening. Benjamin thought he must hate being the little guy with the towering female partner.

"Wait—are you arresting me?"

"No," Detective Rivera said.

"What if I don't want to go?"

"You want to find your children?" Arnal said.

"Shit," Benjamin said, rubbing his eyes. It was hard to think clearly. He was still half in the dream. Did they have important information? Should he ask for a lawyer? "Let me get my clothes."

He closed the door without latching it, so they wouldn't think he was locking them out.

"Is everything okay?" Liv mumbled from the bed.

"Yeah," he said, pulling on his pants. "I'll be right back."

He found his wallet and phone, and started a text to Kenji Kirby. He kept hitting the wrong letters with his thumbs. Finally he got it sent:

> Police picking me up,
> no explanation.

Then he went out and closed the door behind him. The two cops flanked him down the hall. This felt like a perp walk, but why? What did they think? They rode the empty elevator down to the lobby and he got into the back of their car, in the predawn darkness. No reporters were camped out this early, and he was grateful for that.

Then he was in an interrogation room at the police station, just like in a movie. Detective Rivera and her partner sat across from him.

"So what's going on?" he asked.

"You told me when I first interviewed you that you had never been arrested," she said.

"Right."

"But you were. For assaulting a police officer in 1996."

He frowned. "Wait—what does that have to do with my kids?"

"So it's true?"

"No! I mean, the arrest is true. But I didn't assault anyone. And they said it would be expunged from my record."

"Why were you arrested?"

Benjamin sighed. "I thought you really had something."

"We have to follow everything," she said. "We need to understand why you lied."

"I didn't lie!"

"We could send you home," Arnal said.

"Are you fucking kidding me? While my kids are missing?"

They both waited. Benjamin stared at Detective Rivera's smooth, impassive face. She had warm, light hazel eyes, almost golden. He was disappointed in her. She had seemed like she was on his side. He guessed that was her job.

"Okay," he said. "I was in college. I was at a bar with my friends. A guy hit on one of the girls I was with. When she told him to go away, he threatened her, said he was going to rape her. So we called the college cops, and this old white Berkeley cop showed up and was really shitty to the girl, Tracey, who was black. He kept asking where her parents were from and why she wore her skirt so short. I was impatient, because the cop wasn't doing his job. But I was just standing on the street with my friends, talking to him, and all of a sudden I was flat on my back on the concrete. The cop had sucker punched me before I even knew what had happened. But he can't hit a college kid in the face without some reason, right?"

The cops said nothing.

Benjamin sighed and went on. "So he said in his report that I assaulted him, which wasn't true. My father hired a lawyer, who told me it was my word against the cop's, with some drunk witnesses, and I should plead nolo contendere. I didn't want to, because it sounded like 'no contest.' But he said if I did, the incident would be expunged from my record. So I could honestly answer 'no' when asked if I'd ever been arrested for a crime. Which is what I did, when I talked to you. But obviously it wasn't expunged, if you guys dug it up."

Officer Arnal didn't seem to have followed the story.

Benjamin wished he could explain in Spanish. "Sucker punched?" he said. "What's the word for that here? No warning. He cold-cocked me. Punched me in the face, out of nowhere." He mimed it, fist tapping his chin, head turning away from the impact.

He remembered the strange violation of it, the way the pain hadn't kicked in until he was lying on the sidewalk, looking up at a streetlight, watching Tracey in her short skirt yelling at the cops. She later told him that he'd called the cop a racist asshole before he got punched, though he didn't remember that. He'd never been hit before. His face had been tender and bruised for days.

The whole thing had made Benjamin disgusted and depressed. He'd thought about dropping out of school. He lost weight. Everything seemed pointless, if people with power could abuse it like that, and get away with it. Tracey had told him to get on with his life. Shit like that happened all the time, just not so much to white dudes. He shouldn't be so surprised.

"You should have told us," Detective Rivera said now.

"It happened over twenty years ago," he said. "Honestly, I'd forgotten it. And it has nothing to do with my kids."

"But it could make us think you have other things to hide."

"I would never, *ever* assault a police officer," he said.

But the truth was that he might, if he thought he could get away with it. It seemed like a very satisfying thing to do, to leap across the table and throttle them both. The only question was: Which one first? The guy, to be gentlemanly. And also because Detective Rivera could probably take him.

Instead, he said, "Please tell me you've uncovered some information besides this. Please tell me you've investigated the actual, immediate *crime* of this kidnapping. What about Pedro, the guide? Have you investigated *him* this thoroughly?"

"We have," Detective Rivera said.

"And?"

There was a knock at the door and young Kenji Kirby came in, looking neat and cool in a light suit and an open collar, even at this ungodly hour. "What's going on?" he asked.

"There was some confusion," Detective Rivera said. "It's okay now."

"They dragged me out of bed," Benjamin said. "And they've done nothing to find my kids."

Kenji stood looking at the three of them as if they were children fighting in school. "Tell him what you found," he said to the cops.

"We don't have to," Arnal said.

"Just tell him," Kenji said.

"What?" Benjamin said. "Tell me!"

Detective Rivera hesitated. "We think we've identified the people the courier was working for."

"And?"

"We're following up leads."

"How hard can that *be*?"

"We've eliminated one house, at least," she said. "Two officers went to check it out, and the kids weren't there."

"You didn't go yourself?"

"We can't be everywhere," Arnal said.

"No, you have to be here, doing bullshit investigations of my college drinking career." He could feel his blood pressure rising. He was definitely capable of assaulting a police officer now. He didn't care if Rivera could beat him up. "What about the other leads?"

"We're working on it. It's New Year's Eve."

"Bring people back! Pay them overtime! *I* will pay them overtime!"

Kenji gestured toward the door. "Let's get you back to the hotel," he said.

19.

RAYMOND WOKE EARLY and watched his wife's face as she slept. Her hair was coming loose from the ponytail that held it back, in dark wisps around her face. It was the third morning since the kids had gone missing. If an abductor was going to kill a kid, they usually did it in the first five hours. He'd learned that on some cop show. He hadn't said it to Nora. But it meant that if the children hadn't been dead by the time he got to that clearing, they were probably still alive.

He couldn't believe that people were still drinking coffee, making breakfast, going to work, when his kids were gone. He'd had so many worries about his children, because of the melanin in their skin. But their disappearing on a zip-line tour had not been on his mind. He'd been blindsided.

Nora woke and blinked, her eyes wide and green, with tired circles beneath them. He could tell she didn't remember. Then he saw the awareness slowly return, her mind fighting it. Pain took over her face, her forehead crumpled. "Oh God," she whispered. "I can't bear it. I can't."

He put his arms around her until she fell asleep again. Sleep was insulation and armor.

He was fully awake, so he went to the hotel gym to try to work out some of his misery by causing himself pain. If he didn't exercise, he couldn't sleep, he couldn't shit. The gym was a smallish converted hotel room crammed with four weight machines, a treadmill, and a stationary bike, with mirrored walls and fluorescent lights. A TV mounted on the wall played the morning news at top volume. Raymond turned it off, in case he might be on it.

Liv had described the guide pretending to be dragged under the water, at the beach. At that moment, Raymond would've picked up his family and left. He didn't care about being able to take a joke. He didn't care about being cool. He would've walked back to the road and waited for a taxi to drive by.

He had that fantasy a lot: the taxi back to the ship. Just him and Marcus and June waiting by the road. The other families could fend for themselves. He didn't know where Nora was, in his fantasy. Maybe the women had gone golfing, and the men had gone to the zip line. But Marcus and June were very vivid, packing up their beach stuff, leaving that joker of a guide, hiking back to the road. They were hot and sweaty and a little whiny and reluctant. June gave him side-eye in the cab. But they were dumped out safely on the dock, next to the enormous ship. They trooped back to the metal detector at the gangway, and showed their ship cards to José, the Filipino officer at security.

"You're back so soon!" José said.

"Our dad *made* us come back," Marcus said. "Over a stupid *joke*."

Junie said, *"Yeah."*

José gave Raymond a sympathetic grin.

But as soon as they hit the pool, the kids were happy again. June wanted to have underwater tea parties. Marcus wanted chicken fights. Raymond indulged them both, sitting on the bottom of the pool sipping imaginary tea, feeling their slick bodies on his shoulders. His beautiful children.

They were hungry by the time they got to the lunch buffet, and they piled food on their trays. When it was time to leave port, Raymond ordered wildly expensive blue Sail Away drinks from the pretty Jamaican bartender at the poolside bar—virgin ones for the kids— and they leaned over the rail to watch the bow thrusters push the ship away from the dock, the water churning white, the day fading. In Raymond's dream, they'd spent an hour and a half on land in this benighted country, and they would never set foot in it again.

But that wasn't what had happened. Instead, he'd gone golfing with Gunther's friend, that colonial relic. Benjamin had slathered up with sunscreen in the car, smearing it over his face. He'd offered the bottle, but Raymond had turned it down, and wound up getting a black man's sunburn. Dumb.

Meanwhile his wife had tolerated the guide pretending to be eaten by a shark. She'd watched the kids play in the water and had some slushy cocktail. And then she'd gone looking for birds and the kids had drifted away and got kidnapped.

He had thought, growing up in Philadelphia, that his own parents were hard on him. Now he understood how deep their desire to protect him was. He understood their anger when his sister stayed out past curfew, when his brother got drunk, when Raymond skipped school with his friend Tyrell. Their fury stemmed from love and fear. They had been *vigilant*, and had known where their children were, every minute of every day. If they didn't know, there would be consequences. He had never raised a hand to his children—he had tried to be a conscious, twenty-first-century parent—but he had not been vigilant enough.

He'd loaded too much weight on the machine, he was going to hurt himself. He let the stack clang down and put his forehead against the sweaty vinyl pad. He would never forgive Nora, that was the truth. And he would never forgive himself.

20

LIV NEEDED TO get out of the hotel for some air. She couldn't stand the silence in the room. For years, her daily life had been punctuated by the alarm on Sebastian's glucose monitor going off. The high-pitched beep interrupted sleep, conversation, meals, Penny's dance recitals. She had wished, in the past, not to have those constant alarms jangling her nervous system. Now all she wanted was to hear that beep, telling her that Sebastian's blood sugar was high or low, or that the battery was dying, or the sensor signal was lost. But there was nothing, just a rattling fan in the wall from the air conditioning.

She tied a turquoise scarf over her head and put on sunglasses. She felt foolish doing it, like she thought she was some kind of celebrity, but she'd been on the television news with her recognizable hair, too short and too blond. "La madre rubia," they called her. She couldn't face the reporters, or the people who came up to her in the hotel lobby, offering condolences and theories on where the children were.

At first she'd thought real information might come from these strangers. She'd been begging Kenji to talk to people, and here they were! But she soon realized that it was all noise, no signal. People thought they could touch her because they understood her grief. They clutched her arm, patted her shoulder, stroked her hand. It was intolerable.

So she went out in her disguise, through a back door, near the hotel's kitchen. No reporters there. In the alley, she stepped over broken concrete. She heard her mother's voice in her head, saying that people who complained about litigation should see what the world looked like when the law held no one responsible. Gaping holes in the sidewalk. No railings where there should be railings, on stairways that people could tumble off.

Liv had emailed her mother the ship's liability waiver, for legal advice, and her mother said it would be tough to go after them. It wasn't an American company. The ship was registered in the Bahamas, for tax purposes. And the local laws wouldn't help because there was no tort system. Civilization, her mother had told her since she was small, was a series of agreements about what was good for everyone, enforced by law. And civilization was only a thin veneer over the savagery and greed that were the human default.

She had gone on the Internet this morning, which had been a mistake. On Facebook, people had first sent support and good wishes, although there were a few weird comments she wished she hadn't read. Someone had linked to a crowd-funding site to help with a reward, which had seemed touching, but ultimately came with weird comments, too. On Twitter, strangers started sending blame, shame, questions about her judgment, remarks on her hair, offers of sexual comfort, and terrible speculation about her children's whereabouts.

She'd deleted her Facebook and Twitter accounts, and then regretted it. What if someone had actual information, and couldn't reach her? She could create a new account, only for information about the children. But that would bring on more jokes, and more false information. The Internet would not give you what you wanted. She had talked to the endocrinologist at home, and to her doctor friend Meg who'd stayed with them when Sebastian was first diagnosed. Both of them told her to stay off the medical Internet. No more googling.

Her phone rang in her pocket and her heart jumped. She saw her mother's name on the screen and put the phone back in her pocket. Her parents had wanted to get on a plane as soon as they heard the news, and she had told them not to. The last thing she needed was to be taking care of them and their needs and opinions. People regressed, around their families, to the age at which they had been angriest. With her mother, Liv was always fifteen.

The scarf slipped off her hair and she adjusted it, then turned down a side street she didn't know. There was a café with small black tables on the sidewalk. She could get a coffee and keep her sunglasses on without looking weird. And the street was tiny and secret.

She was thinking how secret it was when she recognized Nora at one of the tables. Or she recognized the salmon-colored running shoes, the ones Nora wore every day because she never had to go to work. Her long hair was tucked up under a baseball cap. Then Liv registered Nora's companion. Nora was sitting with Pedro.

Pedro, the joker who'd pretended to be sucked under the river's surface and scared the shit out of them, and then sputtered up laughing at his own hilariousness.

Pedro, who had not warned them that the tide would change and the motionless river would start running inland, fast.

Pedro, who had not known there were crocodiles.

Pedro, who had brought the frozen daiquiris that had put Liv to sleep.

Pedro, who had taken Nora looking for birds, while their children disappeared. Would you like to see a quetzal? Nora had looked Liv in the eye and told her nothing had happened. And now Pedro and Nora were talking intently over the café table. He was holding Nora's hand, leaning toward her.

Liv found herself standing over the table. "Hola, amigos."

Pedro glanced up and gave her an uncertain smile. He didn't recognize her right away: the scarf and glasses. Nora snatched her hand back from Pedro's and looked down at her lap, the cap hiding her face.

"So," Liv said. "The plot thickens."

"There's no plot," Nora said.

"Oh, I think there is," Liv said. "Do the police know about this? I think they might be very interested."

"Please don't say anything," Nora said, looking up and squinting. "It was just a mistake."

"A mistake," Liv said. "That the only two people awake while our children disappeared were *fucking*?" She whispered it, although there was no one in earshot.

"We weren't."

"Oh, no? Everything but?"

"No!" Nora said. Then, accusingly, "You were asleep."

"Because of his drink!" Liv said. She turned to Pedro. "Was it drugged?"

"No!"

"Was it all a plan?"

"No!"

"Please," Nora said. "Do you think I could blame myself any more than I already do?"

"I don't know," Liv said. "I don't understand you at all. Why are you here?"

"I just had to talk it through. See if there was anything we missed. See if he knew anything. Just because he's local."

"And?" Liv said, looking to Pedro. "Any hot leads? Any clues?"

He shook his head, looking regretful.

"Okay." Liv turned to Nora. "So you're having an affair, while our children are missing. That's what this is."

"No!" Nora said. "You would be here, too. Looking for the kids."

"I would *not*!" Liv said. "Because I wouldn't have been off in the trees in the first place!"

"Please don't say anything," Nora said. "I can't bear it if this comes out."

"Then what the *fuck* are you doing meeting in public? Are you *insane*?"

"Yes!" Nora said. "Aren't you? Our kids are gone. Aren't you a little bit insane?"

"Yes! But not like this!"

"Well I *am* like this. And it was your fucking terrible idea, the whole cruise, so back the fuck off."

"We shouldn't be here," Pedro said, in a warning tone.

"I'll leave," Liv said, and she turned.

"Liv!" Nora said.

Liv tugged at her headscarf as she walked down the tiny street, no destination in mind. Her sunglasses were so big they touched her cheeks. Her tears pooled inside the frames, against the lenses, then spilled down her face to her chin.

Pedro had looked as wretched as they were. She realized Nora was right: She would have met with Pedro, too. Nora could be fucking him now, as far as Liv was concerned, if he could provide information about these feudal families controlling the interior, paying the police, killing people, stealing children. *That* was the kind of guide they needed.

She kept her eyes on the ground, watching for holes. She couldn't break an ankle, not now. No tort system, no procedure for wrongs. No recourse for your pain, when it was someone else's fault.

She regretted being ugly to Nora. She had learned that mode of attack from her mother, and she hated herself when it came out. She should have been empathetic, understanding. Maybe Nora was right, maybe Pedro could come up with something. But she couldn't bring herself to go back. And they were more identifiable together, Pedro was right.

Poor Raymond, it would crush him. Embarrass him. A new anger at Nora rose up, for making her part of the secret.

A child selling roses tried to press one on her, and Liv held up a hand in protest. But she fumbled in her pocket and gave the girl a coin. It would go straight to whatever adult was pimping the child out, of course.

"Señora!" another child called after her, but she didn't turn.

21.

GEORGE WATCHED THE children play tic-tac-toe, and thought about his brother. He thought their mother, before she died, had understood that something was wrong with Raúl. She had been repulsed by him, but that made her feel guilty, because a mother should not be repulsed by her son, so she gave him anything he wanted. He was handsome and charming and manipulative and she never punished him for anything. George—Jorge, then—took the blame for whatever went wrong. A broken fence, a wrecked bicycle, a smashed window. His brother deflected all damage and disruption onto Jorge, who got the reputation as a troublemaker. It didn't help that he wasn't as good-looking as Raúl. His forehead was too big. His mother used to smooth his hair and frown at the dome between his temples, so he had taken to wearing baseball caps to hide it.

When Raúl was eight, he caught small emerald green frogs in the forest and cut them up with razor blades while they were still alive. He showed Jorge how they twitched and wriggled until the very end.

Then they got a small capuchin monkey for a pet, and Raúl tormented it with mind games until it went insane, baring its teeth and screaming when anyone tried to get close. The monkey was sent away somewhere, and no one spoke of it again.

An aneurysm killed their mother when George was twelve, and he thought things would shift then. Their father did not understand Raúl well enough to be distressed by his feelings about him, and he tried to treat his sons equally; it was a point of principle. But even equal wasn't right, when it came to Raúl.

George went away to boarding school in Santa Barbara and decided to remake himself as an American. He worked at cultivating his mother's California accent. When he got to Berkeley, he played Truco sometimes with the South Americans, with the Spanish cards and the elaborate system of tiny facial gestures to communicate across the table, but mostly he tried to abandon his past. He tried to become interested in finance, in business consulting, in law, in anything that might create for him a new life.

But there was so much money to be made at home. And Raúl had no business mind at all. He just rode around on his white horse, and got girls pregnant. The daughter of the local grocer almost bled to death delivering Raúl's baby. The grocer called George, who sat with the girl in the hospital all night. She was nineteen years old and looked gray, all the blood and warmth drained out of her. She'd survived, and so had the baby, but Raúl never even went to see them.

Raúl's ruthlessness might have helped in their father's business, except he was not ambitious in that way. He didn't know how to make money. He made mistakes, alienated allies. He bragged on Instagram about his exploits until George made him shut down his account, but then he would start another. He drank too much of the local guaro. Eventually, it would kill him, but that might be twenty years from now. Who could wait?

And then Raúl had shot the Colombian courier. He said Bolaños was cheating them, but George suspected that Raúl owed the man money on a side deal and didn't want to pay. So he shot Bolaños in the head. But this was not Colombia. They lived in a country with almost perfect literacy, with excellent medical care, and they had a profitable little business that the police ignored. You could not shoot people in the head. They were not butchers or desperadoes. The death had been stupid, unnecessary.

George had been in California at the time. Something always went tits-up when he was away. So he'd been flying home to do damage control when Luz Alvaros, working for his brother, brought those fucking kids to the house in the Jeep and caused an international incident.

George did not consider himself a moral paragon. He understood that his father's business was illegal, and that he had taken part in it. He had certainly lived off the spoils. But most business was in some way unethical. Look at DuPont dumping poison in drinking water, look at big pharma, look at subprime mortgages. It was just the nature of making money. Everyone profited at someone else's expense. But Raúl was unredeemably bad.

And stupid. Raúl had decided that the solution was to ransom the children. There had been a reward offered, fifty thousand dollars for information. Raúl thought they could get more. "People kidnap Americans on *purpose*," he told George. "We could make so much money!"

"That is not what we do!" George said. "Do you understand the shit-storm you would bring down on our heads?"

"Your problem is that you have small ideas," Raúl said.

If Raúl just disappeared, no one would miss him. Their father would mourn the loss of a son, but he would get over it.

Their father was in hiding now, and hadn't told George where he'd gone, so it couldn't be beaten or threatened out of him. His dear father, always considerate. He'd taken two of his men with him, and the other two had quit when they realized the shit they were in. Luz Alvaros had bolted, too, after starting all of this with her shitty choice of a grave site. And now two tame cops had heard Marcus pounding on the window. Even Raúl should understand that this was a big fucking problem. But he didn't. When he came in from bribing those cops, he'd smiled an oily, frog-murdering smile, as if everything was under control.

George's first idea had been a return through intermediaries. Find someone to dump the kids outside the Argentinian embassy office. The van that dropped the kids would have no license plate, they would be unhurt. Return the kids unscathed, and maybe the Americans wouldn't come after them in helicopters.

But after he saw that smile on his brother's face, he changed his mind. His new, bigger idea was to take the kids to the capital himself, and turn his brother in. He could rid himself of two problems at once. He would be the hero, and surround himself with the family's lawyers, and they would let Raúl take the fall. He'd caused them enough trouble already.

"Can we go outside?" Penny asked, snapping George from his reverie. He'd been standing over the children, watching them play, and now they were all staring up at him.

"No," George said.

"Why not?"

"Satellites," Marcus said. That kid was not stupid at all.

22.

ISABEL SCRATCHED HER head. It was starting to itch. She still had the salty river water dried on her hair. She'd given up thinking about getting a key to the door, because she was barefoot and wouldn't get far. Instead, she'd been focusing on a computer or a phone. Raúl and George had the outlines of phones in their pockets, but they never took them out, or left them on a table. And they hadn't turned on a TV since the old man turned it off on the first day.

She should have waited for Hector to come back with their parents. It was so obvious. She thought about the crocodile moving on the bank, but then she reminded herself that Hector was such a good swimmer. She wished she could talk to someone about it, but she hated Penny for leading them into the trees, away from the river. And Marcus was kind of weird, always watching her. And the little ones hadn't seen the crocodile, so she couldn't say anything in front of them.

Hector was *probably* safe with her parents, and they probably all thought she was dead by now. She wondered if Hector missed her. Or if, in his secret heart, he didn't mind being an only child. She wondered if he was playing sad songs on the guitar. Having a dead sister was going to make him so romantic and interesting. Girls were probably falling all over him, wherever he was, at a nice hotel somewhere.

Her family had been getting along so well on the ship, where there was nothing to do but play tennis and swim. There were no dishes after dinner, or beds to make. Her friends weren't around for her mother to have opinions about. When Isabel had puked off the back of the catamaran in Acapulco, her mother had kept her hair out of her face and rubbed her back. She'd found a ginger ale and held up a pareo as a sun shade, to keep people from staring at them. Isabel felt bad about some things she'd said to her mother before the trip.

The wind had started up again. Raúl was down at the stables below the house, where the white horse whinnied in protest. Isabel watched through the window as Raúl rubbed its nose and its neck. He must have been saying reassuring things, promising the wind would stop. But it didn't. It tried to reach in through the cracks in the house, and shook the ceiling. Maria called it the Christmas wind. Isabel asked her—*again*—if she could please use a phone.

Maria shook her head. "No, mija." She brought them a plate of cheese quesadillas, cut into triangles.

Penny and Sebastian finished their huddled business with the finger-sticking and the calculator, and the others waited to eat. Sebastian wanted to give himself the shot with the pen. "It hurts less if I do it," he said.

June shuddered. "I couldn't do that."

"I thought you were going to be a pirate," Penny said.

"I could be a pirate," June said. "I just couldn't give myself a shot."

Then they all fell on the quesadillas like animals at the zoo. They were disgusting. None of them had showered since they arrived. There were no grown-ups to tell them to. The little ones smelled stale, in that musty, little-kid way. Isabel was getting grown-up body odor. She'd never gone this long without bathing. Her armpits smelled like vegetable soup. It had been interesting at first, but now it was kind of gross.

She crept downstairs, into the bathroom, and locked the door. She stripped off the ugly cotton clothes and made the shower as hot as she could stand. The shampoo smelled of orange blossoms, and she stayed under the water a long time. In the shower, she could be anywhere. She could be home.

She stepped out and stood in front of the mirror, with her hair wet and clean. She had boobs already, even if they were small ones. That was why Raúl looked at her the way he did. And she had a little triangle of hair. Some of her friends were already waxing, but her mother said it was ridiculous and she wouldn't allow it, even though she had lasered off the hair on her own legs.

The television news, before the old man turned it off, had shown a photograph of Isabel on the ship, leaping into the pool. She'd just been playing, striking a pose in the air, but she looked so good, with one leg kicked up behind her, toes pointed, arms raised like wings, hair streaming out. It must have been on her mother's phone. Her mother only showed her goofy pictures. Isabel had to steal the phone to see anything that looked halfway decent. But that photo was perfect, and it had been on TV. She tried to strike the pose now, but it wasn't the same when you weren't airborne. Her hair didn't fly.

She sniffed the white shirt and put it back on, and pulled on the ugly red shorts. It was New Year's Eve. Her friends at home would be out in shimmery dresses and heels, dancing and laughing at the boys who stared at them hungrily. She wondered what Hector was doing. Sitting with her parents? What would they talk about? She wrapped a towel around her hair and went upstairs, where the brothers were playing poker at the kitchen table. She took her corner of the couch.

George had a beer in front of him, and Raúl had something that looked like a rum and Coke. Maria kept bringing them drinks. Fresh ones before the last ones were finished.

"Marcus," Isabel said. "Get me one of those drinks."

Marcus looked at her, surprised.

"The old ones," she said. "They won't notice."

He hesitated.

She nodded at him. "Go on."

So he sidled over and snagged a half-finished glass and a beer bottle. The brothers didn't pay him any attention. Marcus moved toward the sink, as if he was just clearing the table. He checked that Maria wasn't looking, then doubled back to the couch where Isabel sat. He sank down next to her, breathing hard.

"Good work," she said, and took the cocktail and sipped. Even with the ice melted, it was sweet and strong.

Marcus brought the half-filled beer bottle tentatively to his mouth. He drank, and something crossed his face: not dislike, but surprise. Maybe concern. He shifted the front of his shorts with his free hand.

Isabel laughed. "I get that feeling, too."

His cheeks flushed.

"Don't be embarrassed," she said.

She'd never talked about the feeling, that twinge of unexpected pleasure that came with the first sip of alcohol, the heat in her under-wear. From listening to her friends talk, she didn't think everyone had it. It was oddly comforting that Marcus did.

"They're having a competition, for us," she told him.

"They are?"

"We need George to win." She wondered if they could help him cheat. "Do you play poker?"

Marcus shook his head.

June spotted the beer bottle in her brother's hand. Her mouth dropped open. "Marcus!" she said.

"Shhh," Isabel said. "It's okay."

Marcus put the bottle on the floor.

Isabel sipped her drink and watched the poker game. George still had the bigger pile of chips. Nothing happened for a while. The brothers played in silence. Maybe they were so absorbed that she could get upstairs to a computer and send a message.

They had finished another game when George got up and went to the bathroom on the other side of the kitchen. Raúl put his head down on the table to rest, like he was taking a nap in school. Isabel stood, with a moment's light-headedness from the drink, and moved toward the stairs. June was hunched over the bunny. Penny and Sebastian were playing tic-tac-toe on the floor. Maria was rummaging in the refrigerator. Marcus saw her, of course, but she put her finger to her lips. Raúl didn't look up. She climbed silently.

Upstairs, there was a door immediately on the right. Isabel turned the doorknob and it opened. Inside were two big computer monitors and an open laptop. She eased the door closed behind her. One of the monitors had a screen divided into six parts, with grainy black-and-white images in each box. She recognized a shot of the door they had come in, from outside. And one of the gate at the end of the driveway. A shot of the stables with the white horse. It wasn't even that fancy a security system. Some of her friends had better ones.

She slid into the chair and tapped the laptop keyboard to wake it up. The screen asked for a password. She blew the air out of her cheeks. Her dad always wrote down his passwords. She opened the drawer in the desk. There was junk, paper clips and pens, and a yellow sticky note. It said "panocha" in handwritten letters. She thought of her own triangle of hair and she blushed, but she entered it as a password and it worked. She guessed it was Raúl's password. That guy was a dick. She opened a browser window to message her brother.

The computer was slow and she was still waiting for it to open Facebook when she heard steps behind her on the stairs. Her heart started going twice its normal speed. She typed her login and password but then the door opened. She quit the browser before a hand grabbed her chair and swiveled it around. Raúl was standing behind her, leaning close. His hand was on the back of the chair, behind her towel-wrapped head.

"What are you doing?" he asked.

"Nothing."

If she were a spy caught like this in a movie, she would kiss her enemy, to distract him. Then she would punch and kick and climb on his head to break his neck with her legs. But she didn't know martial arts.

"You have to let us go," she said.

"Do I?"

"Please," she said.

A weird look had come into Raúl's eyes. He wasn't listening to her. He pulled the towel from her wet hair. She grabbed at it, but it dropped to the floor. He put a hand on her breast, through the white T-shirt, and she jumped.

"Please don't," she said.

"It's okay."

"Stop," she said, pushing at his hand. "Stop!"

He pinned her arm to the chair and slid his free hand down over the T-shirt and moved the shorts aside. Then he slid a thumb inside her, as if investigating something. She tried to shove him away but he was so strong. His hand was locked over her pelvis. She couldn't move him.

He lifted her out of the chair with one arm. He was so much stronger than she was. He kept his thumb inside her, fingers splayed across the front of her shorts. She felt frozen, paralyzed. Her throat constricted, and she couldn't scream as he carried her down the hall. And if she did, what would the little kids do? Would Maria help? She felt like a bowling ball in his hand, with his thumb inside her.

They were in a bedroom. She had time to register its messiness, like a teenage boy's room. And then she was face down on a bed and he was peeling off her shorts. She tried to kick him but he pressed her torso to the bed with one arm. She could barely breathe. He kneeled on her leg so her hamstring seized and cramped. She heard him undo his belt and his zipper.

"No!" she said.

He spread her legs, hard, and then there was only pain. It seemed to be ripping her apart. When she turned her head and cried out, there was the suffocating feeling of a pillow over her face, and the heavy weight of his body pushing her into the mattress again and again.

Then she lost track of time, and the next thing she knew another voice was swearing in Spanish. "Son of a bitch. What the *fuck*, Raúl."

There was a stinging between her legs, and something sticky on her thighs, and she rolled painfully, trying to cover herself. George stood in the doorway. Isabel looked around the messy bedroom. There were clothes thrown over a chair, bottles and crumpled paper and trash on the bureau. Raúl lay on the other side of the bed, playing with his phone. She felt sick when she saw him. She pulled her legs up, edged away.

"She came onto me, maje," Raúl said. "I swear it."

"I did *not*."

"She was wet as fuck," Raúl said.

"I can't leave you for five minutes?" George said, his voice high with fury. "I can't go to take a shit? Do you know what you've done?"

"Had a first-class teenage fuck," Raúl said. "Best sleeping pill there is."

"I was trying to *solve* this!" George shouted. "You've completely fucked it up!"

"She was so ready," Raúl said.

"She is a *child*!"

"I'm not a child."

"See?" Raúl said.

"Just her saying that *proves* she's a child!" George said.

Isabel looked under the sheet and saw blood on her thighs. "I have to throw up," she said. She stumbled, half falling, off the bed.

She didn't make it, but puked all over the rug.

"I'll clean it," George said, and he helped her to the bathroom.

She stepped into the shower and crouched under the water, and George left her there. She washed the puke out of her hair, and did a gingerly wash between her legs. It hurt. There was some blood but not a lot. She peed into the shower drain, watching the water between her feet become yellow and a little bit red. Then the water cleared and washed it all away. She pulled a clean towel around her shoulders like a tent, and sat hunched on the bathroom floor, trembling.

There was a knock, and George came in. "Are you okay?"

She stared up at him.

"My brother is a monster," he said. "I'm sorry. Do you want to see the doctor?"

"No!"

"The doctor's safe," George said.

But she didn't want any more hands, any more investigating. "I just want to go home."

George closed the toilet and sat on the lid. He put his head in his hands. "I told you to stay away from Raúl," he said. "I told you to stay with the little kids."

She winced. "I was trying to help them."

"This makes it so much harder. You understand that, right?"

"I won't say anything."

George laughed. "Yeah, right."

"I promise!" she said. "I won't let any doctors near me."

"That will be proof enough."

"You can't keep us forever."

"Yeah, I know." He sighed. "Raúl says you were on the computer."

"I wanted to send a message to my parents."

"Did you?"

"I didn't have time. Raúl came in."

George looked at her, and she thought he was trying to tell if she was lying. "Okay," he said. "Okay."

"I want to go downstairs."

"I don't want you to scare the little kids."

"It will scare them more not to see me," she said. She didn't know if that was true, but she couldn't stay up here. She felt her stomach churn again.

George sighed. "I'll go get your clothes."

She put a cold, wet washcloth over her eyes. That was what her mother did after she cried a lot, to make the puffiness go down. George brought her yellow bikini from downstairs and she put that on first. Then she pulled on the too-big shorts, the cotton T-shirt. Her wet hair made the shirt stick to her back. Her legs were wobbly.

She walked down the hallway past a bedroom that was cleaner than Raúl's, with a big framed baseball poster. George's room. Then there was a bedroom that she could tell was the old man's room, the father's. It was neat, the bed was made, there were a few old leather books between bookends on the long low bureau. An upholstered chair with a little footstool.

Her legs shook on the stairs, but she made it to the bottom and slid onto the red couch beside Marcus. He was watching her, as usual. She knew her eyes were red. Penny had the cards back and they were playing Crazy Eights. How much time had passed? None? Had they heard her cry out? *Had* she cried out?

"What happened?" Marcus asked.

"Nothing."

She was losing track of time again, because Raúl had come downstairs, and was yelling at George in Spanish.

"What are they saying?" Marcus asked.

But she couldn't tell him, because George was shouting that he'd been going to take the children back, and now he couldn't. Because now the cops were going to crawl up George's ass and they were going to prison and it was all Raúl's fucking fault, he was a fucking psychopath and a fucking idiot. George shouted other things, insults, curses.

Raúl took a beer bottle by the neck and smashed it on the table with a bright crash. He lunged at his brother with the jagged, broken end, but George stepped deftly away. When Raúl came at him again,

George grabbed his brother's arm and took the bottle, dropping it in the kitchen sink, where it clattered. They grappled, clumsily.

The other children drew close to Isabel in the corner of the sofa. Marcus took her hand. The brothers looked like dancing drunks. There was broken glass on the floor, and spilled beer. Raúl hit George hard in the stomach and he wheezed and staggered. Isabel's heart tripped over itself. Raúl couldn't win.

But then George had his brother in a headlock, and Raúl's face turned red as he struggled, his windpipe cut off. Raúl reached for the table, for anything to give him leverage. Her heart was pounding. She thought George might kill him.

Then George released his brother's head. He told him to go to bed, to sleep it off, they would talk about it in the morning.

Isabel thought Raúl might take a swing, but he seemed to accept that he was beaten. He gave Isabel a long, reproachful stare. Then he staggered upstairs, wheezing, muttering something she couldn't understand, except that "puta" was in there. George started to clean up the kitchen, picking up pieces of broken glass in a cupped hand. Maria appeared, and together they swept up the glass, and wiped away the spilled beer.

George seemed to notice the kids in the corner for the first time since the argument had begun. "Watch your feet in here," he said.

23

NORA WANDERED THE halls of the hotel in the middle of the night, taking the stairs from one floor to the next, thinking about depression.

Her mother had probably had a serious bout of postpartum, from her description of the time after Nora was born, although no one called it that at the time. It was just "feeling blue," listening to too much Joni Mitchell, locking herself in the bathroom sometimes. Nora's earliest memories were of sitting by the bathroom door listening to her mother cry, not knowing what to do.

As an adult, Nora had thought her mother's problem was tricky brain chemistry, but now she wondered if the family depression was just a rational response to the facts on the ground. The brutality of the world. She was standing at the edge of the yawning pit of her hereditary sadness, and might slip in.

She'd been frantic after Liv busted her at the café. She wished she'd told Liv earlier what had happened, and trusted their friendship, instead of startling her into rage. She was sure Liv would go straight to Raymond, and he would never forgive her. He was a man of great moral clarity. Things were right or they were wrong; he had no patience for gray areas. It would be over now.

But it couldn't be over, because they had two children.

Unless they didn't. And if they didn't have their children, then nothing mattered, or would ever matter again.

Nora had started to tremble at the café table and talk too fast, turning it over and over in her mind, and Pedro had guided her down the street and into a cab. She'd cried silently in the back seat, not seeing the streets outside. Then he had led her into a small papaya-colored house where she could talk and pace and regret and rehash without anyone watching. She kept trying to find new words to explain herself to Liv.

Pedro let her rant. He straightened a few things in the kitchen and put on a kettle to boil. Then he led her into the bedroom. He had a rumpled, unmade bed, a surfboard in a rack over the window, posters on the walls.

"I can't," she said. Whatever desire she had once had for him had been blasted by guilt.

"No sexo," he'd said. "Don't worry."

He sat her on his bed and the kettle started to whistle. He went to make tea. A few shirts hung in the open closet. Nora had tipped over in his stale-smelling bed, onto his pillow, and slept for fifteen oblivious minutes, as she hadn't slept in days. When she woke, she drank the lukewarm tea he'd brought her. Then she took a cab back to the hotel and told Raymond she'd been for a long walk.

But now, while Raymond slept, Nora stalked the hotel halls. She thought about how smart her son was. And how good his sense of direction—it went with his love of maps. She used to take him to a park with a blank map of the United States painted on the asphalt, and he could name every state by the time he was three. He used to narrate their drive back from preschool, turn by turn. She truly believed that if the children could escape from wherever they were, Marcus could walk them to safety, he could get them to the police.

On the third floor, she came upon a man in blue coveralls and a woman in a maid's dress, carrying a rolled carpet between them. Nora wondered why a carpet needed to be replaced in the middle of the night. Had something terrible happened?

"Buenas noches," she said.

The man smiled at her. He was missing a tooth. "El terremoto," he said. "Has sentido?"

"Perdón?" she said. Was he asking if she'd heard something?

"Terremoto," he said. "Has sentido?"

"No."

He smiled. "Air-quick." They had stood the carpet on its rolled end, and he made a motion with his free hand, moving his fist back and forth. "Air-quick."

She frowned.

"No ha sentido," the woman said.

"No has sentido?" the man asked, still smiling.

Nora shook her head. She hadn't heard a thing. Except his weird questions.

When she got back to the hotel room, Raymond opened the door in a bathrobe. "Where'd you go?" he asked.

"Just walking. I couldn't sleep."

"You can't disappear on me. I was about to come looking."

"I'm sorry."

"Did you feel the earthquake?"

"When?"

"Just now."

"Oh!" she said, sinking to the bed. "That's what they were saying. They asked if I'd *felt* it."

"It was long," Raymond said.

"I thought this maintenance guy was making an obscene gesture," she said.

"What gesture?"

She made the jerking-off move. "He kept saying, 'Air-quick.' I was so confused. But he was miming an earthquake."

"Maybe," Raymond said, doubtful.

"No, he was."

"That was a serious earthquake. I can't believe you didn't feel it."

"I'm kind of distracted." She felt a cold ache in her stomach as she said it, because it sounded like she was implying that *he* should be so distracted, too, as if it were a competition. But he didn't have all the reasons she did.

"What's up with you and Liv?" he asked.

"Nothing."

"Really?"

She nodded.

He tried to put his arms around her, but she hopped up from the bed.

"I can't," she said. "Not with the kids gone. I just—can't." She moved toward the bathroom, the only private space in this claustrophobic, airless hotel room. She couldn't stand to be looked at.

"What do you want from me?" Raymond asked.

"I don't know," she said. "I'm sorry."

She closed the door and sat on the edge of the tub, trying to breathe.

24

ISABEL WAS NOT tracking time well. She kept losing chunks of it. Somehow she was in her bed downstairs in the house, but she didn't remember getting there. She could see Marcus and June in the other bed, their heads sticking out over the covers. Isabel felt protected by their presence, even though that was stupid.

She fell asleep and dreamed of the river, of floating on the inner tube. In her dream, she tried to swim back upstream after Hector, but the current was too strong. It was impossible to make headway.

Then someone was shaking her awake. She scrambled back in fear, but it was only the housekeeper, Maria, whispering urgently in Spanish. Then Maria moved to shake Marcus and June in the other bed, whispering to them to be very quiet, to follow her. Isabel tried to stand. She could feel the pain between her legs. It stung.

Penny and Sebastian were in the entryway, rubbing their eyes.

"Where are we going?" Penny asked.

"A mi casa," Maria whispered. She unlocked the deadbolt with the key around her neck and guided the little ones outside.

Then June's high, piercing voice cried, "The bunny!"

Isabel froze. So did Maria. They stood listening to the quiet night. But no footsteps came running.

"I'll go get it," Isabel whispered, and she stepped back in and closed the door, in case June made any more noise. This was a moment for decision. Was it smart to run off with the housekeeper? George was supposed to be her rescuer, her protector. He had beaten his brother in the fight for them. He had a plan. And now Maria was going to mess it up.

Barefoot, she climbed the stairs to the main floor, then climbed the second flight to the third floor, where the brothers slept. Everything was quiet. She tiptoed past the old man's empty bedroom.

She listened at the next door, then pushed it open. There was the big framed baseball poster on the wall. George's cap hung on a chair. His head was dark on the pillow. If she woke him and told him Maria was stealing the children, he would be grateful.

But what would he do to Maria? And what was his plan? Maybe Maria stealing the children *was* his plan, and Isabel was messing it up. She was back on the third floor, when she shouldn't be.

She would count to ten, and if George woke up, it would be a sign that she should stay. She began to count silently. One, two, three—

She got to ten and he slept on.

She would count to ten one more time. Just in case. One, two three—

He didn't wake up.

She tiptoed back down the two flights to her room and found the bunny huddled between the pillows of June's bed, in the tumbled covers. She scooped it up and went outside, to find Maria actually wringing her hands.

"Oh, mija," Maria breathed.

"What *took* you so long?" June whispered, taking the bunny.

They followed Maria in bare feet over the unpaved driveway. Her car was parked a long way from the house, down by the security gate. As they walked, Isabel felt unsteady and thought the trembling in her legs was getting worse, but then she realized the earth was actually moving.

"Earthquake," Marcus whispered.

They all looked at each other, then looked back at the house. Isabel hoped it would collapse. She hoped a huge chasm would open in the ground and swallow the house and the sleeping brothers. But the shaking stopped. No lights went on in the windows. No one burst out after them.

They hurried to the car. Penny took the front seat. Isabel slid in back with Marcus and the little ones, closing the door as silently as she could.

Maria started the engine, peering up at the house. They drove down the rest of the driveway with the headlights off, to the gate.

"Push it open," Maria said in Spanish. "The power is off."

Isabel got out and ran to the gate, which opened. The car rolled past her and through. Isabel closed the gate quietly and ran to the car.

Then they were on the paved road down the hill. Maria kept checking the rearview mirror, but no one followed them. Isabel lost some more time, but then the car stopped outside a small white house.

They all got out. They were on a quiet street, with one streetlight at the end of the block. Maria jangled her keychain, looking for the key in the dark.

There was a sticker beside the front door that said, *"En este lugar, creemos en Dios,"* with a little drawing of praying hands. Maria led them inside, to a crowded living room with two mismatched couches and an armchair.

Maria knocked at a door, and called, "Oscar!"

After a minute, a teenage boy came out of the room in a T-shirt and boxer shorts, with his hair messy from sleep. There was a picture of him on the wall, as a little boy with his arm around an older girl. A sister somewhere.

"This is Oscar, my son," Maria said.

He was trying to put his glasses on. When he did, he saw the children all standing there in their matching clothes. He put his hand to his forehead. "Ay, Mamá," he said.

She spoke to him in rapid Spanish, saying, "You have to drive them to the American embassy, right now."

"Me?"

"Yes. Get dressed. I have to go back to work."

"You can't go back!"

"I have to," Maria said. "If they see me gone, they'll come straight here."

He looked frightened. "I don't even know where the embassy is."

"In the capital. Ask someone. Take your uncle's car."

"That piece of shit?" he said. "You're not giving me yours?"

"I can't." Maria went to a closet and pulled out five pairs of flip-flops in different sizes.

Oscar stared at the shoes. "When did you buy those?"

June pulled at Isabel's arm. "What are they saying?" she asked.

"We're going to the embassy," Isabel said.

Maria handed Oscar a set of car keys. Then she gave him a small paper bag. "Insulina," she said. "For the little boy."

"*I'll* keep that," Penny said in English, and she snatched the bag away.

"What do I tell the Americans?" Oscar asked.

"Say these are los niños del barco and you need protection."

"What about you?"

"I'll be fine, mijo." She kissed his sweaty forehead and cupped his cheek with her hand. "This is the thing we have to do."

25

PENNY SORTED THROUGH the flip-flops Maria had pulled from the closet and found her size. Maria had done a good job guessing. It was nice to have shoes again. The boy, Oscar, came back out of his room in jeans and a T-shirt.

"Hijo de puta," he said, rubbing his hair. "Qué hizo mi mamá."

June, in her new flip-flops, put her hands on her hips. "Do you speak English?" she asked.

"Yes," Oscar said.

"I'm hungry," June said.

"No time."

"Can you bring something?"

He handed her a banana from a wire basket.

June made a face. "It has brown spots."

"So don't eat it." He went to the refrigerator and pulled out a block of cheese and some apples. He put the food in a nylon backpack and added a jacket and a flashlight.

June peeled the banana, grimaced, and took a bite.

Oscar opened the front door and waited for them to file out. The other houses were dark. It was strange to be outside, and free.

Oscar unlocked a very old car parked on the street, and they all got in. Penny had never been in a car so old. It was even older than her dad's Volvo. There was dust all over the windshield and the windows. When she pulled the passenger door shut, the handle felt sticky, like the plastic was breaking down. "Whose car is this?"

"My tío's," Oscar said.

"Will he care?" she asked.

"He's dead."

"Oh."

Oscar turned the key in the ignition and there was a straining, chugging noise. Then it stopped.

"What was that?" Penny asked.

"We don't drive it," he said. "It doesn't have the right papers." He tried to start the car again: the click, the tinny *chug, chug, chug*, and then nothing. "Hijo de puta," he said, and put his head on the steering wheel.

He took his phone out of his pocket and made a call. Penny heard the tiny recording of a girl's voice, against his ear. He hung up. "Vámonos," he said.

They got out of the dusty car and walked down the dark road, past the other houses. The flip-flops slapped against the sidewalk. They wouldn't be able to sneak up on anyone. June carried the bunny in a makeshift pouch in the front of her T-shirt.

"Where are we going?" Penny asked Oscar.

"To find a car."

"How old are you?" she asked.

"Sixteen."

Penny blinked. Her cousin Winston was sixteen, and he still played "Jump or Dive" in the swimming pool, contorting himself in midair to obey the commands. He had a soft pale body, and pimples on his shoulders, and he refused to eat anything but turkey sandwiches and junk food. "Oh," she said.

26.

RAYMOND LAY AWAKE in the hotel. He had a travel alarm clock that projected on the ceiling, and the red numbers said 3:03 A.M. New Year's Day. He liked the projection, usually, but now it just reminded him that he couldn't sleep. The earthquake had unsettled him. What was next: Pestilence? Famine?

He was disturbed by how paralyzed he'd been, during the earthquake. He should have known what to do. Had someone disproven the "triangle of life"? They didn't even have an earthquake kit at home. They had some big bottles of water, and a lot of flashlights, and some bags of rice and quinoa that Nora had overbought. Pantry moths had gotten into the last stash.

A movie director had once bragged to Raymond about keeping a "ditch bag": a backpack filled with dried food, antibiotics, a space blanket, and $20,000 cash, for when the big one came and all hell broke loose. Also a dirt bike. The director was a fiftyish English guy who lived in Santa Monica Canyon.

Raymond had laughed. "I give you three minutes. Someone'll shoot you and take your ditch bag and your bike."

"I have a .38," the director had said.

"I hope you're a good shot."

"I should practice more," the director had admitted. "It's a hassle to get to the range."

Raymond could store more water, if they ever got home, but there was no preparing for what actually happened. A ditch bag was not going to protect you. Nothing was going to protect you.

He got up to pee, and walked around the bed. Nora seemed to be asleep, after her obsessive pacing of the hotel hallways, oblivious to the earthquake, and her forty-five minutes in the bathroom, doing her best imitation of her crazy depressive mother. It was the thing she always talked about, the thing that had scarred her most as a kid: her mother holing up in the bathroom and crying. It was worrying to see her do it herself.

When he came back, Nora's phone screen was lit up on the night table. Who was texting her at 3:15 in the morning? Four white lines glowed on the screen. She didn't wake up.

He moved closer. The screen went dark. He pushed the button to light it up again. The sender was "Pedro." The fucking guide. He picked up the phone to read the text.

> I haven't herd anything ether.
> Sorry. I would tell You if I did.
> Hope your doing OK or good
> as possible. Con . . .

The notification cut off there. Raymond thought about unlocking the phone to see the whole thread, but then Nora would know he'd read it. His sister kept an eye on her husband's phone. She said it would be naive not to, if you could. But he was not someone who snooped, that was not part of his sense of himself. He could ask Nora about it, but then she would know he'd been looking. The screen went dark again.

He put the phone back down on the night table. It made a light click. He waited, but Nora didn't move, and her breathing was steady. He stepped back around the bed and climbed under the sheet, careful not to bounce the mattress. The projection on the ceiling said 3:19 A.M.

So what did he know?

That Nora was looking for information. Fair enough. She must have asked the guide if he'd heard anything about the kids.

That Pedro knew nothing, and had pretty good English, even if his spelling wasn't great. "I would tell you if I did" was not something Raymond could say in Spanish.

That Nora was depressed, but of course she was depressed. Their kids were missing.

That he could pretend to be a cop, he could make a living doing it, but he had no idea what to do in an emergency, when the chips were down. No idea at all.

27.

OSCAR LED THE children down the quiet street. Under his breath, he cursed the fucking Herreras, and the fucking luck that led the kids to that grave, and his mother's fucking conscience, and his uncle's car that wouldn't start. *Five* kids, who had been all over the television! And no car! What kind of magician did his mother think he was? And why did she even still work for those assholes?

When they had fought about her job in the past, she'd cried and said she had to put food on the table. He told her never *ever* to use him as an excuse. He said he didn't want her food, he would buy his own, he would live on tortas. But she'd worked for the Herreras so long, she was afraid to leave, and they were both used to it. He got hungry and ate what she cooked.

He tried Carmen's number again, but she didn't answer. The kids' flip-flops slapped against the sidewalk.

After another block, they stopped outside a party to which he had not been invited. He knew that it shouldn't matter, when bigger things were at stake. But it would've been easier if he'd been invited. Carmen's shiny red Fiat was parked on the street outside the house. Reggaeton boomed from the windows, loud enough to piss off the neighbors. It would be morning soon. But it was New Year's Eve, it was allowed.

"Are we going in there?" Penny asked. She was the one who talked the most.

"No," he said. "You wait here."

The littlest girl sat down on the sidewalk with the bunny in her arms and said, "There's dog poop on this grass."

He tried to remember that he was more scared of the Herreras than he was of this party, and he walked up to the front door, knocked, and waited.

"Just go in," the Argentinian girl said. "It's a party."

He pushed open the door. The music got louder.

Carmen had been his friend since they were little, when she had thick glasses and a long braid down her back, and he'd thought they would always be together, doing their math homework at his kitchen table. But then she got beautiful all at once, some kind of quinceañera magic. She got boobs and hips and contact lenses, and took out the braid to have masses of wavy hair, and he stayed a skinny nerdy kid. She'd been nice to him about it, but she'd also acted like she *had* to go hang out with the beautiful stupid people at school. And she started acting dumb, which was the worst part. She wasn't dumb.

He moved through the drunk, dancing people in the dim living room, and found Carmen on the back patio with her boyfriend, Tito. Oscar had known Tito since fourth grade, when he was fat and his name was Norberto, but Tito had gone through the magical process, too, and got tall and muscled. Fucking Norberto. He and Carmen were dancing slow. Her head with its beautiful hair was on his chest and her eyes closed.

"Carmen," Oscar said.

She didn't hear him.

"Carmen!"

She opened her big eyes. He could see, in the patio light, her contact lenses floating on the surface. She was at least a little bit drunk. She stared at him. "Oscar."

"I need to borrow your car."

She blinked. "Why?"

"I just do."

Tito said, "You can't," leaning in close and threatening.

"This is none of your business, Norberto."

"It is when she's driving me home."

"This is really important," Oscar said to Carmen. "You shouldn't be driving anyway. I'll bring it back."

Carmen blinked again, and Oscar remembered the girl with the braid, who'd been better than he was at math. She could've been gorgeous *and* smart! "*Please*, Carmen," he said.

"I have to drive Tito home."

He imagined Raúl pulling up outside and grabbing the children from the sidewalk. Were they still even out there? Had they run away? He gave up on Carmen and made his way back through the living room, defeated, feeling the bass pound in his chest as he passed the speakers.

But then he saw Carmen's bag on a side table, the shiny red patent leather that matched her car. He looked over his shoulder and saw Carmen and Tito dancing again.

He unbuckled the bag and reached inside: lipstick, wallet, something round and flat, *keys*. He took the keys and slid the bag back onto the side table, then dodged the drunk and dancing people between him and the front door.

Outside, the air was fresh. He hadn't realized what a smoky, beery funk he'd been breathing. His kids were all sitting on the sidewalk, watching the front door. They perked up when they saw him. One, two, three, four, five: all there.

He held up the keys and they smiled at him, and he felt like a hero.

"You did it!" the tiny one with the bunny and the braids said.

He unlocked Carmen's shiny red car. They all piled in and he called his mother, triumphant, to tell her that his uncle's piece-of-shit car wouldn't start, but he had figured it out.

28

MARIA DROVE BACK to the finca with her headlights off. Maybe she shouldn't be going back to the house. But she needed to give Oscar time to get away. That was all she could think of. And her job was at the house. It had always been her job, since she was twenty years old. She hoped that somehow she could keep it.

She pushed open the gate and parked in her usual spot, then shut off the engine and listened. The house was dark and quiet. The brothers should still be asleep, drink-sick. She went back to close the gate, then walked up to the door and let herself in. Still no sound.

She hated to ask so much of her son. He'd had enough trouble in his life already. He'd been the one to find his sister dead of an overdose, when he was nine years old. He'd tried to shake Ofelia awake.

Maria thought that a small part of her son would be frozen forever in that moment. Her remaining child, her baby.

She took her shoes off and crept upstairs to the kitchen, and was just going into her little bedroom when she remembered that she had to turn the power back on. Then she heard a pounding on the door downstairs. A muffled woman's voice shouting. Maria ran back down in her stockings as quietly as she could. Who had come at this hour of night? How had they gotten through the gate? She had confused thoughts of Isabel, who had taken so long getting the bunny. But why would Isabel come back?

Maria unlocked the door with the key around her neck and blindly put a hand out to stop the shouting voice. It wasn't Isabel. It was a woman, and she'd been crying.

She pushed Maria's hand away from her mouth. "Let me in!"

"Shut up!" Maria whispered. "Stop it!"

"They owe me," the woman whispered back, matching Maria's undertone. She had dyed red hair and she seemed to be drunk. "I saw you drive in."

"Who are you?"

"Consuelo Bolaños. They took my husband."

Maria understood. The Colombian courier was called Bolaños. The widow must have followed Maria in through the unlocked gate. It was such terrible timing that Maria wanted to sit on the stoop and weep.

She heard footsteps on the stairs and prayed it was George. Please, God, let it be George.

He came downstairs shirtless, in pajama pants. "What is this?" he asked.

"Consuelo Bolaños," Maria said.

"You took my husband," Consuelo said. "You owe me money."

But George was looking at Maria. "Why are you dressed?"

"I couldn't sleep."

He focused on Consuelo again. "How did you get past the gate?"

The woman opened her mouth and Maria stared at her, willing her not to tell him that the gate had been unlocked, that she had watched Maria drive through. But Consuelo didn't notice. She was preoccupied with her own story.

"You killed my husband," she said, pointing at George. "I have nothing now."

"I didn't kill anyone," he said.

"My child's father is *dead*."

But George seemed to be listening to the room, to the silence. He held up a finger to Consuelo to wait, then went to the first of the children's bedrooms and opened the door. Maria felt her stomach clench. Moving faster, he ran to the other bedroom.

"Where are they?" he demanded.

Maria made her voice calm. "Not in bed?"

"Where are they?" he said, his voice rising, frantic.

"I don't know!" she said. "I thought they were here!"

George turned to Consuelo. "Did you let them out?"

"*What?*" she said.

Maria heard Raúl upstairs. He stumbled down to the entryway, shirtless in jeans. He had a mark on his face from the fight. "What's going on?"

Maria could smell the booze on his breath from six feet away, and feel his foul mood. "I don't know."

"Who's she?" Raúl asked, pointing his chin at the woman in the doorway.

"This is Consuelo Bolaños," George said, his voice rich with meaning.

"Bolaños," Raúl said, as if it rang a distant bell. Then his face shifted, and he glowered at Consuelo.

"Also the kids are gone."

"Gone?" Raúl turned his glower to his brother.

"Yep."

"Where are they?" Raúl asked the intruder.

Consuelo shook her head. "I don't know."

"*How* did you get through the gate?" George asked.

"She was pounding on the door," Maria said quickly, before the woman could answer.

"Was the door locked?" he asked.

"Yes," Maria said.

George was clearly trying to think it through.

Raúl was staring at Maria. "I saw the boy talking to you yesterday," he said.

"About nothing," she said. "We talked about the bunny."

"Nothing else?"

She shook her head.

Raúl took a pistol out of the back of his jeans and stepped toward Consuelo. He held the barrel to her forehead, pressed against her skin. Consuelo gasped. Raúl looked to Maria. "Tell me where the children are or I kill this woman."

"Stop it, Raúl," George said.

"I don't know!" Maria cried. If she told the truth, he would go after her son, and he would kill Oscar. The children needed more time to get away. She wished Consuelo hadn't come. "Please put the gun down."

"Tell me where they are," Raúl said.

"Please," she begged. "This woman has a little boy."

Maria thought he couldn't kill the mother of a child. And because of that tiny sliver of decency, because Raúl would let her live, Consuelo would give Maria away, and tell him she had just seen Maria driving through the gate. And then they would know everything.

The report of the gun made her jump. Consuelo's body jerked and slumped to the terra cotta floor. A red circle bloomed on her forehead.

Maria fell to her knees at the woman's side.

"What the fuck did you do?" George shouted at his brother. "Why did you do that?"

Maria grabbed Consuelo's limp hand. It was warm. "I'm so sorry," she said, sobbing. "I'm so sorry."

Raúl shouted, "I have to do everything around here!"

"You can't just kill people for no reason!" George shouted back.

"There was a reason!"

"Oh, what was it?"

"To get Maria to talk!" The gun was against Maria's forehead now. "Where are the kids?"

"I don't know!" she cried. He could kill her, but he could not go after Oscar and the children.

"She doesn't know!" George said. "And now we have another fucking body to deal with! That's how we got into this mess in the first place!"

"Please," Maria begged, "give her to her family. She has a son."

"We can't," George said wearily. "Not with a bullet in the head."

Raúl dropped the gun from Maria's forehead to turn to his brother. "You do nothing but criticize me!"

"You do nothing but give me reasons!"

Maria was panting with nausea. She thought that George should not speak to his brother that way, not when Raúl had a gun in his hand. Her phone vibrated in her pocket. She put a hand there to muffle the sound, but George heard it and crouched beside her.

"Who's that?" he asked.

"I don't know."

"Give me the phone."

Maria stared at him, paralyzed.

"Give it to me!"

She handed it over, but not before seeing Oscar's name on the screen. George accepted the call and put it to his ear. "Hello, Oscar," he said calmly. "I'm here with your mother. Where are the kids?"

Maria waited.

"You sure?" George said, eyes on Maria. "You have no idea?"

Dark blood was pooling on the stone floor around Consuelo's head.

"You're a bad liar," George said. "You will return the children to me *now*, do you understand?"

Maria could hear Oscar's tinny voice, pretending ignorance.

"Don't fuck with me, Oscar," George said, and his voice was all threat.

She heard Oscar say he didn't know anything, and then he must have hung up. Maria prayed that he wouldn't be lured back here by worry for her. She'd had her life. She couldn't bear to lose her son.

George stared at her with wonder. "So *you* took the children."

She shook her head. "No."

"I was trying to help them," he said. "And now this woman is dead, because of your stupid plan, because of your lies. Is that what you wanted?"

She shook her head. "No."

"Where is Oscar taking the children?"

"He doesn't have them."

Raúl shouted, "We've always been good to you! And this is how you repay us? We even paid for the funeral for your slut daughter!"

Maria started to weep. But Raúl didn't shoot her. He stomped upstairs.

George reached out and flipped a light switch. Nothing happened. He flipped it again. She watched him, holding her breath, and she saw him understand. "You turned the power off," he said.

"It went out. It goes out."

"You turned it off," he said, amazed.

She said nothing.

"For the gate!" he said. "And that's how Consuelo got in." George laughed, and leaned back against the wall, and the laugh became a groan. "Tell me what you did, Maria. I want to help the children. As much as you do. Just tell me what you did."

She shook her head. "Nothing."

"You can't do this alone," he said. "You need my help. You couldn't save Ofelia alone."

Her breath caught at the pain and truth of that.

George crouched beside her in his pajamas and looked at her with the frustrated, thwarted brown eyes she had known since he was a child, as he watched his brother get away with everything. "Maria," he said. "Tell me. You can tell me. Raúl isn't here."

"Oscar is taking them to the embassy," she whispered.

He nodded, and put a hand on her shoulder. It was warm. "Good," he said. "That's good. That's what I was going to do, in the morning. Does he have a good car?"

"No," she said. "His uncle's Impala. I'm worried it won't run. Don't tell Raúl."

George nodded and squeezed her shoulder.

Raúl came back downstairs with a shirt on, boot heels striking the stairs. "I'm going to find them."

George stood, stretching his knees. "Oscar's driving them to the embassy."

"No!" Maria cried.

"Oscar?" Raúl said.

"In an old Impala," George said.

Maria stared up at him. The good brother.

George pointed his finger at her. *"That's* for fucking with me, Maria," he said. He had a strange look in his eye, one she had never seen before.

Raúl stepped over Consuelo's body in the doorway and staggered out into the night. There was the sound of the Jeep engine starting up.

Maria had always thought George was better and nobler than his brother. But it turned out he was worse. There was something missing in Raúl. He felt nothing, he couldn't even help it. But George *knew* he had just cleaved her heart in two.

"The children," she said. "My son."

"They have a long head start," George said. "They'll be fine."

"Please stop your brother," she said. "Please."

"Raúl's drunk. He'll roll over in a ditch."

"I thought you wanted to help the children," she said.

"I did!" he shouted, right in her face, a fleck of spit in the corner of his mouth. "But you fucked that up for me, didn't you? I was going to turn him in, with the children!"

"You still can!" she said. "Go after him!"

He seemed to think about it for a moment, then shook his head. "No," he said. "He's fucking crazy. I'm getting out of here, before he comes back."

"Oh, God," she moaned.

George stopped pacing and studied Consuelo's bleeding body draped over the threshold. He asked, "Do we have a tarp?"

29

MARCUS SAT BEHIND Oscar in the red car. It was not a very big car. They were four in the back, with Isabel squished next to Marcus, which made his heart skip and tumble over itself. June and Sebastian were buckled under the other seatbelt, next to them. Penny had grabbed the front seat, of course.

Oscar hung up the phone. "They have my mother," he said.

They all sat silent. Then Isabel said something urgent in Spanish. Marcus guessed she was saying that Oscar couldn't take them back to that house, not even for his mother. That's what Marcus would have said if *he* could speak Spanish. They needed to go to the embassy.

Oscar nodded. He was trying to act calm. "Okay," he said, and he started the engine. It caught and purred lightly. "Okay, okay."

Marcus heard a shout, through the window. A girl and a boy had come out of the house with the party in it. The girl had long black hair and a red bag slung across her chest.

Oscar swore, and the car leaped forward and stalled. It was a stick shift. Marcus's dad had taught him how they worked. You had to let the clutch out, as you pressed the gas.

The boy and the girl ran toward them, across the lawn. Marcus hoped they would step in dog poop.

"Go!" he said. "Slow on the clutch!"

Oscar restarted the car, and gunned it. It jerked once and then pulled miraculously away, swerving down the block, almost taking off the mirror on a parked car. Oscar shifted to second and third. Marcus looked out the back window and saw the couple running behind them. Then they jogged and slowed and receded. Marcus turned forward, his heart pounding.

"Did you just steal this car?" Penny asked.

"It's my friend's," Oscar said.

"Was that your friend chasing us?"

"Yes."

"Do you even have a driver's license?"

He said nothing.

"Oh my God," Penny said.

"It's okay," Oscar said, but his voice was shaky. "We go to the embassy now. Let's not look like the lost kids."

"We are the lost kids," Penny said.

"Do you know how to get to the capital?" Marcus asked.

"There's only one road," Oscar said.

The sun was coming up, glowing behind the mountains in the east. They left the neighborhood and headed south. Oscar drove in silence for a long time. He might not have a license, but he was an okay driver, once he didn't have to start and stop. The sky glowed brighter, and lightened to blue. The trees looked dewy and wet. They passed a sign that said INTERSECCION ADELANTE.

June, in a quiet voice, said, *"A."*

Marcus was going to tell his sister that this was no time for a game. But it would keep her from being afraid or carsick. And he couldn't help scanning the signs outside the window for his own *A.*

"B," June said after a minute. "Banos."

"Ba*ños,*" Penny corrected.

After a while, they passed a roadside restaurant with a chalk sign. "Arroz con pollo," Marcus said. *"A."*

"Con!" June said. *"C!"*

"Can I play?" Sebastian asked.

"You have to find your own word that begins with *A,*" June said.

Marcus scanned for a *B,* but now they were on a stretch of empty road with no signs. He leaned his head against the glass of the window and wondered if they were going to get breakfast. Arroz con pollo was rice with chicken. There was a car behind them, following too close.

Then the car had pulled alongside them. The road they were on had only two lanes, and it was dangerous to pass. But the car wasn't passing. It was a Jeep with an open top, and Marcus looked straight into the eyes of the driver.

"It's him!" he cried.

Oscar must have seen Raúl at the same moment, because they shot forward, leaving the Jeep behind. Isabel grabbed Marcus's hand.

They sped down the road, but the Jeep caught up. A car came at them in the opposite direction, and Raúl dropped back to let it by. There was a long, annoyed, receding honk from the other car. When the road ahead was empty, the Jeep pulled alongside them again.

"Go faster!" Marcus shouted.

"I can't!" Oscar said.

Marcus leaned forward and looked across Isabel to see if his sister was okay. June sat clutching the bunny, looking terrified, the alphabet forgotten.

Raúl was shouting something at them from the Jeep. Then Marcus saw him waving something.

"He has a gun!" Marcus shouted.

June screamed.

"Hijo de *puta*," Oscar said.

Another car was coming toward them. Oscar swerved to the shoulder, and Raúl fell back, to let the car go by. But the Jeep was faster than their little red car, and was beside them again. Marcus ducked, and heard the crash of glass. He put his hands over his ears. June screamed again. Oscar's window was out. Raúl had actually *shot* at them. A man had shot a gun at them, like in a movie. Marcus revised the seriousness of everything in his mind.

Raúl sideswiped them, and Oscar fought to keep the car on the road. Then he swerved toward the Jeep, clipping off its mirror. Marcus heard another shot.

The two cars approached a blind curve together. As they rounded it, a truck came toward them. There was a blaring horn and squealing brakes. Marcus still had his hands over his ears. Oscar spun the wheel, and the car flew sideways. Then they were rolling off the road. It was too loud. Things were crunching and crashing. The world spun. There were trees. Bright, dark, bright. Isabel was flung against Marcus, and Marcus was flung against her. Then everything stopped, and was silent. Marcus, hanging upside-down in his seatbelt, wondered if he was still alive.

Isabel said something in Spanish under her breath. Her hair hung toward the ceiling, which was now the floor.

"Are you okay?" Marcus asked her.

She nodded. He opened his door, unbuckled his seatbelt carefully, and rolled out. He went around to his sister. He couldn't get her door open, but her window was gone. Sebastian looked okay.

"Where's the bunny?" June cried.

"We'll find him," he said. "Climb out through the window."

In the front seat, Penny unbuckled her seatbelt and landed on her head, saying, "Ow!"

Marcus was afraid that Oscar might be dead. Raúl would come with his gun, and there would be no one to save them.

But Oscar was breathing, hanging upside-down in his seatbelt with his eyes closed. He moaned when Marcus touched his shoulder through the broken window. There was a bloody spot on his forehead and little scratches on his cheek. His glasses hung crooked on his face.

"Oscar? Wake up."

Oscar opened his eyes and looked around. Then he closed them.

Marcus shook his shoulder again. "We have to get out."

"Where's Raúl?" Oscar's voice was hoarse.

"I don't know."

"I found the bunny!" June said. "He's okay!"

Marcus tugged at Oscar's door until it opened, and Oscar unbuckled his seatbelt and did a bad somersault out of the car. He straightened his glasses, then rubbed his head and cursed. Blood came away on his hand.

They were surrounded by trees, but somehow they hadn't hit one. The Jeep was also upside-down, closer to the road. Oscar limped toward it, and Marcus followed him. The other kids hung back.

The Jeep's windshield had shattered. Marcus squatted down and saw Raúl's upside-down face staring at him, tilted grotesquely, with part of his forehead scraped off so his eye socket was bare and bloody. One of the eyeballs was hanging out.

Marcus felt a hand on his shoulder and he lurched back.

"It's okay, it's okay," Oscar was saying.

"It's not!" Marcus said. "It's not!" He had imagined seeing a dead body before, but he hadn't thought it would look like *that*. He started to hyperventilate.

"Shh," Oscar whispered.

"He's dead!" Marcus said. "His face!"

"I know."

Marcus heard a noise and jerked around, expecting to see Raúl's twisted body, staggering up behind him like a zombie. Instead he saw Isabel. "I want to see," she said.

"Don't!"

"I have to."

Isabel moved toward the Jeep and crouched down to look in the window at Raúl. Marcus held his breath, picturing that bloody eye socket. His sister was walking toward him with hesitant steps.

"Don't look," he said.

"I want to see, too!"

"No you don't." He held her back.

"I'm not afraid!" June said.

The others were drawing closer.

"Can I see?" Penny asked.

"No," Oscar said. "We have to get out of here."

"Why?" Penny asked. "Raúl is dead, right?"

"There's still his father," Oscar said. "And George. They'll come after us. We know too much." He limped back to the red car and reached in through the window to pull out his backpack.

"How did Raúl find us?" Marcus asked. "Did he track your phone?"

Oscar fumbled with his phone, tore the back of it open, and took out the battery and the little card. His hands were shaking. He bent the card in half and threw it into the trees.

Isabel watched it go. "You said there was only one road to the capital," she said. "It was easy to find us."

Marcus realized that was probably true. He shouldn't have said anything about the phone. Now Isabel would hold the destroying of it against him. "We could hitchhike to the embassy," he said.

"We're not hitchhiking," Oscar said. "It's too dangerous."

"You could have let us call our parents," Isabel said.

"We haven't had breakfast," Penny said.

"I don't know what to do about any of that, okay?"

They all stared at him.

"I'm sorry," Oscar said. "We have to go."

"Do you have sunscreen?" Penny asked, squinting up at the climbing sun.

"No," he snapped. "Let's go."

30.

LIV WOKE, AMBIEN-GROGGY, with only a vague sense of dread and foreboding. Something was beeping, and her heart started to race. She sat up to listen. The beeping was outside in the hotel hallway, and then it passed by. It wasn't the right tone for Sebastian's glucose monitor. It was someone carrying some other device. The memories came flooding back, and the pain.

She reached for her phone and peered at the blurry screen. It didn't used to be so blurry. She'd gotten old, in the last few days. No messages. 7:00 A.M.

She pressed her hands into her eyes and wished she could go back to the unconscious forgetting. She needed coffee. There was a club room on the top floor of the hotel, with food. She pulled on clothes at random and took the elevator up, reading the engraved panel with the emergency instructions in English:

IF THE ELEVATOR DOORS FAIL TO OPEN, DO NOT BECOME ALARMED.
PLEASE USE BUTTON MARKED "ALARM" TO SUMMON HELP.

She remembered the first time Penny had pointed out the instructions in the elevator at the UCLA Medical Center and explained how funny and contradictory they were. Liv remembered the building because Sebastian had been having big blood sugar swings, and was leaning exhausted against her hip, so the elevator advice had seemed particularly poignant and impossible.

In the club room, she surveyed the coffee and pastries. It was a pale imitation of the ship's buffet, but it would have been very useful for feeding children. Penny would have loved the tall Plexiglas cylinders of cereal, the little knob to fill your bowl. Sebastian would have peeled himself a hard-boiled egg.

Camila came in, looking haggard and tired. She no longer looked like she'd stepped out of a glossy ad for the cruise ship.

"Coffee?" Liv asked.

"Thank you," Camila said.

Liv poured two cups. "Is your embassy being helpful?"

"I suppose."

"Any news?"

Camila hesitated. "Isabel logged in to her Facebook account."

Liv put down the coffee pot and stared. "She did?"

Nora had appeared in the doorway, her dark hair unwashed, scraped back in a ponytail. "Did what?"

Nora looked—Icelandic. That was the word that came to Liv. Like a character in a saga, living alone on a windswept crag, trying to survive against the elements, battered by cold and want. She didn't belong in the club room of an equatorial hotel. Liv hated her cousin for whatever was going on with Pedro, but she did feel a pang at how miserable Nora was.

"Isabel logged in to her Facebook account," Camila repeated.

"Did she write a message?" Liv asked.

"No," Camila said, taking a seat on a couch. "She just signed in."

"Are they sure it was really her?"

"I suppose they can't be," Camila said. "But who else? Someone with her password? And why not send a message, if it is someone else? I mean, what do they want?"

"Maybe she was trying to give her location," Nora said.

"So why not *give* it?"

"But this is good news, right?" Liv said. "I mean—she's alive. They're in a place with a computer."

"Unless it was a phone," Nora said.

"They say it wasn't," Camila said. She looked at the coffee cup on her knees. "There is something else. They found a photograph."

"Where?" Nora asked, in a strained voice.

"Instagram. They have been tracking the account. They thought it might be her."

Liv didn't want to know. Her legs felt weak.

"You cannot see her face," Camila said. "But I know it is her. They are searching the—metadata, I think it is called."

"But is she okay?" Nora asked. "In the photo?"

"It is a trophy, I think," Camila said. "A boast, you know."

"Oh, no," Liv said, sinking to the couch. A trophy. She could not think about what that meant for her own children. She *would* not. She put her arms around Camila, whose shoulders felt like a bird's wings. Slight, hollow bones. "I'm so sorry," she said.

Camila submitted to be held.

Liv kept stumbling over blank spots in her mind. She remembered reading about mad cow disease, how prions ate holes in the brain, left it like Swiss cheese. Her brain felt like that. There were places where fear had created a gap, places she could not go.

Nora sat across from them, perfectly still. "Do you have the picture?"

Camila pulled free from Liv. She produced a phone and touched uncertainly at the screen. An Instagram post—or a screenshot of one—appeared. She offered the phone, then looked away as Liv and Nora leaned over it.

The photograph was of a girl in a bed, face down. She seemed to be naked, but only her back was visible. Her long hair was loose and damp over her face. It looked horrifyingly postcoital, but there were no identifying marks. No moles, no scars. Nothing on the smooth, lovely skin to prove that it was Isabel. The photograph had a filter on it, fading the edges dark, and Liv thought about the person who had taken it choosing a filter, trying Clarendon, X-Pro, Lo-Fi.

"How do you know it's her?" Nora asked.

"I know," Camila said stiffly, taking the phone back and putting it in her pocket, as if her privacy had been violated, which it had. "I tell you, I do."

Liv imagined a similar photograph of Penny or Sebastian and nearly tumbled down one of the Swiss cheese tunnels in her brain. Of course she would know their backs, recognize the shoulders she had bathed and toweled and covered in sunscreen. "Will you tell us, if they learn anything?" she asked.

Camila nodded and sat for a moment with her hands clasped on her knees. "Isabel loves photographs of herself looking sexy," she said. "I always try to keep them from her. But now I look at those photographs and they look so innocent. A child's pictures. Her body is like a new toy." Her jaw was shaking. "But this one—" She faltered.

"Camila, I'm so sorry," Liv said.

They sat in silence for another moment, and then Camila stood. "Thank you for the coffee."

Liv imagined that polite reserve was the only thing holding Camila together. She seemed to carry herself carefully. Any minute the shell of her formality might break.

"You'll let us know what you find out?" Liv asked.

Camila gave an austere little drop of her chin and left the room.

31

PENNY STALKED DOWN the trail, nursing her resentments. Oscar had yelled at her, when all she'd said was that they hadn't had break-fast. But then he seemed to feel bad about it, and cut up the apples and cheese, and passed them out on the trail as they walked. Penny did the calculation, watched Sebastian give himself his shot, stuffed the calculator back in her pocket with the paper bag of insulin cartridges, and ran to catch up. If Oscar were a babysitter, her mother would fire him.

They walked a long time. Oscar was limping badly. They saw a tree made of tiny trunks and a long sloping neck like a giraffe's. Oscar said it was called a walking tree. They all stopped and stared at it. Penny's legs were tired.

"Where are we?" she asked.

"I don't know," Oscar said.

"We should find a road and stop a car."

"Okay. Where?"

"There *was* a road," she said. "We were on it."

"It was too dangerous there."

"Is there another one?"

"In this country? Yes."

"I could get us back to the road we were on," Marcus said.

"That's so *far*!" June said.

"I'm hungry," Sebastian said.

"He could collapse, without food," Penny said. "Then you'll have to carry him."

Oscar looked miserable. "We keep walking," he said, but he grimaced when he put his weight on his bad leg.

They trudged on. Penny considered the benefits of complaining some more. But then the trail through the trees opened up into a cleared area. There were train tracks running through it.

"Come on," Oscar said. He led them toward the tracks.

"What are we doing?" Penny asked.

"Waiting," he said.

They sat on the ground near the tracks, and Penny looked at the big tarred railroad ties. Her mother used to put pennies on the rails when she was a kid, so they would get flattened by the train, but you weren't supposed to do it now. It was like not wearing a seatbelt, and climbing from the front seat to the back, and other things her mother had done when she was little that no one was allowed to do anymore.

Penny didn't really like taking trains. First you had to find the right track at the station, and it was always confusing. Then you didn't have an assigned seat. Penny got sick if she sat facing backward, so she had to guess which way the train was going to go. Her parents were always looking for four empty seats facing each other, and people glared at you like they were afraid you would sit next to them, and it was stressful.

June, sitting on the ground, sang softly, "Una vieja-ja—mató un gato-to—con la punta-ta—del zapato-to." She brushed her hands back and forth across her bent knees and clapped her legs. Then they heard the noise of a train in the distance.

It was moving slowly. Penny could see the engineer's face in the window, shiny with sweat. Penny thought maybe he would recognize them from the TV, but he didn't seem to see them. It was a freight train, not a passenger train. The first few cars were closed up, but then one passed with an open door. Oscar stood and peered in as it went by. Penny knew about riding trains because they'd done a unit on immigration in school. Some people were so desperate to get to America that they paid strangers called coyotes to take them. Her mother had let her watch a movie about it even though there were things in it that weren't appropriate. Penny always thought of the actual coyotes that yipped in the distance and sometimes ran down their street at night, skinny and gray-brown and purposeful. The people called the train La Bestia.

Two more closed cars. Then an open one.

"That one," Oscar said. "Go, go, go!"

It all happened so fast. Isabel and Marcus, who looked as startled as Penny felt, scrambled up onto the bare metal of the train car, with their long legs. Oscar handed June up to them, and they caught her by her elbows and lifted her in. It was too high for Penny to climb. She ran alongside. Oscar grabbed Sebastian and passed him awkwardly up. Then he threw the backpack in.

Penny had always suspected that this moment would come. They would abandon her because she was slow and bossy and annoying. "Don't leave me!" she screamed.

"*Run!*" Oscar shouted. His face looked desperate. The train rumbled and creaked, metal on metal.

It was hard to run in flip-flops, and she had never been fast. Oscar grabbed her hand and pulled her forward, limping. She stumbled and went down on her knee.

The others were all shouting, and she heard Sebastian scream her name. Finally Oscar picked her up and heaved her into the train with a grunt. She landed painfully on her side.

"Come on!" June screamed at Oscar.

He ran and struggled to climb up, the others pulling at his clothes. Then he was in. He collapsed on his back, breathing hard and moaning. June unzipped the pocket on the backpack and peered inside, then reached in and pulled out the bunny, like a magic trick. Its nose twitched and she hugged it to her face.

The train jostled its way down the track, with all of them aboard. Penny sat up and looked at her knee. Sticky blood ran down her shin. She wanted to cry, but that didn't seem right when they had done something so impossible. "Where are we going?" she asked.

Oscar shook his head, still out of breath.

"We're going northwest," Marcus said.

"What's there?" June asked.

"Nicaragua," Marcus said.

"We're going to *Nicaragua*?" his sister said.

"No," Oscar said. "We're just resting, and getting to somewhere with food."

"Will they have insulin, too?" Sebastian asked.

Penny had a terrible thought, and she put her hand on her pocket and felt no paper bag. An icy flush passed through her body, even in the heat. The bag must have fallen out of her pocket when she ran for the train. "I thought we were going to the embassy," she said.

"We *were*," Oscar said. "But people are trying to kill us. And we can't keep walking. I can't keep walking. We need to rest."

Isabel was watching Penny, with flat eyes and a tiny smile—she knew she'd lost the insulin. Penny hated her.

Sebastian unscrewed the pen and took out the old cartridge. "This one is empty," he said. "Can I have a new one?"

"Just a minute," Penny said.

He rolled the empty cartridge between his fingers. "Do you think Mom and Dad will find us?"

"Of course."

"Can we call them?"

"We don't have a phone."

"We *had* a phone," Isabel said, "but Oscar threw it away." Penny's mother would have told her she didn't like that tone of voice.

"How far is Nicaragua?" June asked.

"We're not going to Nicaragua," Oscar said.

"But how far is it?"

"I have no fucking idea."

June blinked at him.

"Probably about a hundred miles," Marcus said.

"See, he knows," Oscar said, and he closed his eyes. "He can be leader now, okay? I quit."

32.

THE TRAIN HAD a different motion from the truck, and Noemi woke to the new rocking, trying to figure out what was different. It jostled in a different way: more rhythmic.

Chuy had chosen their car and they had climbed in at night in the dark, and then realized it wasn't empty. A woman and a little boy were inside, hiding against the wall. But Noemi was tired, and she had shrugged her backpack off. She didn't want to have to go find another car. Her once-pink backpack was scuffed and grayish with dirt. So was the plush pig.

The woman in the train car had seemed nervous. Noemi had tried to be friendly to the little boy, she had showed him the pig, but he didn't want to talk. She thought maybe in the morning these people would see that they didn't have to be afraid of Chuy, and then she and the boy could be friends.

Now, as she woke, with her pig as a pillow, she saw that the woman and the little boy were gone. It was light out, and the train was crawling.

"Why does it go so slowly?" she asked Chuy.

"You in a hurry?" he asked. He was rolling loose tobacco in a piece of paper.

"I just wanted to know."

Chuy licked the paper to seal the cigarette.

She sat up and watched the trees go by, thick and green and tangled. After a while, she asked, "Where do you think the woman and the little boy went?"

"To find another car."

"She was afraid of you."

Chuy lit his cigarette. "Not my fault."

"Did you talk to them?"

He nodded.

"Where are they going?"

"Texas."

"Maybe we'll see them there."

"They won't make it."

"Why not?"

He shook his head and blew out smoke.

Noemi searched Chuy's broad face. "Why didn't my parents want me to know about you?"

"They think I went bad."

"Did you?"

He paused, then said, "For a while."

"So why did they change their minds?"

"Because your grandmother couldn't keep you."

"What did my father say then?"

"He thought you should stay with your grandmother," Chuy said. "But she's an old woman. She can only do so much."

They heard something outside the boxcar: voices. Noemi got up and went to the open door.

"Careful," Chuy said, and he came to stand beside her.

Some people were climbing into the train, two cars ahead. Kids. A lot of them. They all struggled into the train, an older boy climbing in last.

Noemi couldn't see them, now that they were in the train car, but she kept watching. They'd all been wearing the same kind of clothes: red shorts, dirty white T-shirts, flip-flops. The oldest boy had a backpack, which he'd thrown into the train. Then he'd helped a girl in. Noemi had seen her face as she grimaced and rolled inside. "That girl," she said. "I thought I knew her."

Chuy grunted, stamping out his cigarette.

The recognition shimmered somewhere in the back of her mind, then burst forward, where she could see it. "They're the kids from the ship!"

Chuy said nothing, so she knew she was right.

She looked out the door again. They weren't in their swimsuits from the television, but they wore matching outfits. They'd appeared, and she'd been here to see it. She wished she could tell Rosa, but did Rosa even know who the kids were? "Do you think they were on TV at home?" she asked.

"Maybe," Chuy said.

"Can we go talk to them?"

"No."

"I want to meet them."

"Not a good idea."

"Why not?"

"They have bad luck," Chuy said. "We don't want to catch it."

Noemi looked out again. She couldn't hear the children over the clank and rumble of the train. Then she saw something emerge from the car. It was a boy's hips, pushed forward with his red shorts lowered, to pee out the door. Noemi could only see his hand, the arcing stream, and the splash on the rocks below. She pulled her head back inside, giddy with shock. "One of them is peeing," she whispered.

"Everybody has to," Chuy said.

33.

WHEN GEORGE wanted help moving Consuelo's body, Maria refused.

"Do you know how much we pay you?" George demanded. "For making scrambled eggs and sweeping the floor? Help me!"

So she did. There were tiny shards of Consuelo's skull on the bloody tile floor. It was hard to get the plastic tarp under her, and the body was heavy and awkward. Finally they pulled the tarp out of the doorway and against the wall, and they could close the door again.

Maria mopped the floor, filling buckets with bloody water, dumping the buckets in the bathroom, trying to keep herself from retching. When she was finished, she told George she needed to go home. She wanted her phone.

He said she wasn't going anywhere.

"Am I a prisoner?"

"As soon as I leave, you can go," he said.

He went up to the office and she heard him opening drawers and cabinets. A hammer blow, a breaking of glass, the sound of a power drill. She had lived so long in fear of the Herreras, in the habit of loyalty to them, in the habit of fear of the police, that she could not make herself leave when George said she couldn't. It was as if something physical was stopping her.

She heard his phone ring. She climbed the stairs to listen to George talking, and looked into the office.

George dropped the phone to his side. "He's dead."

Her heart pounded. Oscar. "Who?"

"Raúl."

Maria didn't know what to say to that. She had thought Raúl was indestructible. "How?"

"Car accident."

"And the children?"

"I don't know."

She slumped down on the stairs.

George seemed dazed. He went to his bedroom and came out with a duffel bag. Then he stepped around her. "Good luck, Maria," he said. "You should get out of here, too. The police will come."

"My phone!" she said.

"Sorry. No."

He was downstairs and out the door. She collected her handbag and a few small things of her own. She left poor Consuelo alone in the entryway, and Sancho in the dog kennel, and the white horse in the stables. The police would come, and someone would look after them all. She locked the door when she left, out of habit.

She eased her car down the driveway and out the gate, as tired as she had ever felt. She could not think of where to go except home.

34.

LIV HAD SAT hunched over her phone in the club room, looking for suspicious Instagram posts, trying different hashtags while her coffee went cold. Now she forked an English muffin into halves. Crumbs dropped onto the table in front of the toaster. That was her, she reflected: soft, white, torn, crumbling. The karmic bus had mowed her down. She was being punished for living in a false world, spongy and insulated from the reality around her. For living in a house with an alarm system, in a neighborhood where the only Latinos were gardeners and day laborers. For sending her kids to a private school that was almost entirely white in a city that wasn't.

She told herself that she wasn't being rational, she was being self-aggrandizing. The universe didn't care what she did. But their life was obscene. Her kids didn't see anyone except kids like themselves, and kids who were richer.

And now her kids were where? Seeing what? With Sebastian so fragile and dependent on first-world medicine. Sebastian, who, if he was in *Treasure Island*, would run home when the first scary thing happened. The thought nearly buckled Liv's knees and sent her to the floor in the middle of the club room.

She waited for the toaster. The kitchen had no reason to change up the food, because most people didn't stay this long. Tourists were here overnight before going somewhere beautiful. Business people stayed for a meeting. If you stayed long enough to notice that the breakfast-makings never changed, something was deeply wrong.

Her phone buzzed in her pocket. A text from Kenji, at the embassy:

> On my way to hotel with news.
> You there?

Liv's hand started to shake, holding the phone. She hit the microphone and dictated a text. "Good or bad news—question mark." She waited for his answer, and it popped up:

> Gather the others?

Fuck you, Kenji, she thought. "GOOD OR BAD?" she wrote, with one thumb.

The three little gray dots appeared, pulsing on the screen. She waited. Then the reply:

> Good I think.

The English muffin popped out of the toaster. She left it there and texted the others.

They gathered in the empty club room, and Benjamin took her hand. Raymond sat opposite them, clearly jittery. Nora stood, with that Icelandic saga air. Gunther, so outsized and jovial a week ago, seemed to be shrinking, his spine compressing day by day, his face graven with lines.

Kenji Kirby arrived, polished and hale. He sat in a leather chair and clasped his hands together. The parents mirrored him instinctively, clasping their own hands, leaning forward on the couches. They were praying, in their way.

"They've narrowed down the Facebook login to one area," Kenji said.

"Why is it taking so long?" Camila asked.

"The computer had good security."

"Also the police are incompetent," Gunther said, his voice startlingly loud. Liv wondered if he was drunk.

Kenji ignored him. "The police have also been tracking down the contacts of Luis Bolaños. Bolaños is the dead Colombian man who was found—"

"We know," Gunther said.

"The Herrera family lives in the right area for the login and had contact with Bolaños," Kenji said. "That's a house they thought they'd ruled out, but now a tactical team is going back with a search warrant."

"Wait, like a *raid*?" Liv said.

"Something like that."

"And you think our kids are there?"

"We certainly hope so."

Benjamin said, "Couldn't a raid put them in danger?"

"Not more danger than they're already in," Kenji said. "In the official estimation."

"When's the raid happening?" Benjamin asked.

Kenji looked at his watch. "Right now."

"Oh *fuck*," Nora said.

"*Now?*" Liv said. "No one thought to *consult* us about this? What if the kids become hostages, or—or human shields?"

"You've been urging speed and action all week," Kenji said. "And now you've got it."

"But we thought you'd let us know!"

"Can we go to the house?" Raymond asked.

"It's too dangerous," Kenji said.

"Our *children* are there."

"The team will keep us apprised."

Liv leaned into her husband's side, and he locked his arms around her. She tried not to think about Penny and Sebastian seeing men with masks and guns and bulletproof vests rushing into a house. Or about the lengths to which desperate kidnappers might be driven. How did hostages ever survive? It seemed unlikely, impossible.

"This took a lot of work on a lot of people's part," Kenji said, sounding peevish.

"You might have told us," Camila said.

"That's what I'm doing, right now."

They glared at him and sat in silence.

Kenji's phone rang, and Liv jumped. He turned away for privacy, but they all watched him. He spoke in monosyllables, in Spanish, and hung up. Then he stared around at the parents as if he didn't quite see them. "The children weren't there," he said.

"What does that mean?" Liv asked.

"I don't know." Kenji looked stunned.

"Who *was* there?" Raymond asked.

"No one." This wasn't the outcome he'd expected.

Liv wondered if Kenji had imagined himself some kind of action hero, directing his armored team to the villain's lair to rescue the adorable children, who would be huddled in a room full of toys, frightened but unscathed.

"Was there evidence that the kids were there?" Benjamin asked.

"I don't know." He looked down at his phone.

"Find *out*," Raymond said.

"Okay," Kenji said, backing out of the room. "I will."

35.

EVERY TIME PENNY closed her eyes, she saw herself running for the train, tripping over rocks, stumbling in flip-flops, losing the insulin, the paper bag disappearing behind her. Then she opened her eyes again. The train rumbled along.

"I'm hungry," Sebastian said.

"We don't have any food," she said.

"Can I have a new cartridge, for when there is food?"

"No."

"Why not?"

"Because your sister lost them," Isabel said, from across the train car.

Penny glared at her. "Shut up, Isabel."

Sebastian looked up. "Is it true?"

"I was running for the train," Penny said. "They fell out of my pocket."

There was a mortified silence.

Marcus asked, "Why didn't you let Oscar carry them in the backpack?"

"Because we don't even *know* him."

Oscar had his eyes closed and seemed to be pretending they weren't there.

"You let him hang your butt out the train door," June said.

"I had to pee!"

"That's crazy!" June said.

"Well, you went in your pants and I can smell it!" Penny said. "*That's* crazy!"

There was another silence, in which June looked shocked and betrayed. "Hanging your butt out the door is dangerous," she finally said, very quietly.

"Everything is dangerous," Penny said. "I want to go home *now*."

"Don't be a child," Isabel said.

"Shut *up*!" Penny felt the tears coming. But tears would just prove Isabel right. Penny wiped her wet cheeks with the back of her hand. "Our parents would have found us at that house."

"Don't say that," Marcus said.

"It's true! We should have stayed there. We only had to leave because of *her*." Penny knew she was onto something, because Isabel's face had turned a weird color. "We had a doctor there, and food, and bathrooms. But Isabel wouldn't listen to George and stay downstairs."

"Leave her *alone*," Marcus said.

"You just don't want to admit it, because you're in love with her."

"Shut *up*!" Marcus said.

"But she's not in love with you. She was in love with Raúl."

"I was not!" Isabel hissed.

"Shut up, Penny!" Marcus said.

"*Stop!*" Oscar said.

"You don't understand anything," Isabel said, low and threatening.

"I understand!" Penny said. "I understand it's your fault that we're on a stupid train in the middle of nowhere!"

"So go, then."

"Fine," Penny said, getting up. "I will."

She stood, her split knee stinging, and went to the open door. She couldn't stand to be with Isabel another second.

"Penny, no!" Sebastian said.

"I have to find the insulin." She sat down at the edge, so she wouldn't have so far to jump to the ground. It was still alarmingly high, and the ground was moving. She could tell she was about to make a terrible mistake, but she couldn't help herself.

"Don't go!" June cried.

"Let her," Isabel said.

Penny pushed off, hit the ground hard, and fell sideways. The loud wheels of the train went by, too close to her head. The others were shouting. But they couldn't tell her what to do. Her mind had gone blank with rage and indignation. She stood and brushed off her legs.

"Penny!" Sebastian said. "Wait!"

And he jumped out of the train. He took the landing pretty well, bending his knees, but he still fell over. She ran to help him up. No one had ever risked so much to join her.

"Sebastian!" June shouted.

For a moment Penny thought June might jump, too. But she didn't. Penny was not as magnetic as all that. June in the train car's doorway was getting farther away.

Penny took Sebastian's hand and they set off walking back along the tracks. They would find the insulin, and then they would figure out the next thing. It was good that Sebastian had jumped, because she didn't know how she would have gotten back to him. It hadn't been a great plan. The train rumbled alongside.

"Penny?" Sebastian said.

"What."

"Remember the man with the white horse?"

"Yes."

"Did he die?"

"Yes."

"Are you sure?"

"Yes."

They walked. "Do you think we'll die, too?"

"No."

"Look," Sebastian whispered, pointing at the train.

Penny turned and saw a little boy peering at them from one of the cars. He was younger than Sebastian. He drew back into the dark and then the car was past.

Penny wondered if the little boy was with his family or with a coyote. *Pollos*, she remembered they were called, the travelers trying to get to America. Thieves robbed them.

The train's caboose came past, and a sweating man looked out the window.

"Hey!" Penny shouted up at him. "Can you call the police? La policía?"

The man frowned down at them.

"We're the kids from the ship!" she shouted. They watched the back of the train pull away, and get smaller. "Los niños del barco!" she said, but there was no way he could hear her.

The world grew quieter, with the train gone. They stood together in the silence.

"Do you know where we are?" Sebastian asked.

"No," she said.

"Will someone find us?"

"I think so."

They kept walking. Penny scanned the ground for the paper bag, even though it was probably miles back. There was a wall of green trees on either side, and no sign of a trail.

"Did you hear that?" Sebastian asked.

"What?"

"That," he said, and he looked toward the trees on their right. It was an engine noise, a car or a truck on a road. The last time they had followed an engine noise, it had been a bad idea. But they couldn't stay alone here.

They left the tracks and made their way into the trees. It was darker there, and they had to climb over branches. A giant buzzing bug flew at Penny's face. She swatted it away and wanted to cry.

"Do you think there are snakes?" Sebastian asked.

"Probably not," Penny said, though they couldn't even see the ground.

She thought about the time she'd been on an overgrown trail in Colorado with her mom and then reported to her dad that they'd been swashbuckling through the forest. Her mom had laughed and said, "You mean bushwhacking." They still teased her about it, and would call this swashbuckling if they were here.

She wished they were here.

Abruptly they came out on the side of a narrow dirt road, but there were no cars.

"Should we walk?" Sebastian asked.

"Yes."

"Which way?"

Marcus would know. But she'd left Marcus in the train. If they turned right, they would be going the same direction the train had gone, and she wasn't sure that was a good idea. She didn't want to go to Nicaragua. So she turned left, and Sebastian followed her.

An old red truck came toward them and Penny instinctively stepped back into the trees. Sebastian followed her. There was a man in the cab of the truck, who didn't seem to see them. When it was past, Sebastian said, "Why didn't we wave?"

"I don't know," Penny said.

"Someone has to find us," he said.

"I *know*."

They walked. Penny felt sweaty and miserable. Now that they had left the tracks, she would never find the bag of insulin.

A small yellow car came along and slowed when it passed them, then stopped. A woman looked back. Penny jogged toward the car.

The woman rolled down the window. "Por dónde van?"

"A mi casa," Penny said, because she couldn't remember how to say *parents*.

"Eres americana?" the woman asked. She had her hair up in a scrunchie and wore no makeup.

"Sí," Penny said. There was something about speaking Spanish that made this feel like a game, like a test she could pass. "Somos los niños del barco."

The woman looked startled. She looked around, into the woods. "Dónde están los otros?" she asked.

"On the train," Penny said.

The woman reached over and pulled the handle to open the car's door, but Penny moved toward the back seat.

"Can we sit together? In the back?" Sebastian was moving slowly, but Penny got him in. "Will you call our parents?" She mimed a phone at her ear. "Mis padres?"

The woman made an apologetic face. "No tengo teléfono. No podía pagar. No phone. No pay. Me entiendes?"

"Oh," Penny said. "My parents will pay you."

"I don't feel good," Sebastian said.

The woman looked worried.

"We need a doctor," Penny said. "Please."

The woman turned in her seat and started to drive.

36.

NORA TEXTED PEDRO to ask if he knew anything about the Herrera family. It was a perfectly rational, understandable thing to do. He might know something now that they had a name. But texting him still felt compulsive and shameful.

He didn't respond, and she took the stairs down to the lobby and stepped into the heat.

Outside, it looked like some catastrophe had happened, and for a moment Nora was confused. It was as if her inner life had been suddenly externalized. The streets were deserted, postapocalyptic. The sidewalk was sticky with dried liquid. There were pieces of paper everywhere, stuck to the pavement, blowing down the empty street in the hot wind. Nora looked at one and saw it was a Page-a-Day calendar. Everything smelled like old beer. A man staggered up the block. New Year's Day.

At least there were no reporters. A cab cruised by, the driver eyeing Nora, the only person on the street who might not puke in his car. She climbed in. She didn't have Pedro's address, but she had paid attention returning to the hotel, the last time. And her high school Spanish had come back to the surface. She explained where she thought she was going. They found the papaya-colored house together, no trouble, and she asked the cabbie to wait. She knocked at the barred door of the house. No answer.

She got back in the cab. "Momentito," she said. "Por favor."

They watched the house. No one came. The cabbie was playing American oldies on the radio. He turned up the volume and said he liked this song and asked her to translate it.

"Caballeros en satina blanca," she began, then realized it probably wasn't "knights" in white satin. "Nights" made more sense. "Wait, *noches* en satina blanca. Nunca llegando al fin." She'd lost some lyrics and tried to catch up. "Lo que es la verdad, no puedo decir—um—de nuevo. Porque te amo. O, como te amo."

"It's a love song," the cabbie said.

"Exactly."

They sat in silence for a while, listening. Sappy mustache rock, it never died.

"Can I say something, señora?" the cabbie asked.

"Yes."

"Maybe he's married."

She had to think about the word he used, *casado*, before she understood it. *Housed*. To be married was to make a home together. "I don't think so."

"A lot of men are married," he said. "But they don't say it to a woman."

"He's only a friend."

The cabbie said, "Oh, yes?"

"Let's go back to the hotel," she said.

"Can I say something more, señora?"

"Okay."

"I hope you find your kids."

Her face got hot. She thought of denying that she was that person. She only *looked* like the American woman who had lost her children.

She knew that cab drivers in LA sold stories to gossip sites, and she wondered if there were local news outlets that would pay for the story of the mother of los niños del barco waiting outside a man's house. She thought of asking the cabbie not to tell, but that would be admitting that she was doing something wrong. So she was looking for her friend, so what? "I hope we find them, too," she said.

The driver pulled a U-turn on the quiet street, and left the little papaya-colored house behind. "He is not worth it, señora," he said.

Her phone whistled with the arrival of a text and she felt a dopamine jolt, the thrill of Pedro responding. But the text was from Liv:

Where ARE you? Call me.

Nora put the phone in her pocket and sat back in the cab with her shame.

37.

OSCAR DIDN'T KNOW what to do about Penny and Sebastian jumping out of the train. Was he supposed to go after them, and abandon the other three? Having three kids was better than having two, right? His knee ached, and the stress made it harder to breathe. He knew he was panicking, but he couldn't help it. The adrenaline in his body made him feel sick.

He'd had throat infections when he was little, and his mother had taken him to the hospital to have his tonsils out. He was to stay overnight. She'd kissed him and told him she would see him in the morning.

Then someone had made a mistake, and put him on the children's psychiatric floor. The kids were all older than he was, screaming and violent, or silent and catatonic and staring. It was like something from a nightmare. He'd begun to scream, which convinced the nurses that he was supposed to be there. They put him in restraints, gave him a sedative, bound him to a bed. He was seven years old.

When his mother showed up in the morning, the hospital told her she couldn't see her son yet. She thought they meant he was still recovering from the surgery. She'd been up all night long, hauling his chaotic teenage sister out of some shitty drug house where Ofelia had gone as soon as they left for the hospital. So his mother had been grateful that the doctors were keeping Oscar and she could sleep.

Three days he'd stayed in that medieval crazy ward. The drugs wore off and they untied him, but then a child had bitten him, and another had hit him in the head with a tray. He'd started to scream and thrash again. The more he said he shouldn't be there, the more the nurses thought he should. They'd seen it all before.

His defense had been to withdraw into himself. He made himself as small as possible, against the headboard of his bed. He kept his terror inside his chest, said nothing, closed it all out. By the time his mother was able to navigate the hospital bureaucracy—people assuming she was wrong, telling her administrative lies—he almost belonged on the psych ward. He was completely unresponsive. He could not stand or dress or unfold his knees from his chest. His mother carried him to the car in a ball, shivering with fear in his hospital gown, his swollen tonsils still in his throat. After that, he didn't speak for weeks. Even Ofelia, appalled at what had happened, briefly sobered up. She tried to take care of him, heated soup on the stove, drew him out with games.

Oscar felt himself going back to that state of unresponsive immobility now, sitting in the train car with his knees pulled up. The remaining children shouted at him to *do* something, but he couldn't do anything. He couldn't move. His heart raced, but his muscles were locked down.

Marcus was yelling in his face, telling him to wake up. But if Oscar woke, he would have to live in this world in which he had fucked everything up. From here, the voices were muffled, the problems unreal. June was standing in front of him, staring dolefully, holding her bunny. Isabel sat against the wall, as withdrawn as Oscar was. *She* understood how bad it was. She knew there was no point yelling. She just watched him with hollow eyes.

38.

IT TURNED OUT the police had found a dead woman at the Herrera house, in their raid, which a week ago would have made Liv lose her mind, but how many times could you lose your mind? Eventually you had to adjust to the out-of-body experience that was the worst possible thing happening. Your lost mind followed you around on a tether, floating above you, reporting on each new outrage. *The police are raiding the house where the kids are, with guns*—Fuck! That sucks! *Oops, no kids there. But a dead body!* Okay! Let's discuss what that means.

The body at the house belonged to Consuelo Bolaños, the widow of the Colombian courier. She'd been shot through the head and rolled in a tarp, like her husband. That meant that Consuelo had figured out who killed her husband before the police did, and instead of going to the police, she had gone to the house to—what? Complain? Take vengeance? Demand recompense? No one knew, because she was dead. Whatever she'd done, it had pissed off the Herreras.

The police found Penny's and Sebastian's swimsuits at the house, and Marcus's and June's, but not Isabel's yellow bikini or Hector's madras shorts. They'd also found two computers, but the hard drives had been destroyed.

Most important to Liv, they had found the empty boxes for a finger-stick monitor and an insulin pen, which meant that someone had wanted the children to stay alive. That was the hope she was clinging to.

Next they learned that one of the Herreras had been killed in a car accident, on the road between the house and the capital. There was another car involved, but no sign of the kids. Raymond got permission to go to the accident site, and Kenji sent another Suburban for them. The press must not have learned of the new developments yet, or else they were all still drunk from New Year's, because the street outside the hotel was deserted, shiny and tacky underfoot. There were white squares of paper everywhere and the air smelled of hot beer.

Camila still had that careful stillness, like she was holding herself together with great effort. She slid into the middle row of the Suburban, next to Liv.

"Are you taking something?" Liv asked.

Camila nodded. "Xanax."

"Can I have some?"

Camila handed over a metal pill case with painted roses on the lid. Liv shook out a pill and swallowed it dry. They were still waiting for

Nora. No one had seen her since the morning in the club room and she hadn't answered any of Liv's texts. The husbands were debating leaving without her when a cab pulled up and Nora got out. Liv heard Fleetwood Mac playing on the cab's radio until Nora slammed the door.

"Where were you?" Raymond asked.

"I went for a walk." Nora took a seat in the back of the Suburban without looking at Liv.

Unbelievable.

The men got in and Benjamin took shotgun. Penny liked to claim the front seat, and Liv kept seeing her in the passenger seat of a car rolling over. Penny's desire to assert herself was fine at a progressive LA school with feminist teachers, but was it working for her now? Liv could imagine it not going so well. The obscene jungle rolled by. Liv was so sick of this fucking country, the humidity, the endless green. At least Sebastian had insulin. *Sebastian had insulin.*

As they drove, Kenji told them what he knew. The dead guy in the Jeep was Raúl Herrera, and he lived at the house where they'd found the swimsuits. His Jeep had collided with another car, which was empty when the police arrived at the scene.

"It belonged to a teenage girl, who reported it stolen by her friend Oscar," Kenji said. "She said he had a lot of kids in the car."

"And who's Oscar?" Raymond asked.

"The son of the Herreras' housekeeper."

"I told you!" Liv said. "I said there has to be a woman, who'll have a conscience."

"We don't know yet what the scenario is," Kenji said. "Here's the kid." He passed his phone around, the photograph on the screen of a teenage boy with short dark hair, unfashionable glasses, and a scruffy bit of untended mustache.

"How old is he?" Benjamin asked.

"Sixteen."

"You're fucking kidding me," Raymond said.

"Nope," Kenji said.

"And he's made six kids disappear?" Benjamin said.

"Not for long, let's hope," Kenji said.

They drove. Camila fell asleep.

"Monkeys," Benjamin said listlessly, and they all looked out the window at some black shapes in the tops of the trees. One swung by the arm from one tree to the next. Liv heard a faint hooting through the window. The monkeys seemed to be mocking her, for once having wanted to see them on a zip-line tour.

The Suburban pulled abruptly across the road, onto the opposite shoulder, then bumped over uneven ground. There was police tape marking off an area in the trees. The Jeep had already been removed, its position marked with police tape, but a small red Fiat remained, upside-down. A police officer stood guard.

Gunther looked at the red car. "You're saying six kids, plus this Oscar, were in that little thing?"

"I told you," Kenji said, "we don't know the scenario."

"Five in the back?" Gunther said. "Or three in the front?"

"Where did they go?" Raymond asked. "Has there been a search?"

"The police combed a mile radius this morning," Kenji said.

Liv looked around. "Five minutes into a nature walk, my kids are complaining."

"Could they have hitchhiked from here?" Benjamin asked. "After the accident?"

"I think we would have heard from a driver," Kenji said. "Someone would've seen them."

"What of the housekeeper?" Camila asked.

"They found her at home. She's asked for a lawyer."

"Can we look inside the car?" Liv asked.

Kenji spoke to the police guard, and said, "You can look, but don't touch anything."

They moved closer to the turtled red car. Liv crouched to peer through the windows. She tried to focus, to pay attention, without being overwhelmed by the idea that her kids had been inside. She had a sudden clear memory of the last book she'd read aloud to Sebastian. Benjamin usually did the bedtime reading, but he'd been out of town, and they had started one of those wish-fulfillment kids' adventure books, where the boy hero has exactly the qualities he needs to triumph, at every moment. You could feel the next beat coming, like the kind of country song where you can guess the next rhyme. She'd been bored and annoyed, and at one point she tried to explain to Sebastian why it wasn't her favorite of his books. But Sebastian had loved the book unreservedly. Why hadn't she just read the thing with gusto, and relished every moment with her son? Why had she brought her adult judgment and her professional story opinions to a book her kid loved? Of course the child hero should always triumph! Who wanted a kids' book to feel like real life? Real life was fucking intolerable.

The windows of the red car were broken but she didn't see any blood. Something dark moved inside, and Liv jumped backward and fell. The police guard lunged forward. The shadowy thing darted out of the car. It was a striped mammal with a long tail, a little bigger than a house cat. It ambled away.

"Oh, shit," she said, her heart booming in her ears. "That scared me."

"It's just a coatimundi," Kenji said.

"*That*'s a coatimundi?" Benjamin said. "*That*'s what we came ashore for? It's a fucking raccoon!"

"Please don't start blaming me for the zip line again," Liv said.

Her tailbone was bruised. She felt woozy and confused, on a cocktail of adrenaline, Xanax, regret, leftover Ambien, and coffee.

"No one is blaming anyone for the zip line," Benjamin said.

"You are," she said. "And I'm sick of it."

"Liv," he said.

"You all blame me!" she said. "You do! But I'm not the one who was fooling around with the guide, okay?"

There was a silence. She saw a quick look of naked fear on Nora's face.

"What's that supposed to mean?" Raymond asked.

Liv covered her eyes. "Nothing. I just meant they were off looking for monkeys or whatever. Birds."

Benjamin turned away and walked back to the Suburban. So did Nora.

Liv's face burned with shame. She was sure Nora had been with Pedro this morning, but she'd had no right to say anything. Her heart could break for Raymond, but the code of female friendship required her to keep her mouth shut. She had sounded like Penny having a tantrum, blaming anyone but herself. The zip line had been her idea, and she had fallen asleep.

Raymond put out a hand to help her up, and she took it, gasping at the pain in her tailbone. "Oh, fuck," she said. "Hang on. I really hurt myself."

"You okay?" Raymond asked.

"Yeah. I will be." She straightened carefully.

"What happened with the guide?"

"Nothing," she said. "I got scared by that animal. I took a Xanax with coffee, I'm not used to it. I'm talking shit."

"You sure? Nothing happened?"

"Positive."

He studied her face. She turned from him and limped back to the Suburban, wincing with every step. Nora was in the way back, earbuds in. Liv had not thought she could feel more miserable, but here it was. There were always lower circles of hell. Welcome to the next level down. She climbed in.

39.

IT HAD GOTTEN dark outside the train. Isabel sat against the wall as the car rumbled and swayed, and she bit at the skin along her thumbnail. It hurt and bled. If her mother saw her, she would tell her to stop. But her mother wasn't here. She hadn't protected Isabel. She'd let her swim in a river that had taken her away.

She tried not to think about Raúl. The pain, or the blood after, or even his eye hanging out and his head half scraped off. She found she could only push him away with another painful idea, so she thought about how much she missed her brother. If they had only waited for Hector to come back, then none of this would have happened. But no one had listened to her.

The brakes of the train screeched, metal against metal. It ground slowly to a halt. Oscar didn't move, so Isabel stood and looked out into the dark. Men were shouting up ahead.

"There's a car on the tracks," she said.

Someone in a striped shirt appeared outside the train car, a small girl with black hair, a little Mayan-looking kid.

"We're friends!" the girl said breathlessly, holding up her hands to show they were empty. "My name is Noemi. This is my uncle, Chuy."

A man emerged from the dark beside her. He had a square, solid face. "You have to get off the train," he said quietly, in the same strangely accented Spanish as the girl's.

Isabel looked to Oscar to confront these people, but he sat curled up and frozen, after leading them thrashing through the woods. He was so useless. She turned back to the man. "Who stopped the train?"

"Thieves," Chuy said.

"We don't have any money."

"They'll recognize you. Rich Americans are looking for you."

"You're on television," the little indio girl said shyly. "You're *famous*."

Isabel had heard about these migrant kids, and she'd seen pictures. When she hadn't wanted to go to the passport office, her mother had lectured her about what a privilege it was to have a passport, to be able to go anywhere you liked. Those migrant children would do *anything* for a luxury like that. The passport office would be *exciting* to them. It occurred to Isabel that if she made it home, her mother would never lecture her ever again. She looked ahead, to where the car had stopped on the tracks. "Maybe they'll take us to our parents," she said. "For the money."

"You want to trust those men?" Chuy said.

Isabel felt a roiling in her empty stomach. She remembered the weight of Raúl's body, the tearing feeling, the blood. She couldn't have it happen again, and her legs started to tremble.

Oscar spoke up. "Where would we go?" His voice was small and whiny, but at least he'd snapped out of his silence.

"Into the trees."

"But my knee."

"You'll be dead if you stay here, ñaño," the man said. "They don't need you."

"Okay," Oscar said, and he started shoving things into his backpack.

June handed him the bunny, saying, "Don't hurt him!"

Oscar's yellow folding knife was on the floor of the train car, forgotten. Isabel stuck it in her pocket.

Chuy lifted June down from the car, as if she weighed nothing.

Marcus edged out and dropped. Then the man helped Oscar down, so he wouldn't land so hard on his knee, but Oscar still grunted with pain. Isabel slid out after them, and then they were all outside in the dark.

40.

ON THE DRIVE back to the capital, Raymond made a point of sitting next to his wife in the Suburban. Nora kept her earbuds in, and stared out the window at the trees going by. Raymond didn't buy that Liv had made up what she'd said about the guide. You didn't get two children to school age together without knowing a thing or two about a person's moods.

He had taken all the shit about marrying a white girl. He would catch, from black women, a barely raised eyebrow, a subtle reproach. He felt it in airports, on subways, any time he was in a not-all-white public setting with his wife. And he thought they were right to hold it against him. But you didn't get to choose. Love seized you, or it didn't. He wouldn't say that aloud, not even to his own sister, who would laugh at him. She and his brother had both found black partners, and he'd ceded the moral high ground to them. But he knew Nora was the person he was supposed to be with. They fit in some chemical, physical way.

Aside from girls in high school, which hardly counted, he'd never loved anyone else. He loved the smell of her, the sight of her getting out of the shower. Twelve years and two kids later, he still craved her. When he jerked off, it was Nora he thought about.

He'd had other offers, of course. There was always someone flirting on the set. The black-man roles he got didn't usually have a love interest, so he'd been protected from too much gazing into each other's eyes while the whole crew watched, the kind of gazing that made your brain chemistry start saying *THIS IS LOVE*. When he did get a part with a romance, or when someone hung around his trailer during the endless downtime, his brain had never fallen for it. He'd been faithful, a hundred percent, and now Nora had not. At the precise moment when it mattered most.

The sun had gone down in that abrupt equatorial way, and now it was late. At the hotel, Camila and Gunther went off to the bar, and the rest of them rode the elevator in silence. Benjamin and Liv, shifting uncomfortably, got off on five. Then it was just Raymond and Nora in the steep fluorescent light and the unforgiving elevator mirrors, riding up to their room on six.

"You want to tell me what's going on?" he asked.

She didn't answer. The elevator door opened on their floor, and he held it for her, but she stayed where she was. "I'm going up to the club room," she said.

"First we talk."

"I need something to eat."

So Raymond let the door close.

"You don't have to come with me," Nora said.

"Oh, yes, I do."

When the door opened again on the top floor, she stepped out past him. She was wearing the white shorts she'd worn on the day the kids had vanished. He'd thought she might not wear them again, although he was wearing his stupid golfing shirt, the stress stink washed out of it by the hotel laundry.

In the empty club room, lunch was over. Tea had been laid out: little triangular sandwiches and cookies, a silver urn of hot water. Small white ceramic pitchers of milk.

"So," Raymond began, and he cleared his throat. "What Liv said."

He saw a flash of anger cross his wife's face. He could tell she wanted to attack Liv, but that would give weight to the accusation. Nora was seriously pissed.

"What did she mean?" he pressed.

"How should I know?"

"What happened with the guide?"

She shook her head.

"Nora."

"What."

"What aren't you telling me?" he asked.

"Nothing!" she said. "Nothing! I went looking for birds. The tide changed. None of us was paying attention. That's what happened. That's all."

She was lying. He absorbed the blow, and the room seemed to spin. Tea sandwiches and milk pitchers caught in a slow cyclone. Was she going to say more? Was she going to cave and tell him the truth? He didn't want her to speak. And he did.

"You have to tell me, if we're going to get through this."

She said nothing.

The silence went on too long and finally he said, "My mother is coming."

"She's *what*?"

"She's on her way. I couldn't hold her off anymore. But I need to know what's going on, before she gets here. I need to know where we stand." He needed to know how humiliated he was, before his mother arrived. He waited for Nora's answer.

"Oh, Jesus," she said. "That's the last thing we need."

He felt he had offered her his exposed chest and a knife, in exchange for information. And instead she was acting wronged. As if *he* had let *her* down. He had been so lucky in his life, but his good fortune had somehow run out. The love of his life, the mother of his vanished children, walked away from him, out of the room.

41.

CAMILA TRAILED GUNTHER to the hotel bar, which was dim with dark green walls. "Let's go upstairs," she pleaded. "Please."

"The minibar is empty," he said. He slid onto a stool and ordered a scotch.

The young bartender, balding in his twenties, glanced at Camila, then turned away for a glass. The bar was deserted, everyone worn out from the night before. Nursing hangovers, making resolutions.

"Just one," Gunther said.

She climbed onto a stool beside him and ordered a gin and tonic.

Gunther's drink arrived, and he nodded at the bartender. "I keep thinking," he said in English, for privacy. "This photograph, on the Instagram."

Camila closed her eyes.

"It could not happen, with Hector there," he said.

Camila had thought the same thing.

"So either they have done something to him," he said, "or the two of them are not together."

The bartender slid Camila's gin and tonic toward her. It was cold and bitter and lovely: quinine, juniper, lime.

"Their bathing suits were not at the house," Gunther said. "Why is that?"

"Perhaps they're still wearing them."

"And this tiny car," he said. "I do not believe they were six, plus the housekeeper's son, in that toy car. It makes no sense. They have been separated."

"You think Isabel is alone?"

He drank. "I don't know."

"I have to believe they're together."

"No." He shook his head. "If they are together, and if Hector could not protect his sister, he can never live with this. It will be terrible for him." He drained the scotch and pushed the glass toward the bartender.

Camila knew Gunther was really speaking of himself. The bartender poured him a second scotch. "You said just one," she said.

"Please don't begin this," Gunther said.

Camila sipped her drink and felt the beginnings of the numbness she knew Gunther was looking for. But there was no numbing this pain, this fear, not truly. She could only smooth the edges.

"This tortillera detective, she has done nothing," Gunther said.

"Don't call her that."

"It's what she is."

"She seems very good, to me."

"Incompetent. Five days they have been missing." He drained his new drink, blinked and grimaced, and pushed it back across the bar.

The bartender looked to her. Gunther tapped the base of the glass on the wood to retrieve his attention.

The bartender poured.

"These American women," Gunther said. "They are at fault."

"I was there, too," she said quietly.

"No," he said. "Their children are small. They should have stayed watching. It was their responsibility."

"Perhaps."

"They know it," he said. "This is the reason they attack each other now. Nora was with the guide today, I promise you."

"I don't think so," Camila said.

"Taking a taxi, to go for a *walk*," he said, with contempt.

Camila knew he was often right, when he took the dark view. He had no illusions about other people. She suspected that his habit of suspicion came from knowledge of his own character. He saw himself clearly, and knew his own impulses were not as reconstructed as people might wish them to be.

The bartender brought the third drink. Gunther raised it to him in a mock toast. "Salud!"

The young man lifted his beer soberly, then moved away to clean something.

"El patán del río," Gunther muttered.

It took Camila a moment to understand what he was talking about. *The lout of the river.* He meant Pedro, the guide. And Nora.

"She has no right to do this to her husband," Gunther said.

"We don't know anything," Camila said.

"I do know that," Gunther said. "It's the only thing I know."

42

PENNY SAT IN the back seat of the yellow car with her brother, watching the woman with the scrunchie drive. The woman's knuckles were white on the steering wheel and she seemed nervous, but Penny wasn't sure why. She remembered the nervous doctor at the big house, who was a drug addict, but this woman didn't seem like a drug addict. She wasn't skinny like the doctor.

"Are you okay?" Penny asked Sebastian.

He nodded. Tears had cut rivulets in the dust on his cheeks.

"Do you have the finger-stick?"

He seemed confused by the question.

She dug into his pocket and found the little device, poked his finger for him to draw blood, and waited for the numbers. He was really low, lower than she had ever seen him. "Do you have any sugar?" she asked the woman. "Candy?"

The woman reached for a purse on the passenger seat, then rummaged in it with one hand. She came up with half a roll of mints, the foil uncoiling, and passed them back. Penny studied the mints. SIN AZÚCAR! the label said.

"These don't have sugar," she said. "Necesito azúcar." She gave two to Sebastian anyway, and he stuck them in his mouth.

"No tengo nada más," the woman said. She passed back a water bottle that had probably been sitting in the car a long time, getting cancer toxins from the plastic. Their mother never let them drink from a plastic bottle that had been in the car.

Penny unscrewed the lid and Sebastian drank. She stuck one of the sugar-free candies in her own mouth, feeling the tingling mint. She hadn't brushed her teeth in a long time. It had gotten dark very fast, like a shade pulled down over the world. Penny had barely noticed, but now the headlights lit up the gray asphalt.

"My stomach hurts," Sebastian said.

The woman looked at them in the rearview mirror. "Hay una recompensa, verdad?" she asked.

"I don't know what that means," Penny said.

"Dinero?" the woman said.

"Sí," Penny said. "Mis padres pagar." Of course her parents would give the woman money. They'd already been over that.

"Pagan," the woman corrected.

"Pagan."

The woman's eyes in the mirror looked thoughtful.

Penny wished she would watch where she was going, and drive faster. "You're taking us to the doctor, right?" she said.

The woman nodded. "Claro," she said, and her eyes shifted back to the road.

43

OSCAR COULD BARELY see anything as he stumbled for the trees. His glasses were fogged, and fear had reduced the visible world to a tunnel. The pain in his knee shocked him with every step. In front of him, the strange man, Chuy, carried the little girl, Noemi. Oscar expected to hear shouts behind them, but everything was distant, muffled.

They reached the woods and stopped, in a place that was sheltered and obscured from the view of the train. Oscar, panting, just wanted to be still, to keep the blinding bolts of pain from shooting up his leg.

In the distance he could see the dim forms of people running. Others had fled the train, too, and were here in the woods, afraid. Pollos. Oscar heard a scream.

"Can you keep moving?" Chuy whispered.

He shook his head. "Not yet."

"Stay here," Chuy said, and he ran off, staying low.

Oscar could tell by the kids' breathing that they were terrified. What was he going to tell his mother? He'd done everything wrong.

"Are people coming to hurt us?" June whispered, huddled against her brother.

"Yes," Isabel said.

"Shh," Oscar said. "No."

"I won't let them hurt you," Marcus said.

Noemi was silent.

They waited, trying to interpret the sounds coming from the night. There were more shouts, then three gunshots, and they all flinched. Then the car must have rolled off the tracks, because the idling train started moving again. A moan of protest went up from the trees. People had hoped to get back on the train. Now they would be stranded.

Oscar heard footsteps running toward them. "Shit," he said. He cowered and shrank into the undergrowth. June whimpered.

A dark figure grabbed Isabel, then Noemi. Oscar braced for someone to grab him, too, but instead he heard a terrible noise. A high grunt of effort and then a kind of choking. He could just make out the shape of the intruder, who had fallen to his knees in the dark clearing. Isabel faced the man. She looked feral, half-crouched. In her hand she held Oscar's folding knife, with its sharp four-inch blade.

The intruder let Noemi go. From his knees, he slumped sideways to the ground.

Oscar crawled toward him, his mind blank with horror. The wounded man was Chuy, and there was dark blood beneath his chin. His throat had been opened from side to side, an extra mouth. He made a gurgling noise that might have been a command. Oscar could still hear people moving through the trees. When he grabbed Chuy's wrist to look for a pulse, his own blood was pounding too loudly in his ears for him to feel anything.

"He wanted us to run," Marcus said.

Chuy's throat was slashed wide open. You couldn't press on a wound like that.

"We have to go!" Marcus said.

The kid was right.

Oscar staggered to his feet and took Noemi's hand. He felt dizzy and sick. The bright pain shot up his leg with every step.

Marcus darted through the woods ahead of them, his sister in tow, as if he knew where he was going. Oscar managed to limp after him, pulling Noemi, who seemed strangely listless. Had she seen? Did she understand? Isabel followed, an ominous presence. Oscar half feared she would leap on him and cut his throat, too. He was more deserving of it than Chuy was. Chuy had tried to help them, and Oscar had only made mistakes. He limped on, dragging Noemi by the hand.

44

PENNY WATCHED THE road in the yellow car's headlights as they came into a town. Sebastian had fallen asleep, his head heavy against her arm. There were streetlights and other cars. They passed businesses that looked like shops and restaurants, closed up with metal shutters. Then she saw a little store with a glass door and a light on.

"There!" she said. "Candy. Phone. Stop!"

The woman slowed the car and parked beside the store.

Penny jostled Sebastian. "We have to get you something to eat."

Sebastian rubbed his eyes and mumbled a protest. His hair was damp. They climbed out onto the sidewalk and Penny's legs felt stiff. Sebastian stumbled like he was still asleep. Penny took his hand so he wouldn't walk right off the curb into the street.

The store was tiny, with unfamiliar packages crowded into racks hanging from the walls. She picked a bag of candy that looked sugary. "These, please," she said. "And can you call our parents?"

The old man behind the counter was looking at Sebastian, who let go of her hand and slid to the floor. His whole body started twitching. There was foam around his mouth.

Penny kneeled beside him. "Help!" she said. "Get a doctor!"

But the adults just stared down. Sebastian's body kept jerking on the floor.

"Help me!" Penny screamed.

Finally the man behind the counter spoke. Penny heard him say the word "hospital." He came around the counter and crouched to lift Sebastian in his arms. The woman ran to her car and threw open the back door.

Penny climbed in beside her brother. The woman got in front and the car peeled out, and Penny clutched Sebastian's head to keep him from rolling to the floor. She must have dropped the candy, but she didn't think he could eat it now anyway.

The woman was driving fast. Sebastian had stopped jerking. Penny shook his shoulder. "Stay awake."

They drove past two hotels, some more closed storefronts, and a swimsuit shop with mannequins in the window. The woman was crying as she drove. "No es mi culpa," she said. "No es mi culpa."

Then they stopped under a bright fluorescent light. The woman jumped out again and helped Penny pull Sebastian out of the car. "No quiero problemas," she said. "Lo siento. Lo siento."

She backed away with her hands up, then got in the car. The tires squealed in protest as she pulled away.

Penny was alone with her limp brother on the concrete at her feet. She couldn't lift him, so she got her arms under his head and shoulders and started to drag him. She thought of playing Light as a Feather, Stiff as a Board, willing her brother to be lighter, but that would mean he was dead.

She walked backward, dragging Sebastian, struggling to keep her hold. His flip-flops came off on the concrete, so she left them behind. Someone was going to come help them, any second now. A doctor, a nurse. And those people would finally, *finally* call her parents.

"It's okay," she said, to herself as much as to Sebastian. "It's okay. It's okay."

45

NORA WOKE TO Raymond's phone ringing in the early hours of the morning. She tried to swim up out of sleep, through the dark water of unconsciousness, into the painful light. The hotel room. The wreck of her marriage and her life. Raymond was awake and dressing. He said they were going to a hospital on the coast.

"Why a hospital?" Nora asked. "What happened?"

"No idea," he said, pulling on a shirt.

"Should we pack? Are we staying there?"

"Don't know."

She pulled on jeans, threw some things in a bag—a toothbrush, underwear, her phone—and climbed into the black Suburban with the diplomatic plates waiting outside the hotel. If she never saw another Suburban she would be happy. Benjamin and Liv were in the car. Benjamin said good morning, Liv said nothing. Raymond got in and read a text from Detective Rivera aloud, saying that two of the kids had turned up at an emergency room in a resort town.

"Which two kids?" Nora asked.

"She doesn't know," Raymond said.

"How do they know they're *our* kids, if they don't know which ones?"

"They saw them on TV."

"But then, which ones? Are they white or brown? Do they speak Spanish?"

"She doesn't know."

Nora sat back in her seat. Of course she should be happy that any of the kids had turned up. But why only two? How could the police not know which ones? People were obsessed with physical descriptions here. They called each other negra, gordo, flaca, chino, morena. If they hadn't specifically said it was the moreno kids, then it wasn't. But maybe brown was the default here? Either way, two parents had won the lottery, and four had lost. Unless the kids had split up. It could be Penny and Hector, or Marcus and Sebastian. That was too complicated to think about.

Camila and Gunther hadn't answered any calls or texts, and there was a question of whether to wait for them. Raymond was texting with Kenji about a car to pick up his mother at the airport. He told the driver it was okay to go. Nora had forgotten, in the depth of her sleep, about Raymond's mother. Her heart sank anew.

On the drive, she tried to think of a question that would produce information, whichever kids were at the hospital. Like those logic tests, trying to figure out who the liar is. *What had the kids who'd been found said about the kids who hadn't?*

But what if the kids said that the others were dead? She thought of Schrödinger's Cat, a problem she had never understood, because the cat was either dead or it wasn't. It didn't matter if you looked in the box. Now she finally understood it. Until they got to the hospital, her children were alive. And they were dead. But once they got to the hospital, it would be one or the other. She didn't want to arrive.

What she knew for certain was that she had brought this punishment on her family. She didn't know what the punishing entity was—God? Karma? The Furies?—but its sharp talons were shredding her heart. She wanted to bargain, to promise sacrifice or good behavior, but what more could she sacrifice than her children? How could she imagine living righteously without knowing what she had to live for?

The drive was endless, and Raymond sat beside her, as wretched as she was. His mother, a woman Nora admired, was on a plane somewhere overhead, about to witness their failure as parents. Benjamin and Liv sat close together and seemed to be leaning slightly forward, as if that might get them to the hospital faster. They couldn't wait to open the box.

When the Suburban finally parked, the morning was oppressively sunny. Benjamin and Liv climbed out.

"I don't know if I can go in there," Nora said.

"You can," Raymond said.

"Come back and tell me who it is."

"You're going with me."

So she climbed down into the parking lot, her legs weak. Benjamin and Liv were already halfway to the door. Nora gripped Raymond's arm. "Someone would've said it was our kids, if it was," she said.

"If that's true," Raymond said, "you're going to be happy for Benjamin and Liv, do you hear me?"

"I can't."

"Yes, you can. She's your family. Her kids are your family. And whoever's in there, they're going to know something. They're going to have information, and we're going to get it."

She held his arm and they passed through the doors, just in time to see Penny fly into Liv's arms. Liv was kneeling, laughing, kissing her daughter's face, holding her head as if she couldn't believe Penny was real, as if she might be an illusion or a dream. Then hugging her again, so tightly that Penny laughed and said, "Mom!"

Nora felt a physical revulsion, and turned to go back out the door, but Raymond blocked her way. She looked up into his eyes. They were hard.

"Happy," he said.

"I can't."

"You can."

So Nora followed Liv into a hospital room where Sebastian was hooked up to an IV. He looked angelic and wan. Liv was sobbing. It was hard enough to keep Sebastian alive at home. Of course if there were two kids in the hospital, it would be the kid with the chronic illness and his self-important sister. Nora had been insane to hope at all.

Penny seemed healthy and fine, radiant from the attention, no surprise. She'd apparently carried Sebastian into the emergency room, like some sort of kiddie pietà, and she'd been petted and praised for it by nurses and doctors. Nora remembered that Raymond had said the kids would have information, and she crouched down in front of the child she had held as an infant in her arms.

"Where are your cousins?" she asked.

Penny looked at the floor. "I don't know."

"Where did you last see them?"

"On the train."

"What train?"

Penny blew her bangs off her forehead in exasperation. "The train we were on. Before we went to the road and the woman left me here with Sebastian, who was *really* heavy."

Nora recognized this for the humblebrag it was, and thought she had never known a more slappable child. "Were Marcus and June alone on the train?"

"No," Penny said. "They're with the others. It's not my fault."

Nora felt a cold certainty that it *was* Penny's fault, whatever "it" was. But the detective had arrived, and she took Nora aside. She said that a social worker was coming so they could do a proper debrief of the children. Could Nora wait? It was easy for kids to get confused or dug in about details.

"A social worker," Nora said. "Why?"

"She's specially trained to do these interviews."

Something about her tone was odd, and Nora moved to make sure they were out of earshot. "Are you looking for sex crimes?" she whispered.

"We're just being careful."

"Did you *hear* Penny? Have you *ever* seen a child who's been assaulted be that smug?"

"Please, just wait," Detective Rivera said. "She's not the only child involved."

So Nora sat on a bench on her hands, to keep them from trembling. When the social worker arrived, she was slight and gray-haired, in a lavender dress.

"You've had a terrible time," she said, holding Nora's hand in hers. "I'm so sorry."

"You're American," Nora said.

"I came here in the Peace Corps and never left," the woman said. "My name is Allison."

Nora asked if she could listen during Penny's interview.

"Are you the mother?" Allison asked.

"No, I am," Liv said, raising her hand.

Nora had a sudden flash of Liv at nine, always having the right answer in class, always getting the best grades. "But I've known Penny all her life," she said. "And my children were with her."

"It's up to the mother," Allison said, apologetic.

Liv said, "I think maybe we should talk as a family first."

Nora stared at her cousin. Liv wouldn't meet her eye.

"All right," Allison said, all business.

"Sorry, Nora," Benjamin said, putting a hand on her shoulder.

"Actually," Allison said, smiling brightly at him, "it can be easier for children with just the mother there, at first. Do you mind waiting out here?"

Benjamin blinked. Nora thought he would object to being shut out, but he didn't. He seemed too shocked to protest. It was like childbirth in her parents' generation: Dads wait outside.

So Liv, Penny, the social worker, and Detective Rivera went into a little room. Nora could see blue plastic chairs and some dolls and stuffed animals inside. They shut the door behind them.

"Fuck," Benjamin said.

"No fucking kidding," Nora said.

46

RAYMOND SAT ON a bench in the hospital hallway, feeling numb. The press hadn't found them yet. His manager had been trying to work with a local PR person to stem the tide of stories, but it hadn't worked. The astronaut picture was still running on the news. And the reporters would find them soon. Liv and Benjamin would be on TV, with their kids safe in their arms, and his kids would be gone. He had tried to be big about it. He had tried to see any of the kids' return as good news, but it was getting hard to keep the optimism going.

Liv came around the corner with her arms full of vending machine snacks. She seemed to consider turning back when she saw him, but it was too late. "Hey," she said.

He nodded, not trusting himself to speak.

She sat beside him on the bench, arms full of chips and pistachios. "How's it going?"

"How do you think?"

"They're going to find your kids," she said.

"Sure."

"I know it doesn't seem fair that ours are back."

"I'm glad they're back."

"How's Nora?"

"You could ask her."

"She's not really talking to me."

"I thought you weren't talking to her."

Liv adjusted the snacks in her arms. "Listen, I lost my mind, when I said that thing. I'm so sorry. We've all lost our minds a little."

"I haven't."

"Well, I'm sorry," she said.

He had to assume he had been cuckolded, and he knew that if Liv had said nothing, it still would have happened, he just wouldn't know it. Could you be humiliated if you didn't know it? He thought you could, and it was worse, because other people knew. So you were a cuckold *and* a fool. "I'm glad you said something," he said, though the words felt like ash in his mouth.

They sat in silence. "So your mom is coming," she said.

"Yeah. Nora's dreading it."

"Nora's in a terrible place," Liv said. "She just lost her mom, the kids are missing, she thinks she's lost you. I mean, *imagine*."

"I don't have to imagine," he said.

"Oh, Raymond." Liv dumped the snacks, slid close to him on the bench, and put her arms around him. Her short hair brushed his face and he smelled rosemary shampoo over the disinfectant smell of the hospital. "I'm so sorry," she said.

"I don't know what we do now," he said. "Where do we go? What do we try next?"

"We'll figure it out."

"You should take Penny and Sebastian home."

"Absolutely not," she said. "We're staying with you."

"That's crazy."

"I mean it," she said. "Then we're gonna sue the shit out of the cruise line."

He laughed. He sometimes forgot that he'd known Liv as a movie executive before he ever met Nora. She'd fought to cast him and to keep him, working around his schedule. She'd introduced him to his wife. She was reliable, brash, sometimes aggravating. Just now she'd put her arms around him only to comfort him. But with her body close against his, with Nora freezing him out, something seemed to shift, the ground moved beneath his feet. He sensed that Liv felt it, too. A stirring.

"I should go," she said.

"Okay." But she didn't leave. His arm was still around her, her head still resting against his chest.

Then Liv stiffened and pushed away from him, staring down the hall. He followed her eyes and saw Nora and his mother silently watching them. His mother looked road-weary, her handbag on a shoulder, her hair smoothed back.

Liv, her movements jerky and agitated, gathered up her snacks from the bench. But nothing had happened! There was a way to play this, to make it explainable—and of course it *was* explainable, it was fine—but Liv wasn't doing it. She was making everything worse. She dropped a bag of chips. "Fuck," she breathed.

Raymond leaned over to pick up the bag from the polished linoleum, placed it on the top of the bundle in Liv's arms, then stood to welcome his mother to this world-class shit show.

47

IT STARTED TO rain as they stumbled through the woods. Noemi had a plastic slicker in her backpack, but she didn't know where her backpack was. Had she dropped it? Chuy would have picked it up, but she wasn't sure where Chuy was. Something had happened. She felt dizzy. Water squelched in her shoes.

The others were silent, run-walking ahead of her. The toy pig was lost somewhere in the rain, and this made her sadder than it should have. She stumbled on a root and caught herself.

There seemed to be a weight pressing down on her head. The older boy with the glasses, who'd been so afraid on the train, told her to keep up, until he saw that she couldn't. He'd been carrying the littlest girl, but he put her down and picked up Noemi. It was an uneven ride because he was limping.

They reached a road. Noemi's eyes felt gummy, her head confused. A pair of headlights came out of the gloom and blinded her. The other children looked like ghosts on the roadside. There was a long wait and another set of headlights went past, red taillights vanishing into the dark again. A third car stopped, and the boy with the glasses leaned over to speak into the window.

Noemi lost track again, because now she was inside the car and she was sweating. The woman driver was talking about Jesus. Maybe they were all on the way to heaven, maybe this was how you got there. In a car in the rain. Noemi fell asleep.

Then they were in a building, but she couldn't tell what it was. She heard Isabel tell someone that they needed dry clothes. Noemi was afraid of Isabel, but only a little, because the older girl seemed more afraid than she was. They were in a bathroom and Noemi's fingers didn't seem to be working, so the older girl helped her undo her pants and steadied her while she sat on the toilet, and helped her change. Noemi watched, dazed, as the girl stuffed Noemi's clothes, the clothes her grandmother had washed and folded, into the garbage in the bathroom. She stuffed something yellow in, too—the bikini from the TV. She gave Noemi strange new clothes, a blue sweatshirt and a dry pair of jeans with an elastic waist. Noemi remembered asking where the clothes came from and the girl saying something about a church. So maybe they were in a church. It didn't look like the church at home.

Then they were in a car again.

Noemi dreamed that the white bunny grew as big as a house. She was sweating again, and then she was shivering. Someone put a jacket over her. The car was moving. She woke up enough to think that she would never see her grandmother again.

She heard the littlest girl ask, "Will she be okay?"

"Shhh," the girl's brother said.

That seemed to go on, the dreaming and sweating and shivering and the voices, for a long time. She thought she was in her friend Rosa's dollhouse. In her dream, the kids from the ship were the tiny dolls, all in white shirts and red shorts.

She knew a phone number where someone would go and get her grandmother, but she couldn't remember it. And what could her grandmother do? Travel through all these countries to find her? It wasn't possible. And her parents couldn't come get her. If they did, they couldn't go back to Nueva York. So would someone put her in an orphanage? In this country? What country was she in?

She wondered if the bunny had been lost in the woods, like the pig. Maybe it was alive in the underbrush, foraging for grass and seeds, its coat dirty, its fluffy tail gone gray with dust. The wild rabbits would sniff at it with suspicion. Or an owl out night-hunting might eat it. She was the bunny, hiding in the brush, hoping that no one would find her.

48.

MARIA SAT WITH her lawyer in a small room at the police station. The police had promised they would tell her if they learned anything about her son. The lawyer had dyed black hair in a tight ponytail, thick mascara, and eyebrows drawn on. Maria felt faded by contrast.

"I'm not in contact with my son," she said. "I took the children to my house, and told him to take them to the United States embassy. I don't know what happened after that. I couldn't reach his phone. We were trying to rescue the children."

"But you didn't know anything about the Herreras' criminal enterprise," the lawyer prompted.

"Right," Maria said, chastened.

"So what were you rescuing the children from?"

Maria hesitated. "Raúl."

"You feared he would abuse the children."

"I think perhaps he did." She remembered George shouting at Raúl, the girl upstairs.

The lawyer shook her head. "You don't know that. If you'd known that, you would have taken the child to a hospital, or to the police."

Maria hung her head. She had been so afraid, and there'd been all the other children to deal with, and so little time. Why had she gone back to the Herreras' house? Out of habit? No, she was afraid that Raúl would discover her and the children missing, and come after them.

"You only had a *fear* that Raúl might abuse them," the lawyer said.

"Yes, okay."

"And why didn't you go to the police?"

"Because the Herreras pay the police."

The lawyer dropped her pen to her yellow notepad in exasperation. "But you don't know that."

"Everyone knows," Maria said tiredly.

"*You* don't," the lawyer said. "Because you didn't know the Herreras had a criminal enterprise, as you have told me. And you are not involved or complicit in that criminal enterprise. I'm just trying to help you account for your unaccountable actions."

Maria nodded, and began again. "They are American children, so I was trying to get them to their embassy."

"Okay," the lawyer said, picking up her pen.

"I knew I could trust my son. Oscar is a very responsible boy."

"Okay," the lawyer said. "And Oscar knows the Herreras?"

"Yes. They have been my employers for many years."

"Was your son involved in their work?"

"No!" Maria said. "Never."

The lawyer raised a painted eyebrow. "You sure?"

"Yes."

"And will he ask for a lawyer?"

Maria considered. He knew to be wary around the police. But this was a stressful situation, and Oscar would be frightened. He might not remember to ask. "Perhaps."

The lawyer sighed. "And you believe George Herrera has left the country."

"I do."

"Why didn't you tell anyone he was leaving?"

"I did."

"But before, when they could have stopped him at the airport."

"I was in shock," Maria said. "I had seen a woman murdered. I had seen her body. All I could think of was finding my son."

The lawyer nodded and made a note. "You weren't thinking clearly. You were panicked about your son. He's your only child?"

"I had a daughter."

"Had?"

"She's dead."

"How?" the lawyer asked.

Maria could not bear these questions. "Drugs," she said. "An overdose."

The lawyer sighed. "If you get charged, they'll go after that."

"Why?"

"Character."

Maria drew herself up. "What happened to my daughter had nothing to do with my character."

"That's not what people will think. You worked for drug dealers, your daughter died of an overdose. A simple equation."

"That isn't true." Though she did wonder, sometimes. Raúl had called Ofelia her "slut daughter" just this morning.

The lawyer was writing on her notepad. "We'll see what happens, if they charge you. We'll talk about it then."

Maria was astonished at such matter-of-factness about the deepest wounds of her heart.

There was a knock at the door, and a young Caribbean officer came in. "They found the kid," he said.

Maria leaped to her feet. "Where?"

"At a police station, not far."

"Why at a police station?"

"He walked in."

"And the children?"

"Some of them."

"Not all?"

The young officer shrugged. "Don't know."

The lawyer slid her notepad into her briefcase. "I'm going there. No one questions Oscar until I arrive."

"I'm going with you," Maria said.

"Let me handle this."

"Are you keeping me here?" Maria asked the cop.

He looked uncertain.

"Someone needs to take her home," the lawyer said. "She's not under arrest."

The cop nodded. "I'll get someone."

"I want to see my son!" Maria said.

"I'll call you," the lawyer told her. "Right now you need to sleep, and be *quiet*." She said it with a significant look.

The door closed behind them and Maria was alone. She slumped to the table, exhausted. She should have fought harder to go along. But Oscar was alive. That was enough for now.

49

NORA SAT WITH her mother-in-law in the hospital's little café, over coffee. Liv sometimes talked about what a cliché it was to feel oppressed by her own mother-in-law. Someday, she said, Sebastian would fall in love, and when that happened, the person he loved would feel oppressed by Liv, and she wouldn't be able to catch a break. But Nora didn't feel that way.

She loved Dianne, who was sixty-three, with a majestic bosom and an excellent poker face. She was a middle school principal, and Nora had spent her professional life working with middle school principals, trying to please them. She did not want to seem like a failure in Dianne's eyes—in her marriage, in her parenting, in anything. And she did not want Raymond to seem like a failure. Dianne expected a lot of her son, and now Nora had to explain what he'd been doing in the hallway with his arms around Liv.

"It's been really tough," Nora said. "I think we're all in need of comfort."

"You and Raymond don't comfort each other?"

"That's been hard to do lately."

"Why?"

It was impossible to explain. The guide, the disappearance, Liv's blurted accusation, Raymond's baffled hurt. And before that, the way things had cooled between them, incrementally, so she'd barely noticed until it was done. "It's a long story," Nora said.

"I have time," Dianne said.

Nora felt restless and itchy. She wished she could crawl right out of her skin. "Can I tell you what I'm afraid of?" she asked.

Dianne nodded.

"I'm afraid I've taught my children to be too good," Nora said. "I wanted to keep them safe. I taught them that they can't play with plastic guns, ever. And they can't lose their tempers. I wanted them not to draw attention to themselves. I wanted them to be small targets."

Dianne was listening.

"My niece, Penny, her personality is to be a *big* target," Nora said. "And Liv encourages it, because she's a good feminist, mostly. And I know that people are going to hate that quality in Penny, because she's a girl. She's assertive and she wants things, and she doesn't care about being polite, and it comes off bossy and greedy. I want to be a good feminist, and *I* hate it in Penny. But I also know she can get away with it, because she's white."

Dianne drank her coffee and gave nothing away.

Nora took a deep breath. "So Penny got pissed off and jumped out of the train. It was so insanely stupid. But then it got her rescued. I'm afraid that Marcus and June are huddled somewhere being *good*, like I taught them. And they won't take a chance and they would never do anything that dumb, and so they won't be rescued, like Penny was. And it will be my fault."

Dianne considered her for a long minute, then said, "They'll be all right."

Nora was bursting to say that there was no way of knowing that! Kids died and were hurt all the time! Instead she looked at her hands. If Dianne said something about God, about prayer, she didn't know if she could trust herself to be tactful in response. "I do know Marcus will take care of his sister, if he can," she said.

"Of course he will."

"But what if he can't?" Her voice cracked.

"He will. Those children are *strong*."

Nora blew her nose in the paper napkins from her cafeteria tray. "I miss my kids so much," she said, through snotty tears. "And I miss my mom."

"I know, sweetheart," Dianne said. "I know."

Loud voices echoed down the hall, and Nora recognized Liv's. She jumped up and ran toward the noise, with Dianne behind her. They found Liv outside Sebastian's hospital room.

"Get the doctor!" her cousin was shouting at a nurse. "Do something!"

"What happened?" Nora asked.

Liv was frantic. "I can't believe this. After all that. Oh, my God."

A ponytailed doctor ran into the room, and Liv followed her. What had they done to sweet Sebastian? He was supposed to be all right.

Nora turned and walked blindly away, toward the exit. She needed to get some air. She rounded a corner and saw Detective Rivera walking toward her, raising her hand in greeting. Nora wheeled, afraid of the detective, and almost bumped into her mother-in-law behind her.

Dianne grabbed her by the shoulders. "Where are you going? What are you doing?"

"I can't."

"I came to find you," the detective said.

Nora stood still. She wouldn't turn. She wouldn't look. She felt a flush, a prickling of sweat all over her body.

"That woman is talking to you," Dianne said.

"I can't," Nora whispered. "I can't hear it."

"We found them," the detective said.

Nora saw bodies in her mind, and she started to shake.

"They walked into a police station," the detective said. "They're okay."

Nora stared at her mother-in-law. "What did she say?"

"That they're okay," Dianne said.

Nora turned, finally, to face the detective. "What?"

"They're okay."

Nora felt like she was at the bottom of a pool, and the tall detective was standing on the side, trying to communicate. The words couldn't make it down through the water. "How?" she heard herself ask. But that wasn't the right question.

"They just walked into the station."

"Where?" Nora mouthed. She couldn't hear herself.

"They're coming here. One of the officers is driving them, in a police car."

"No!" Nora cried.

The detective looked confused.

Nora couldn't find the words to explain that the car would crash, that cars kept crashing. She remembered the scene she'd been running from. She had the terrible thought that she had hurt Sebastian, by wanting her own children to be safe instead of Liv's. She had wished it into being. The power of prayer. "Sebastian," she whispered.

The detective frowned. "What happened?"

Nora was hit with a wave of vertigo so strong that the hallway spun. The floor moved to her left beneath her, the ceiling moved to her right. She tilted with the motion and put a hand out. Her mother-in-law caught one arm and the detective took the other.

The three of them staggered down the hallway to Sebastian's room and found Raymond standing outside it. Nora managed to say, "Marcus and June. They're coming here."

"An officer is bringing them now," Detective Rivera said. "But I'm worried about your wife."

White lights flashed at the corners of Nora's vision. "I'm okay," she said. "I'm okay."

They lowered her to a bench.

"Put your head between your knees," Dianne said.

That just made it worse. Nora put her elbows on her knees and her hands over her eyes, willing the room to stop moving.

"They gave him too much insulin," she heard Raymond say.

She tried to breathe. Sebastian was in a hospital with his parents, where he was supposed to be safe, and they were going to kill him. And Marcus and June were in a car with a cop and they would never make it here alive. And she—she was not responding well, she was becoming yet another patient, she needed to get her shit together. But instead everything whited out and she slid off the bench to the floor.

50

ISABEL WAS FAIRLY sure that the Jesus woman who'd picked them up on the road hadn't recognized them as the kids from the ship. She'd dropped the five of them off at a church shelter where they got bad soup and dry clothes. Noemi was so feverish that Isabel had to dress her. But Isabel was able to ditch her bloody shirt and the bikini bottoms, and now wore a secondhand T-shirt with a rainbow decal.

A priest drove them to the police station. He *did* recognize them, and kept talking to the cops about the reward money, and how it would benefit his mission. All of them were stringy-haired, Noemi was sick and slumped over, and Oscar was limping. The cops looked disgusted, like they were homeless people or criminals.

Which Isabel was.

But she hadn't meant to be.

Finally they got in a car with a fat cop. The cop said their parents were waiting at a hospital but he didn't say why. Isabel was afraid to ask. She thought it might be a trick, to get a doctor to examine her. But she wouldn't let a doctor near her. The cop was a bad driver, he kept gunning the engine and braking, gunning and braking. Her father would have told him to stop it.

Her father couldn't know about Raúl. He was going to be so sad and disappointed, she didn't think she could stand it. She wondered if she could tell Hector, and then Hector could tell him.

But there was also the other thing that had happened, in the trees.

When they got to the hospital, where their parents were supposed to be, the cop stopped the car in the parking lot. Terror dimmed Isabel's vision. Marcus cupped his hand around her ear and whispered. At first she felt only his hot breath. It took a few seconds before she could separate the urgent gusts into words. But then she understood. He said, "We don't have to tell." She nodded and climbed out of the car. The cop had to carry Noemi inside.

The scene in the hospital lobby was crazy. Hospital people swarmed around. Noemi was taken away, shivering and semiconscious, and Oscar was, too, in a wheelchair. A black woman gathered Marcus and June into her arms, and their handsome father was there, crying. Marcus looked back at Isabel as he was led away down the hall.

But Isabel didn't see her parents. She was left alone with a tall woman with spiky hair who said her name was Detective Rivera.

"Your parents are on their way," the detective said.

"I don't want to be examined."

"That's up to you."

"Really?"

"Yes."

Isabel eyed the machona detective, wondering if she was telling the truth.

Another woman appeared, thin and pale and old. Detective Rivera said she was a social worker, who had some questions.

"I don't want to talk to her," Isabel said.

"You have to, for me to interview you," the detective said. "Because of your age."

The social worker gave Isabel a tentative smile, like an unpopular girl trying to sit at her table at lunch. Isabel couldn't imagine telling her *anything*.

"Can you take me to a bathroom, please?" she asked the detective.

As they walked down the hallway, Isabel said, "I have to talk to you alone. I can't do it in front of my parents, or that woman."

"Your mom and the social worker only?"

"No."

The detective pushed open the bathroom door and looked under the stalls for feet. "Okay," she said, leaning against the sink. "Go ahead."

Isabel's throat felt dry. "I have to pee first." She went into a stall and sat. It still hurt to pee. She listened to the stream hitting the water in the bowl, and she knew the detective could hear it, too. "I want to tell you something," she called through the stall door.

"I'm listening."

But before Isabel could bring herself to speak, someone else pushed open the door from the hallway.

"Can you wait outside a minute?" the detective asked.

"No," a voice said. "I have patients waiting."

"It's important," the detective said.

"So are my patients." The doctor went into the other stall. Isabel listened to her pee, then leave the stall and wash her hands.

"You okay in there?" the detective called.

"Yes."

"She's gone. What do you want to say?"

Isabel held her breath. She heard the social worker say, from the hall, "Isabel's parents are here."

"We'll be right out," the detective said. The door closed. "Last chance."

Isabel went out and washed her hands. "What's the social worker going to ask me?"

"What happened to you."

"I can't say it," she said. "Not in front of my parents."

"They have dolls," the detective said. "You can show her on the doll."

"I'm not a baby."

"It's hard for everyone," the detective said. "It's hard for grown-ups."

"Two cops came to that house," Isabel said. "Before—before everything."

The detective watched her. "Go on."

"They came to the house and Raúl gave them something and they went away." She hadn't wanted to cry. "You didn't protect us. You could have protected us!"

"Can you describe these cops?" the detective asked. She had gone very still.

"Yes," Isabel whispered.

The detective nodded. "Good."

"Marcus can, too," she said. "He saw them. He's smart."

"Good."

The door started to open again. Detective Rivera pushed it shut with one hand, then leaned back against it. "Just a minute," she called over her shoulder.

Isabel's throat seemed to be closing up again. "I was so afraid."

The detective nodded.

There was a pounding on the bathroom door. "Isabel?" her father's voice called. "Are you in there?"

"Mija!" her mother's voice said.

Isabel remembered Marcus whispering in her ear, his hot breath. He'd said they didn't have to tell. They didn't have to say anything about the man in the woods, from the train, or what had happened to him.

The door was shoved open from the other side, and her father was in the women's bathroom, then her mother.

"Mami!" Isabel said. She fell into her mother's arms.

"I'm taking my children home, right now," her father said.

"We just have a few questions," the detective said.

Her mother held Isabel by the shoulders and looked into her eyes. "Isabel," she said. "Where's your brother?"

"He's not with you?" Isabel said.

"Where's our son?" her father asked. "Where's Hector?"

"That's one of the questions I'm trying to answer," the detective said.

"He swam back," Isabel said. "He swam back to find you!"

There was a stunned silence.

"*Hector!*" her mother cried.

Detective Rivera was already on her phone in the hallway, holding her hand over her other ear. Isabel heard a low moaning and realized it was coming from her body. The social worker tried to guide them into a room with blue plastic chairs and stuffed animals.

"No!" Isabel cried. "I won't go in there! I want my brother!"

No one had done anything to help, from the very beginning. They hadn't found her, they hadn't saved her. They hadn't found Hector.

"Stop looking at me like that!" she screamed at the social worker. She kept thinking of Hector directing the game on the inner tubes, Hector swimming away for help. How many days ago had that been? Five? Six? "Go find my brother!" she screamed.

51

A YOUNG DOCTOR who introduced himself as Dr. Patel told Nora she was dehydrated and in shock. He wanted to put her on IV fluids. But she was not letting them put *anything* into her body, not after what they'd done to Sebastian. She locked her hands over her elbows in the hospital bed. "You're not putting any needles in me."

"You need fluid."

"I'll drink water. I'm fine. I fainted because I'm allergic to medical error. I want to see my kids."

"We have to treat your head."

She seemed to have split her forehead when she hit the floor. Or had she hit the bench? She wasn't sure. She reached for it.

"Please don't touch the wound," the doctor said.

"How's Sebastian?" she asked. "The kid you almost killed?"

Dr. Patel frowned. "He's much better."

A nurse came to dress her head and brought Nora an electrolyte drink. "Donde están mis niños?" Nora asked her. The nurse said they were coming.

And then, like something from a dream, Raymond steered Marcus into the room. Dianne was carrying June, who dived to the bed and latched on to Nora's side. Nora felt joy knocking her senseless.

"Don't cry, Mama," June said.

"I can't help it," she said, laughing. "I'm so happy."

June's braids were coming undone. They both wore strange, ill-fitting clothes. Had Penny looked like this when she arrived? Had she been cleaned up before Nora saw her? She'd seemed so sleek and triumphant, where Marcus and June were a mess. Marcus wouldn't come close to the bed.

"What happened?" he asked, his eyes on the bandage on her forehead.

"I bumped my head, that's all," she said. "Come here. I'm so happy to see you."

Marcus accepted a quick hug, then slipped away to pace the room. June remained at Nora's side, sucking her thumb—a habit she had given up years ago—and curling a lock of loose hair around her finger. Nora would have gently dislodged the thumb under normal circumstances. They'd been gone for six days and she felt as if she'd woken up on a strange planet. She wasn't sure it had breathable air.

Marcus circled the periphery of the room with his elbow bent, his fingers tracing the molding, the doorjamb, the glossy paint. "I'm hungry," he said, his eyes sliding to his grandmother.

"All right," Dianne said. "I'll go get some food."

"Can you go with her?" Marcus asked his father.

"I'd rather stay here," Raymond said.

"We're okay," Marcus said.

"I know," Raymond said.

"You don't have to worry," Marcus said.

Raymond gave Nora a look over their son's head, but she remembered that the detective said sometimes it was easier for children to talk to their mothers first. "Come right back," she told him.

Raymond reluctantly followed his mother out the door.

"C'mere, baby," Nora said, patting the bed. "Talk to me."

"I'm not a baby," Marcus said.

"I know. You've been so brave. Just come talk to me."

He moved to stand beside the bed, staring at the blanket. June, still sucking her thumb, watched him.

"Sweetheart," she said. "Did anyone hurt you?"

"No," he whispered.

"Can you tell me what happened?"

"Everything."

"Do you want to start at the beginning?"

June took her thumb out of her mouth. "I want my bunny!"

"Of course," Nora said. "Where is it?"

"In Oscar's backpack," Marcus said.

"Is it a real bunny?"

June started to wail, a high, keening, mournful cry. "I want Oscar! I want my bunny!"

"Shhh," Nora said. "Shhh. We'll get the bunny. We'll get him right away. I promise."

June stuck her thumb back in her mouth like a plug, silencing her own crying.

Marcus said, "Something bad happened. Isabel went upstairs. At the house."

Nora covered June's ears with her hands, which was maybe pointless, but June let her do it. "Then what?" she whispered.

Marcus hesitated.

"Sweetheart?"

"Raúl went upstairs," he whispered. "I should have st-st-st-st-stopped him."

Nora had never heard Marcus stutter before. "That wasn't your job, baby," she said. "It wasn't your fault. What did Hector do?"

June pushed Nora's hands away from her ears. "What did you say?" she asked.

"I asked about Isabel's brother," Nora said. "Hector."

They stared at her. "He wasn't there," June said.

"Where was he?"

"He swam back to you," Marcus said.

"In the river?"

They nodded.

There was a commotion in the hall, a voice screaming, "I want my brother! Go find my brother!" Marcus recognized Isabel's voice and his eyes widened.

"He swam back to you!" June said.

Raymond and his mother returned with orange trays of food. Nora felt her heart reach for her husband. She had not felt that way in such a long time. But she didn't want to be alone on this strange planet. She wanted Raymond here with her, trying out the weird gravity, breathing the possibly poisonous air.

52.

OSCAR GAZED AT his mother's lawyer, who'd turned up out of nowhere and told the doctors not to give him any pain medication. She
said they needed to talk before he got all dopey. But his knee throbbed
in a way he could *see* when he closed his eyes: a pulsing light. He'd
been hobbling and running and carrying children since the car rolled
over. He wished his sister were here, and not dead. Ofelia would've
had great pills. He concentrated on the lawyer's eyebrows, with all
the hair plucked out. Why was the penciled line supposed to be an
improvement?

"Did you see the Argentinian boy?" the lawyer asked.

"No."

"Did the children talk about him?"

"Not that I remember."

"Do you find that strange?"

How exactly was she defining *strange*? Raúl had shot at them from the Jeep, then had half his head scraped off. Oscar had jumped into a moving boxcar with five children and a bunny. No one had told him he was supposed to have *six* kids, not five. "I don't know," he said. "I think they thought he was with his parents."

"You didn't see his picture on the news?"

"No. I wasn't watching the news."

"And your mother didn't tell you about him?"

"I think she was worried about the kids she had."

"All right," the lawyer said, making a note.

"So where is he?" he asked.

"That's the question."

"Did Sebastian get insulin? Is he okay?"

"He will be," the lawyer said. "You're accused of kidnapping, you know."

He closed his eyes, his knee throbbing. "I didn't kidnap the kids."

"You did take them."

"I was taking them to the embassy."

"You chose a roundabout route."

He opened his eyes. "I was trying to help them. I did the best I could."

"By climbing on a freight train?"

"My knee hurt. The kids were so tired and hungry. How's the little girl, Noemi?"

"She's still in a fever."

He didn't know whether to tell the lawyer about Chuy, about Isabel killing Chuy. Should he tell her? Would they arrest Isabel?

But the lawyer had moved on. "A woman was murdered at the

Herrera house," she said. "The widow of the Colombian man whose grave the children found."

"Jesus."

"Your mother says Raúl shot her. And Raúl's brother seems to have left the country."

"I wish I could leave the country."

"Don't even think about it," she said. "You don't have his resources. There's also the car theft for them to charge you with."

"I asked Carmen if I could borrow it!"

"She said no," the lawyer said. "And you destroyed it, in an accident resulting in a fatality."

He pushed himself up in the bed. "He shot at us! He ran us off the road! He could have killed all of us, like he killed that woman!" His head was throbbing now, as much as his knee.

The lawyer stood. "I'll get the doctor. Try not to agitate yourself. And don't talk to *anyone*," she said.

53

LIV WALKED THE hospital hallways to stretch her legs. Sebastian was stable again, and an endocrinologist had been summoned. Benjamin was at his bedside with Penny. Liv had been making plans: to cut back her hours at work, volunteer at school. Go to every school dance, chaperone every date. The kids would hate her, but they would be alive. She'd once felt annoyed when they clung or leaned against her in the heat—now she wanted to feel their warm bodies against her all the time.

She found Nora outside in a courtyard, staring at some palm fronds. Cigarette smell wafted from two women in scrubs.

"I'm pretending I still smoke," Nora said. "How's Sebastian?"

"Much better." Liv looked for wood to knock, but everything was concrete. "And Marcus and June?"

Nora hesitated.

"Are they okay?" Liv pressed.

"I think so. I mean, yes. But there's something they're not telling me."

"What?"

"I don't know."

"Do you have a guess?"

Nora shook her head. "Marcus has started stuttering, and he can barely look at me. He knows Isabel was raped. But there's something else."

An orderly came outside, eyed them, and lit a cigarette.

There was a long silence. Liv realized she didn't know how to talk to her cousin anymore. Their countless hours of batting the conversation back and forth, the examining of small questions, the light Nora shed on everything as they talked it all through—it was gone. Liv wished, fervently, that she hadn't seen Nora with Pedro at the café table.

Nora walked over to the orderly and gestured to his pack of Marlboros. He shook one out and lit it for her as she cupped her hand around the flame. Then she brought it back to where Liv stood.

Liv felt the words spilling out, she couldn't stop or filter them. "I'm so sorry," she said. "I'm sorry about everything. I don't know why I said that thing to Raymond, about Pedro. I don't know what came over me."

"It was really shitty," Nora said.

"I know. I'd lost my mind."

Nora looked at the cigarette. "This is going to make me puke."

"How did Raymond respond?"

Nora tapped the ash loose. "He's sort of catastrophically disappointed, I think. I refused to talk about it, and then his mother showed up, and then I passed out, and now the kids are with us. So I guess it's on hold."

"I'm sorry."

"It's funny," Nora said, "Marcus keeping some secret—it makes me realize how horrible it is, to suspect there's something you're not being told. It's kind of worse than the news itself. I understand why Raymond is so angry and unhappy. And I'm afraid this will be between us forever. I don't know if we can stay together, but I don't know what splitting up looks like. I have no income. Even if I get a teaching job, there's no way I can live anywhere close to the school. I could barely afford my tiny old apartment, and rents are so much higher now."

"You're not really going to split up."

"I don't know, Liv!" Nora cried, exasperated. The orderly and the two women in scrubs turned to look at them.

They stood in silence. "You could keep the house," Liv said finally.

"I can't do that."

"It's a community property state." Liv sounded like her mother and hated herself for it.

Nora shook her head. "Raymond's mother has always thought me unworthy of him. And now I've proven her right. I'm a terrible mother, who cheated and allowed her children to disappear. I'm not going to take the house."

"We all let them disappear," Liv said.

Nora shrugged.

Liv said, "I'm also so sorry Dianne saw that weird thing in the hall. You know Raymond was just being comforting."

The orderly went inside, and Nora bent and stubbed her borrowed cigarette out on the concrete. "Jesus, that was disgusting."

Liv was fairly sure she meant the cigarette, but she wouldn't have put a lot of money on it. "Have you talked to Camila?" she asked.

Nora shook her head. "They're looking for Hector. You know, I keep thinking how we live in this weird ahistorical bubble, a time and place when it seems unthinkable, impossible, to lose a child. But it happens all the time, all over the world. It always has. And people go on. They can't just drop to the floor and scream for the rest of their lives."

"I might have," Liv said. "If we'd lost Sebastian."

"You wouldn't, though," Nora said. "I think my brain has been preparing all week, making the insulation that lets you go on. You know that earthquake the other night?"

"I slept through it."

"I was awake, but I didn't feel it," Nora said. "I was walking around the hotel and these people replacing a carpet asked me if I'd felt the terremoto. I had no idea what they were talking about. It's like I've been in some kind of deep freeze. I keep thinking of that woman who lost her baby to the dingo, and how people thought she wasn't emotional enough. But you can't be emotional enough. How could you be?"

"Lindy Chamberlain," Liv said.

"I was so angry at you when your kids came back," Nora said. "I thought I could never forgive you for *that*. Forget the rest."

"And now?"

"I should go back inside." Nora tossed the stubbed cigarette into a trash can by the door.

Liv had thought, for a fleeting second, that their old connection might be restored. But it hadn't been. She felt intensely sad. And she thought she had no right to her sadness, not when Penny and Sebastian had survived. She'd lost a friendship, but Camila had probably lost a child, and Isabel had lost her childhood. But how could you measure your own pain against the pain of the world?

She passed the room where Noemi slept. Penny had wanted to visit, but Noemi wasn't well enough. There had been other kids on the train. Penny said they had seen a boy peering out. So many kids in peril in the world, in leaky boats, in captivity, trafficked, sick. She remembered her mother talking about the Bhopal gas leak when Liv was—how old? No older than Penny. Her mother at the kitchen table saying that the average payout for Americans killed in plane crashes was $350,000, and that the Union Carbide payout in Bhopal might be a few dollars a life. There had been children killed, pregnant women. She remembered the overhead light in their kitchen, her mother's bleak and outraged expression at the way lives were valued, her father's silent agreement, their reflections in the big window with the dark night outside.

So what would Camila be thinking, now that the American kids— or no, the *estadounidense* kids—were back safely, when Camila's kids were not?

Liv wasn't sure which room Isabel had been given, so she stopped at the nurses' station to ask. The two women at the station kept tapping away at keyboards and didn't look up. The person Liv was a week ago wouldn't have let them ignore her. She would have demanded their attention, and the room number. But she was afraid to see Camila. So she left the women to their work and walked on.

54.

NORA STILL FELT sick from the cigarette. She'd brushed her teeth three times to get rid of the taste. June was curled up in one hospital bed with Raymond's mother. Marcus slept beside Raymond in the other. He still wouldn't tell her what he was hiding. He'd tossed and turned as Raymond whispered into his hair that it was going to be all right. The hospital was letting them all stay until Sebastian could be discharged, when an American hospital would have kicked them out that afternoon. Nora slipped out and leaned against the wall in the hallway.

After a few minutes, Raymond followed and closed the door behind him. Nora didn't know what a normal conversation between them sounded like anymore. He asked, "What's going to happen to us?"

"I don't know."

"What do you want to happen?"

She shook her head.

"When my cousins' baby died, they couldn't stay together," he said. "There was too much sadness between them."

Nora knew the story. "Our babies aren't dead."

"You know what I mean," he said. "Sometimes people don't make it through a thing like this."

She nodded.

"So what do you need from me, to stay?" he asked.

She hadn't formed the question in that way before. She toed the linoleum with her sneaker. "I need to know if you're going to forgive me."

Raymond didn't respond at first, and Nora was afraid he would say he couldn't forgive her, and they would be done. Instead he said, "Do you forgive me for leaving you and the kids, and going golfing?"

She looked up and met his eyes. She wanted to stay steely and ready for whatever might come. But he was a professional, it was his job to stir up emotions with his eyes, to make people feel his warmth or his seriousness or his anger or his steadfastness or his sorrow or his kindness, or all of those things at once, without saying anything. And she felt all those things. "I do," she said.

"Okay," he said. "You know what I did. Now I need to know what I'm forgiving you for."

Nora swallowed. He had to know, to move forward. But if he knew, he wouldn't forgive her. So she was caught. She thought of Pedro kissing her against the tree, before everything happened. His casual speed and skill, how emotionally unentangled it had seemed. She felt a twitch between her legs, a quickening warmth.

She thought of Pedro leading her away from the café after Liv found them, and her deep sleep in the stale bed in the papaya-colored house. She remembered her humiliating wait in the taxi when she went back the next day. Maybe he's married, señora, the cabbie had said. She would never see Pedro again, she did not want to see him, and yet the damp ache and the shame both grew more insistent.

"Did you fuck him?" Raymond asked.

She shook her head. "No."

"Did you suck him off?"

She shook her head again, a little shocked. That seemed impossible, too much of a betrayal. She had not known she had made such distinctions until now.

"Did he go down on you?" Raymond asked.

She shook her head a third time.

Raymond looked confused. "So then what happened?"

A nurse walked by in purple scrubs, glanced at them and strode purposefully on, in case they might want something from her. Nora watched her go, then turned back to Raymond. She was afraid.

"He kissed me," she said.

"Okay," Raymond said. His breathing had changed, the way it did when he was upset. She could see the uneven rising in his chest, hear the stilted rhythm.

"And then he just—used his hand," she said. "His fingers. It took about thirty seconds. I was wearing my shorts." She wanted to tell him that she had thought of the car wash, but it might seem like she was letting herself off the hook. The non-apology apology. He hated that.

"But you came?" Raymond said.

She nodded, miserable.

Raymond's eyes went from confusion to a different look. "Did you like it?"

She hesitated, then nodded.

"What about him?" Raymond asked. His voice had gone hoarse.

Another nurse walked by. They waited for her to pass.

Nora was aware that she was standing closer to Raymond now, so she could keep her voice low. "He jerked himself off," she said. "It was just as fast. He wiped his hand on a leaf."

Raymond stared at her. She could feel a laugh rising, and she tried to hold it back in case it might make him angry, but there was a smile lurking around the corners of his mouth, too, and they both burst into laughter. He put an arm around her waist and pulled her to him and grew serious again. "What was his cock like?"

"Not as big as yours." She felt it flex, hard, against her stomach. She felt dizzy, as if all the blood in her body had gone to her pelvis and was waiting there, pulsing, leaving her light-headed and stupid.

"Where can we go?" he asked.

"There's a supply closet." She'd seen the nurses go in for boxes of latex gloves.

They waited until the hallway was clear. Then they were in the closet, and her back was against the door, and they were tugging at clothes, surrounded by boxes of gauze and toilet paper. Raymond's mouth was hot on hers and he had a hand on her breast. "Did he touch you like this?"

"No."

"No? What the fuck is wrong with him?"

She shook her head. "I don't know."

His fingers went inside her underwear and slid. "Oh, Jesus, you're wet."

"I need you to fuck me."

"First I need to know," he said. "Did he touch you like this?"

"Yes," she said, clinging to him, trembling. "Please," she said. "Please."

"Not yet," he said. "Did he do this?"

"Yes," she said. He had to hold her upright as she came.

Then he relented. She kicked the underwear off and he lifted her by the waist so she could wrap her legs around him. His cock slid inside her and she gasped with relief. Her face was wet with tears and he kissed them away. Someone was going to hear them, against the door. She wanted to ask again if he would forgive her, because he'd never answered, but no one could be held accountable for anything said now.

55.

THE SEARCH AND rescue team was very professional, very organized. They set out through the woods near the river in a row. Two of the men carried rifles for crocodiles. Gunther walked in step with them, looking for his son.

He supposed all fathers thought their children the best, the most delightful, the most attractive. But most of them were wrong. Hector carried himself like a prince, a leader, a man already. So why hadn't Gunther taken him golfing, instead of leaving him with the women and children? They could have fit one more in the car.

Because they'd had a foursome already, he supposed. And Hector wasn't interested in golf: not enough action for him. Plus—and this made Gunther feel craven—it was easier to have a drink or two at lunch without his son's eyes on him. And the other men might also have felt constrained in the company of a boy.

They found no sign of Hector in the woods, so a team of divers arrived to search the river. Gunther found himself speaking of his son in the present tense, as if he were still alive. He couldn't do otherwise. He talked about Hector's swimming ability as if it were a factor. He knew that crocodiles rolled you over, again and again, to drown you. He tried not to think of Hector gasping, drowning, his lungs filling with the half-salt river water. It had been seven days now. He knew the chances of finding his son were infinitesimal. But still he hoped.

The divers, preparing on the bank, had a device on the end of a long spear. It held a .357 Magnum bullet in one end of a tube, and a charge. The bang-stick could be used at close quarters, underwater, in direct contact with an animal. Someone explained that the blast would do most of the damage, not the bullet itself.

They were looking for traces of his son. That was the only point now: to find proof that Hector was dead, and they could stop looking. Gunther's mind resisted such pain. It recoiled. He became interested in the engineering and the innovation—a layer of nail polish painted on the charge as waterproofing.

He had come to despise the American parents, who thought nothing terrible could happen to them, even in these days of debt and war and warming seas, much of it visited on the world by their own rich, childish country. They did not even know what they did not know.

He had joined the search effort not only because he hoped to find his son, but because he needed to get away from the American women, who had let this thing happen. As he watched the somber team with their deliberate movements, no one hurrying, no one thinking the boy was still alive, his hope began to flag, leaving only his hatred. He knew that if he had been on the beach with a drink in the hot sun, he would have fallen asleep. But his children were teen-agers. He and Camila had worked at parenthood longer than the others, and had earned the right to a nap. If your children were small, then it was your job to stay awake, and not to go off fucking strangers in the trees. This was universally understood. And now his daughter had returned traumatized and withdrawn, and he was standing by this brackish river waiting for divers to find scraps of his son. He could kill those women with his bare hands.

One of the three divers was a muscular girl, perhaps twenty-five years old. She looked sleek and amphibious in her black wetsuit. She laid out her gear: mask, fins, bang-stick. A knife, an underwater light, a mesh bag.

A mesh bag.

The divers stood in their wetsuits on the bank where the inner tubes had been found. If Hector had stayed with his sister, everything might have been different. But you made the decision you could make at the time when you made it. The person Hector was at that moment was someone who would heroically swim back. There was no version of Hector who walked to the Jeep. And if there had been, then maybe Raúl Herrera would have killed him, to get to Isabel. Maybe the Fates snipped with their scissors when they wanted to snip.

The girl diver, who had put on her tank, caught Gunther staring at her. She met his eyes for a moment. She was not going to scold the grieving father for staring. But her eyes held a light reproach. She looked away.

He wanted to tell her he had not been thinking of her neoprene-encased body. How could you seduce someone in a wetsuit? You would be exhausted by the time you peeled the thing off. You would need a cold drink. He'd been thinking of his children, and he'd been thinking of murdering two American women, but he couldn't explain. And now, of course, he *was* thinking about her neoprene-encased body. An aquatic, erotic creature. The body responded. It was not a choice.

He turned to peer back into the trees where Isabel and the others had stepped over roots and branches, toward their captors. He imagined them like water sprites in their swimming costumes, flitting through the woods. Their bare footprints obscured now by the boots of the searchers. There was no sign they had been here at all.

There was a splash, then another, three, and the hunters had gone into the water to prove for certain that his son was gone.

56.

CAMILA SAT IN the dark hospital room and imagined the divers killing a crocodile and cutting its belly open, her son stepping out. Gunther, standing on the bank of the river, would welcome his son into his arms. She felt the tears come, at the joy of it. Hector was her secret favorite. Boys were so much less complicated for a mother. They loved you always.

The boy Marcus had come to visit Isabel in their room, the only one of the Americans who had. He seemed to have appointed himself Isabel's protector. Camila had gone to the toilet and come back to find them whispering together. They'd stopped when she entered.

"What is it?" she'd asked.

"Nothing," Isabel said.

She knew her daughter a little bit, and knew she was lying. But Isabel now slept like an innocent, under a spell.

Camila had been raised a Catholic, in a white dress at her confirmation, married by a priest, the whole thing. So now she tried to think about God and his intentions, out of habit. *Si Dios quiere*, her grandmother used to say, about every plan for the future. Shall we meet for breakfast? *Si Dios quiere. Ojalá que venga.* Why would God want to take Camila's son? Who was this deity who willed such things?

Gunther said there were no gods. He said that man was a brutal creature in a brutal world. The human race was barely removed from clubbing one another on the head, stealing women and provisions, getting through the winter with violence and blood. In Camila's lifetime, in her country, people had been thrown from airplanes for being a political inconvenience. Even America, the alleged light of the world, was built on the torture and rape and murder of captive people.

And yet Hector, her son, had risked his life for his sister, and for these children who were near strangers to him. There were noble impulses in this damned species, still. Which meant that they would find him. He would come back, her handsome young river god, reborn.

In the hospital bed, Isabel rolled over and moaned. She needed her brother, as much as Camila needed her son.

In her youth, Camila had a little singing career. It had never been much: a cabaret act, with a boy who played the piano. She sang standards and tango for tourists. Men brought flowers, but not for their love of music. They brought flowers for the dresses she wore, the décolleté, the sway of the hips behind the microphone. And sometimes, to be honest, for the handsome boy at the piano. But then she had married and created this beautiful girl, and she had been replaced. It was Isabel men looked at when they walked down the street. The child was only fourteen but their heads turned, and Isabel felt her power.

It was the most terrifying age. Her daughter was aware of her allure and she was right. And she was convinced of her invincibility and she was wrong. The drifting away on the river, the stumbling onto the grave site, it had all come at a very bad time for her.

Isabel shifted again in the bed, and then was still.

If this Raúl Herrera were alive, Gunther would have wished to kill him, to tear him apart. As it was, Gunther's rage had no target, no outlet. Camila wondered if it would fester. She wondered if he would blame his daughter, see her as ruined, in some primitive way.

Someone was standing in the light from the doorway. Camila looked up and saw Liv through the gap, peering in.

"Camila?" Liv whispered.

"Yes?"

"How are you doing?"

How was she doing? Camila wanted to laugh. What did they know of the gaping emptiness in her heart that would never be filled until her son came back? The American women would be fine. Their marriages might feel the strain. This hellish trip might expose the cracks in their foundations, and they might crumble. But they had their children, intact. That was all any of them wanted. A voice that she did not recognize came from deep in her chest, and she said, "Go away."

57

ANGELA RIVERA LAY in bed, listening to the street outside. Voices from the bar on the corner, a distant siren. A part of her mind was always scanning those sounds for trouble, but she tried to shut that habit down for a little while. She had enough trouble of her own.

She'd been assigned to the missing kids because her English was the best in the department. She'd worked for an uncle in Florida four summers in a row, pumping gas at a marina, making conversation with the boat owners, going out with the local kids at night. Nothing like four beers to loosen the tongue. She'd kept it up by watching American movies, practicing when she could, proud of her fluency. And she'd also, of course, been put on the case because everyone was home with their families for the holiday. Let the dyke work at Christmas—what did she care?

But it wasn't even her beat. No sex crimes involved, at the time they'd assigned her to it. Unless you counted whatever had happened in the trees, with the guide and the pretty American, but she didn't count that.

Lexi moved in her sleep, stretched one leg out and left it there, toes against Angela's calf. Lexi was small and wiry, but she liked to sleep diagonally across the bed or else right in the middle, spread out like a starfish. When she came home from working late, Angela had to push her across the bed with both hands before climbing in. Lexi might mumble a protest but she never woke up. She didn't have Angela's insomniac tendencies, her way of worrying a case, turning it over and over in her mind.

They'd found a body near the train tracks where the train had been stopped. Male, thirty to thirty-five, probably dead two days. Old gang tattoos, inked over. His throat had been cut, and they'd found a yellow-handled folding knife with two distinct sets of prints that matched no one in the database. And a child's pink backpack beneath his body, soaked in blood, with a stuffed pig and some comic books inside.

Angela had asked the older kids, cautiously, about this discovery, and she had gotten the strangest answers. At first, Isabel pretended not to know what she was talking about. Then she said the man had attacked her, and maybe Oscar had fought him, but she couldn't remember. It was all too terrible. She had started to cry. Angela waited, and then tried to ask more questions. Isabel said she should ask Marcus. He knew.

Marcus didn't stall. With his mother beside him, he said in a hushed whisper that a man had attacked Isabel, and that Oscar had fought him.

The little one, June, said it was too dark to see. She said there was a man with Noemi, who came to the train car, but then he wasn't with them anymore. She didn't know why.

June was the only one Angela believed.

Noemi was still in a fever, and Angela hadn't talked to Oscar yet, because she wanted to think some more about what the kids had said, and what they weren't telling her.

Then word had come that the divers found a scrap of the Argentinian boy's shorts on the bottom of the river, snagged on a branch. Pink-and-green cloth. Was it better to see your kid half-eaten, or better not to find him at all, always to have that sliver of hope that he was still out there somewhere, in torn swim trunks?

Lexi rolled over to the middle of the bed, her forehead against Angela's shoulder. It was too hot to sleep so close, each breath on her skin. Lexi ran a rape crisis center, and Angela thought about the way she talked to the women there, how calm and practical she was. She helped them navigate the worst thing that had ever happened to them—except when it wasn't the worst thing, or the first time. She had an evenhanded sensibility, a businesslike response to trauma. And still she slept so deeply, so unafraid.

Angela herself had forty rape cases open, and hundreds more closed. Most of the rapists were relatives. The youngest victim in her current stack was two years old. Sometimes the families didn't want to prosecute. Sometimes the men disappeared across borders and she couldn't find them. It was so hard to get justice of any kind. She thought about Isabel's tormented look in the hospital bathroom, her weeping in her mother's arms. How was it possible to be calm and reasonable about a child's pain? It was a nightmare.

A hundred reporters with cameras had gone to the river. They'd done a special report on the weapon the divers carried for crocodiles, the bang-stick. They'd already interviewed the grieving sister of Consuelo Bolaños, holding the orphaned little boy on her lap. No mystery there: They had the gun that had killed Consuelo, and the gunshot residue on Raúl's fingers and clothes, and an eyewitness. And Raúl was dead. That particular chapter had exhausted its shock value, and the news cameras would be on the prowl for the next one.

The hospital staff had been discreet and compassionate, but they were getting weary of their troubled guests. Someone was going to tip off the media for cash or spite, and the cameras would descend. This unexpected time of privacy would be over. The new body in the trees would keep the public fascination and the television ratings going, make the flames dance higher. Angela wanted to solve the mystery of the man with the pink backpack, but she was afraid of the truth, and of what it might mean.

58.

OSCAR INSPECTED THE bandage on his knee. He guessed it looked like Frankenstein's monster underneath, but at least they'd given him drugs, and the agony was gone. He felt nothing, only the euphoria of painlessness. His mother, terrified of pills, had insisted he could get through the recovery with ice. Ice! When they'd sliced his knee open.

He was thinking about lifting the bandage to see the stitches when a silver-haired man came into his room and closed the door.

"Hello, Oscar," he said. "I'm Isabel's father. My name is Gunther."

Oscar watched him draw close.

"How is your knee?" the man asked. He spoke Argentine Spanish and used the formal *you*. He sounded rich, but Oscar could have guessed that from knowing Isabel.

"I haven't seen it or tried to walk yet," Oscar said. "But it doesn't hurt."

"Good," Gunther said. "I've been hoping to talk to you." He took a seat by Oscar's bedside and crossed one knee over the other. "Did you know that they found a man dead near the train tracks? Throat cut wide open."

Oscar held his breath. He saw Isabel again, crouched and feral in the dark, holding his yellow-handled knife.

"Do you know who this man was?" Gunther asked.

Oscar cleared his throat. He thought about lying. "Noemi's uncle," he said. "His name was Chuy."

"You think he was really her uncle?"

"Sure."

"Was he screwing the kid?"

"No!" Oscar said. "I mean, I don't think so."

"So what happened to him?"

"My lawyer doesn't want me talking to anyone."

"Smart lawyer," Gunther said, smiling. "Shall I leave? Or shall I tell you some things you might wish to know?"

Oscar watched him. "Okay."

"I have spoken with the machona detective," Gunther said. "My daughter told her that maybe you killed this man."

Oscar blinked, startled. "I didn't!"

Gunther paused. "So why did you not mention the dead man before?"

Oscar's thoughts were jumbled now. He hadn't said anything because he hadn't wanted to get Isabel in trouble. "Did you ask Marcus?"

"Marcus also says maybe you did it."

Fury exploded in Oscar's brain. "That's not true!"

"So who killed him?" Gunther asked.

He took a gulp of air. "*She* did!"

"Who?"

"Your *daughter*!"

Gunther's eyes, beneath bushy silver eyebrows, flicked back and forth between his. He didn't seem as surprised as Oscar thought he should be. "Why would she do that?"

Oscar lay back on the pillow. "She was afraid," he said. "The uncle was trying to help us. He went to see who was coming, and then he came back. He grabbed Noemi and Isabel, to run with them. Isabel didn't know who it was, in the dark."

"How do you know this?"

"I saw it."

Isabel's father rubbed his face and looked at the ceiling. "Okay," he said. "Okay."

"What's going to happen?" Oscar asked.

"I don't know." Gunther rolled his neck and Oscar heard it pop. "If my daughter killed this man, as you say, people will want to know why."

"She thought she was defending herself."

"Yes, but they will want to know everything. A beautiful girl, a killer. People love this like flies love shit. You understand this, yes?"

"Yes," Oscar admitted.

"You know my daughter was raped?"

He hadn't, really, but now it made sense. Fucking Raúl. "Yes."

"There will be nothing else to talk about," Gunther said. "It will be a fucking circus."

The door opened and a nurse looked in.

"A moment, please," Gunther said, and the nurse retreated and closed the door. He moved his chair closer and found Oscar's eyes again. "The story the children told is a good, boring, understandable story," he said. "You were defending them."

"But I didn't do it."

"You know that. And God knows it."

"Do you believe in God?" Oscar asked.

"No."

"My mother believes."

"So does my wife, in a way," Gunther said. "She needs to. Our son is dead."

"I'm sorry," Oscar said. "I didn't know there were supposed to be six."

Gunther clasped his hands together, and put his elbows on his knees. He seemed unable to speak.

"My sister died when I was little," Oscar said. "I found her."

"That's terrible also."

They sat together in silence.

"Can I tell you something?" Gunther asked, and Oscar noticed that he was calling him *vos* now. "Two police officers went to the Herreras' house. Before my daughter was raped. They could have stopped everything, right there. But Raúl Herrera paid them, and they went away. And we got a report that no one was at the house."

"Oh, shit," Oscar said.

"If I had a time machine, I know I should use it to kill Hitler, but I would go back one week from today and shoot those three men in the head."

"Did the detective know?"

"Not then," Gunther said. "She knows now. You see, no one protected my daughter. No one, in this whole fucking place. But I think these kids are very smart. And I think, with their lie, they've made it so you, Oscar, can protect them, like everyone failed to."

"By saying I killed someone," Oscar said.

Gunther was silent.

"But I *didn't*!"

"Okay," Gunther said, studying a spot on the far wall. "So it all comes out. The children say you killed a man. You say my daughter did. But you didn't say anything to the police about this terrible murder, when you were questioned. So you aren't the rescuer and protector anymore. You're this strange kid who stole some children with his mom."

Oscar flinched.

"And then," Gunther went on, "you either killed an innocent man for no reason and tried to pin it on a girl, *or* you didn't say anything when the girl killed him. That looks really fucking suspicious to me, my friend."

"Are you *threatening* me?" Oscar asked.

"No, I'm *explaining* to you," Gunther said. "I'm telling you the future, like a fortune teller, except I am telling the truth."

"That guy was helping us!" Oscar said. "And Isabel cut his throat wide open, with the knife I used for cheese!"

"I believe you," Gunther said. "But if you tell this story, it won't end for my daughter, and it won't end for you. It will be a hell on this earth. I'm trying to help you. I promise you, my boy, I am."

Oscar chewed the inside of his cheek.

"I suppose your fingerprints are on the knife," Gunther said.

"Yes, because I sliced some cheese."

"I will get you the best lawyer," Gunther said. "I believe our detective is sympathetic to my daughter. You will back up the children's story, and the death will be a justifiable homicide. There will be no prosecution. I will make sure."

"Can I get that in writing?"

"We will shake hands, like gentlemen."

"But you're not in charge!" Oscar said. "This is my life! I'll never get a job!"

"You will," Gunther said. "People will think you're a hero, very brave. They will seek you out."

Oscar shook his head. "I don't know."

"If not, come to Argentina, and I will hire you."

Oscar studied Gunther's long, tanned, rich man's face. "What about Noemi?"

Gunther shook his head. "She isn't a reliable witness. Out of her mind with fever."

"I mean what will happen to her?"

"She'll go back to her grandmother. Her parents are illegals in New York."

"She was trying to get to them."

"Do you know what happens to these children when they cross into Mexico?" Gunther asked.

Oscar thought of that tiny girl appearing out of the dark, so brave and unafraid when he'd been paralyzed with fear. He was ashamed of his fear, of his inability to act, of his many mistakes. "If you can get the girl to New York, I'll do it."

"That's U.S. Immigration," Gunther said. "Out of my control."

"You're rich, you can pull something. The Americans can."

"I don't know."

"What if her grandmother tries to send her again? Her uncle is dead. She could die."

"Do you know how many children are on those trains?" Gunther asked.

"She's the one I know," Oscar said. "And your daughter killed the guy who was taking care of her. So you owe him."

Gunther sighed. "I don't know what I can do."

Oscar crossed his arms over his chest, trying to look brave. "Then I don't know either."

The nurse knocked and pushed open the door again.

59

BENJAMIN WANTED OUT. Just out. He wanted to hand his family's passports to immigration and go home.

They'd finally escaped the purgatory of the hospital, extracting a reluctant Penny from a new friendship with Noemi. She'd been visiting Noemi in her hospital room, learning songs in Spanish. Penny seemed to be picking up the girl's accent, using words Benjamin had never heard before. They were *amiguis*, the two of them, and Penny had started saying *simón* for yes and calling him *taita*.

But then Kenji got them out, arranging flights to LA through Miami. Miami! Benjamin wondered aloud, in the car to the airport, why Florida was on their way home. What had happened to their simple boat ride south from LA?

"Mexico curves to the east," Marcus said. He approximated the continents with his hands. "And so does the Isthmus of Panama. So South America is much farther east than North America."

Benjamin had always felt a connection to Marcus. The way his mind worked seemed not unlike Benjamin's own—a little spacey, enamored of logical systems. Marcus had barely spoken in days, and Benjamin was encouraged by this sudden volubility. "Do you know how the isthmus was formed?" he asked.

"Volcanoes," Marcus said, and he settled back into a comic book in Spanish. He had broken his silence only to answer an actual question. He was not going to be drawn out by a grown-up's idea of conversation.

An embassy chaperone took them to the airport terminal, and Benjamin felt curious eyes on them. Most people kept a respectful distance, but one intrepid soul in a swordfish T-shirt put a hand on Benjamin's shoulder to congratulate him. He wanted to shake this well-meaning tourist and tell him: *It was luck! Your car didn't crash on the way here. This airport hasn't been attacked. There hasn't been an earthquake or a tidal wave. We've all been really fucking lucky, for one more day. That's it! That's all!*

The plane took off, separated itself from the tarmac. A motherly flight attendant brought warm nuts in a ceramic dish, and a Bloody Mary. Benjamin didn't usually drink, but what the hell? Beside him, Liv looked out the window at the retreating country. She and Nora seemed to have reached a détente, and she'd stopped talking about lawsuits. They had all given statements that they didn't think Oscar should be prosecuted, to be used in the inquest, because Oscar had been protecting the children. Benjamin was secretly glad that Penny had gotten herself and her brother off the train, that his kids hadn't been there to see the man killed. Not that he wished it on Marcus and June.

There'd been no word of Raúl's brother yet, except from Penny, who said George was really nice. Hard to judge about that.

So now they would all have to reenter their life, carrying this beast they'd picked up on vacation: a hulking creature of reproach, grief, fear, guilt, and untoward luck, shaggily cloaked in the world's lurid interest. He didn't know how they were going to move forward, dragging the thing on their backs.

But then he thought of Gunther and Camila, and the grief that they were taking home with them. He kept thinking of old news footage of the fall of Saigon, those last-minute helicopters off the roof. He and his family had escaped, leaving chaos behind them. It was the American way.

60

THE COUNSELOR, MS. HONG, led a very nonjudgmental discussion at a school meeting in the big hall, and Nora sat reluctantly in a folding chair in a big uneven circle, with kids on the floor and parents in the bleachers and in other chairs. It was the culture of their small school to have meetings like this, and it would have been considered strange to refuse, but she found herself wishing the teachers were a little less dedicated to processing everything, and they could just move on.

She kept waking in the dark of her own bedroom and "seeing" the hotel room where she had spent the worst week of her life. In her mind, she was still there, and so were the bedside tables, the credenza. She moved carefully around them to the door where she knew the hotel bathroom to be, and then she stood there, feeling the blank wall in Los Angeles with her hands, trying to understand where she was.

Raymond had refused to go to the all-school meeting, but his mother came, and sat with Marcus in a far corner. Dianne kept her handbag on her lap, as if she might have to bolt any second. Nora smiled when she caught her son's eye, but Marcus looked away.

Junie sat beside Nora. She didn't like to let her mother out of her sight. She followed her to the bathroom, clung to her at the supermarket. Nora had been staying at school all day, experimenting with leaving the classroom once June was engaged, but never going farther than the hallway outside the door.

Sebastian told the assembled circle the story of how his blood sugar had crashed after they left the train, and how he'd had a seizure while a woman was giving them a ride. He was unselfconscious about it, matter-of-fact.

Penny seemed utterly unscathed, enjoying the attention. Nora wondered if the trauma was in hibernation somewhere inside her, if she would have a delayed breakdown at twenty-three. If the rest of them hesitated before answering a question, Penny would jump in.

But then a girl in June's class, Sunita, asked about the boy who died. Sunita was six years old. What to tell her? Nora expected Penny to speak, but Penny only blinked, and looked as if something had short-circuited in her brain.

Nora turned to the little girl. "You mean did we know him?"

Sunita nodded.

"Yes," Penny blurted finally. "We knew Hector."

"Was he nice?" Sunita asked.

"He was the nicest boy I've ever met," Penny said, her eyes filling with tears.

There was silence in the room. Nora realized how struck Penny must have been by Hector—as struck as Marcus had been by Isabel. They had both lost their hearts to the Argentines.

Finally a mother asked, "What about the Ecuadorean girl?"

Liv said, "She's in New York with her parents. They all have papers."

A satisfied murmur passed through the room. Nora wanted to shout that there were lots of kids who *didn't* get to their parents, who *didn't* get papers. But then they had to sing the "Ode to Joy" in Spanish.

As soon as the meeting was over, Nora tried to flee with Dianne and the kids, but people kept stopping to hug her. Finally she made it out of the building, only to end up walking to the parking lot beside Liv.

Penny had recovered from her moment of public grief and was now angling for a puppy. "But we were *kidnapped*!" she said.

"You have to stop playing that card, Pen," Liv said, spraying hand sanitizer on her hands.

"It's not a card!"

"It is if you try to trade it for a dog."

"I would just feel *safer* with a dog."

"I think you get this from my mother," Liv said. "The lawyering."

"If I can't have a dog," Penny said, "at least let me invite Noemi to visit."

"That's more complicated than it sounds."

"Because the tickets are expensive?"

"Yes," Liv said. "Among other reasons."

"But they aren't expensive for *us*."

"Actually, they are."

"Do you not want them to come because they're poor?" Penny asked.

"No," Liv said. "We're ending this discussion."

Nora knew she would have craved this moment, when they were stranded in the hotel in the capital with no leads. It would have seemed like paradise, to be picking up her beautiful children, and attending a weird, over-sharing, well-meaning school meeting. She would've welcomed the offensive questions and the awkward conversations.

And there *had* been enormous joy, and enormous relief. But here Nora was, desperate to get away from Penny. One aspect of human resilience, in all its marvelousness, was the ability to recalibrate, to adjust to new circumstances with astonishing speed.

"How are you doing?" Liv asked her.

"I'm okay."

Penny had dropped behind to talk to some girls her age, and now Sebastian was yelling at his sister in the parking lot.

"Stop telling that story!" he said. "Just stop!"

"It's my story, too!"

"It is not!"

"Guys," Liv said. "Let's go."

"He's totally freaking out for no reason!" Penny said.

"Because you won't stop talking about me!"

"You need to stop telling stories about your brother," Liv told Penny.

"It's about *me*. He wasn't even *conscious*."

"I was *there*," Sebastian said. "And I already *told* it!"

Liv slid open the door of their minivan and gave Nora a drowning look over the children's heads. "Dinner sometime?"

"Great," Nora said, with a quick smile, and she moved away toward her own car. She buckled June into her booster seat in the back, even though her daughter could do it herself.

"When can I stop having a booster seat?" June asked.

"When you're eight," Nora said. "Or if you get really tall."

"We didn't have them on the trip."

315

"One of the many things wrong with that trip."

"Do you think Penny will really get a puppy?"

"No."

"Oh, she will," Dianne said from the front seat. "Liv doesn't know how to say no to those children."

"I wish I could've kept my bunny," June said.

"I know, sweetheart," Nora said. "I'm sorry."

Even brilliant Kenji, who'd gotten Noemi the papers to go to New York, hadn't been able to get them permission to take the bunny, so it was living with Oscar. If the inquest went badly and Oscar went to prison, Nora guessed the bunny would stay with his mother. Unless Maria went to prison, too.

"Mom," June asked, as Nora backed out of the parking space, "do you think Noemi will come visit?"

"I don't know."

"I hope so," June said. "What about Isabel?"

Nora saw Marcus stiffen in the back seat. "She's with her parents now," she said. "I think it's important for all of us to be with our families for a while."

"That poor woman," Dianne said.

Nora remembered Camila leaving the hospital on Gunther's arm. She'd looked like a husk of herself, as if she'd been caught in a giant spiderweb and drained of blood. Nora could not extract her gratitude that she was not in Camila's shoes from her ability to imagine Camila's pain.

"What are we having for dinner?" Marcus asked.

Nora caught his eye in the rearview mirror. She had talked to Ms. Hong about the way Marcus changed the subject whenever Isabel's name came up. It was as if he'd put up a force field around himself. He went to see Ms. Hong because they asked him to, but he didn't like to talk about the trip, and he avoided Penny and Sebastian at school. Ms. Hong said they had to trust his process, and follow his lead.

"Pesto pasta with chicken," she said.

"I'm making a key lime pie," Dianne said.

"Hooray!" June said.

Marcus nodded and looked out the window, and Nora drove home.

61

MARCUS SAT IN the counselor's office and stared at a puzzle on the table. It was made of wire and wood with a loop of cord, and you had to get the cord off. He'd already solved the puzzle in his head, without picking it up. He went back to looking at the map of the world on the wall behind Ms. Hong's head.

"Did your grandmother go home?" Ms. Hong asked.

"Yes."

"How does that feel?"

"It's okay," he said. "She likes to take us to church."

"Do you like to go?"

"It's okay," he said. "They have codes to live by."

"Like what?"

"Like the Golden Rule. And that you shouldn't lie. That map is wrong."

"Oh?" Ms. Hong said, turning to look. Her hair was perfectly straight, and the tips of it brushed her shoulders.

"It still has Yugoslavia on it," he said. "And Samoa is now on the other side of the International Date Line."

"I guess it's old."

"There are other mistakes, I just haven't found them yet," he said. "Some of the city names I can't see from here."

"You like geography."

"They skipped December thirtieth, when they moved the date line."

"Who did?"

"Samoa. Also Tokelau, that's another island."

"So December thirtieth just didn't happen for them that year?"

"Right."

Ms. Hong smiled. "There are some days I would have liked to skip over, in my life."

Marcus narrowed his eyes at her. She was trying to get him to talk about stuff, but he wasn't fooled. On December 30 of this year, he had been in the house with the red couches and the wooden tic-tac-toe board, and he had not meant to bring up that house. "Everything still *happened* in Samoa," he said. "It's not like they could skip stuff that happened. They just called it a different day."

"I know," she said. "I was using the idea as a metaphor."

"I don't like metaphors."

"Why not?"

"Because they aren't real."

She hesitated. "But maps are metaphors. The world isn't really

319

laid out flat. Imagining our world seen from above is a way of abstract thinking."

"Satellites see it from above."

"True."

"But not with a Mercator projection," he admitted.

They sat communing with those facts.

Then Ms. Hong said, "There's a tribe in the Amazon that has compass points built into their language. I learned this in an anthropology class in college. When the people there are talking to someone, the way they address that person includes their spatial relationship to the speaker—I think I'm remembering this right. So if I were talking to you, I would say, 'You, Marcus, who are northeast of me, what do you think?'"

"I'm not northeast of you," he said. "I'm almost exactly south."

Ms. Hong laughed. "I think you would pick up that language really quickly," she said. "You always have that bird's-eye view in your head. Most of us don't. What I meant was that for those people in the Amazon, the fact that you are almost exactly south of me would be built into the word *you*, when I was talking to you. And in this conversation, you would refer to me as being almost exactly north of you."

"I like that language," he said.

"I thought you would."

"Where in the Amazon? Brazil or Peru?"

"I'm not sure."

"Noemi is from Ecuador," he said. "Maybe she can do it."

"Maybe," Ms. Hong said. "But I think it's a very isolated tribe, and languages there are pretty distinct."

"Penny wants Noemi to come visit," he said. "With her parents."

"Oh?" Ms. Hong said. "How do you feel about that?"

He shrugged. "June wants it, too."

"And you?"

"I barely know Noemi," he said. "She doesn't even speak English."

"I bet she's learned some in New York. And you've learned some Spanish."

"We were just on a train together for a little while," he said. "And Penny wasn't even there. And then we saw Noemi at the hospital, but she had a fever for half the time."

Ms. Hong picked at a thread on her skirt. "Sometimes—when we have a very intense experience, we feel close to the people who were there, even if we only knew them for a short time."

Marcus said nothing, thinking of Isabel.

"And people have different responses to an intense experience," Ms. Hong said. "I know sometimes it's hard for you to be in school with Penny, when she's had a very different response to what happened than you've had."

"She was so mean to Isabel," Marcus said.

"Tell me about Isabel."

He shook his head.

"Please, Marcus," Ms. Hong said. "I think it will help."

He said nothing.

"I saw that photo of her jumping into a pool, on the news," she said. "It looked like she was really happy."

Marcus nodded. "She still posts a lot of pictures looking happy."

"You follow her?"

"On my mom's phone."

"If someone has great capacity for joy, I think they can find it again. Even after something terrible happens."

"She got a puppy," he said.

Ms. Hong smiled. "Dogs can be very comforting. I think all of you lost a sense that the world is always safe. That you're always protected. A dog might help her with that."

Marcus traced with his eyes the path the loop of cord would take through the wire puzzle. "Actually I think everyone is being kind of overprotective."

"Well," Ms. Hong said, "can you understand that, in them?"

"I think they were always like this," he said. "I just didn't notice it before."

"That might be true," she said. Then, "Do you think Isabel would ever come to Los Angeles to visit?"

Marcus shook his head. "She doesn't want to see us."

"And that makes you sad?"

"I guess." He feared that Ms. Hong could read his mind, and wished she wouldn't.

"It's okay to have feelings about what happened," Ms. Hong said. "In fact, it's really important to have those feelings."

"It doesn't do any good."

"I think it does," Ms. Hong said. "Not everyone gets to choose how they respond to a trauma. Isabel might not be able to choose, right now. But you have a really strong mind. She does, too. I think you can decide how you're going to respond."

His eyes stung, unexpectedly. "I can't control it," he said. "I can't control *anything*."

"If you let yourself have your feelings," she said, "then I believe you can control what comes next."

"You don't *know*," he said, angry at her for making him cry. "You don't know anything!"

"I can make some guesses," she said.

"You don't even know that Samoa is on the other side of the International Date Line!"

322

"I learn something new every day."

He stood. "I want to go back to class."

"Please stay," Ms. Hong said. "I think we're just getting to the point where you can start feeling better. I really do."

She was almost exactly north of him. If he spoke that Amazonian language, he would say so when he was talking to her. "You—" he said. "You don't know anything about it."

62.

LIV DIDN'T KNOW what to do about Penny's constant begging for a visit from Noemi, a child they hardly knew. Benjamin had suggested they go to New York for spring break, and invite Noemi's family to his parents' apartment for a nice noncommittal lunch.

But Liv couldn't face another family trip. She had dreams of Sebastian letting go of her hand and disappearing into Times Square—past Batman, the Naked Cowboy, a million strangers. She would wake up drenched in sweat, tangled in damp sheets. Obviously this was an area to work on.

A friend had invited Sebastian to take the Expo Line to downtown LA and the Science Center, but when Sebastian realized the Expo Line was a train, he'd said no. He was *not* getting on a train. So New

York subways were out. Again: something to work on, maybe after a little more time had passed.

So they gave in, and invited Noemi's family to LA, and bought three plane tickets on JetBlue. It seemed worth it to get Penny off their backs. Liv hoped that seeing people who'd been separated from their daughter for so much longer than she had would help with the anxiety and remind her that everything was relative. Noemi's parents hadn't chosen the poverty and violence of the place they came from. They'd been trying to do the best thing for their kid. But to send a child illegally through all those countries—Liv couldn't imagine it.

She'd invited Nora's family to join them all for dinner. She hadn't seen Nora since the all-school meeting. This time of year was busy anyway, with school and sports and work. And there had been so many emails from people she hadn't talked to in years, who were appalled at such a thing happening on a family vacation. They seemed to expect reassurance from Liv that it would never happen to them. When she responded with a few lines, they wrote right back. But she didn't have time for an ongoing conversation with everyone she had ever met. So the emails piled up. The best thing she'd done was to leave her Facebook account deleted. The idea of all those messages from half strangers made her feel faint.

She'd said no to all the interview requests, without mentioning anything to the kids. She hoped that Penny would never find out that she could have danced on TV with Ellen DeGeneres but Liv had said no.

They were still waiting to hear what would happen to Oscar and Maria. Sometimes at night, before the Ambien kicked in, Liv wondered if the police might have found the children earlier if Maria hadn't smuggled them out of the house. But it was impossible to know. Maria had clearly felt the situation was untenable. What would have happened if they'd stayed was the other path, unknowable. Liv just hoped they hadn't left Maria and her son to suffer for having made the choice.

She'd brought home a pile of scripts to read, and sat with them in her office at home. She heard Sebastian's plinking piano exercises begin, and felt a flood of love for him. He had a new glucose monitor that sent information to her phone and to Benjamin's. So even when he was at school, she could see what his levels were. She didn't think she could function, otherwise. She couldn't have gone back to work.

Penny marched in, without knocking. "Grace is getting a schnoodle puppy," she said. "It looks exactly like a teddy bear."

Grace was getting a schnoodle because her father was having an affair, but Grace didn't know that, and didn't know about the impending divorce. "You have lots of teddy bears," Liv said.

"She's also getting a phone."

"You'll get one for sixth grade graduation."

Penny draped herself over the Aeron chair. "If I had a phone, you would always know where I was." A transparently deceitful tactic, when Penny didn't *want* Liv to know where she was.

"Are you excited to have your cousins over?" Liv asked.

Penny lifted her feet in the chair and spun. "I see them every day."

"How are they?"

"June's better. Marcus is still pining for Isabel. He's dying of love. It's like *Rent*."

"They were dying of AIDS in *Rent*."

"Well, that's what it's like."

"No one dies of love at eleven."

"He's twelve."

"What?" Liv had forgotten the birthday. "He didn't have a party?"

"We had cupcakes at school."

"Well, no one dies of love at twelve either."

"Romeo and Juliet were thirteen," Penny said.

"Thirteen was different back then."

"Thirteen is always the same," Penny said. She pushed herself out of the chair. With a triumphant little kick of her foot, she was out the door.

Liv wondered if Nora hadn't had a party for Marcus so they wouldn't have to invite her family, and be reminded of everything that had happened. She remembered Nora saying, "It was your fucking idea, this whole cruise!"

The halting notes of "Für Elise" came from the piano in the living room. Liv was trying not to cry every single day. She didn't want the kids' childhoods to be divided into pre-cruise and post-cruise, although she supposed they already had been. She picked up the script and tried to focus on the swimming words on the page.

63.

ISABEL LAY BY the pool with her puppy on her chest. He was sleeping, his velvety jowls draped over his oversized paws. Her heart was so filled with love for him that it hurt. She held up her phone to take a picture. You could tell she was wearing a bikini, if you looked carefully. Her mother let her post bikini pics now—her mother let her do anything she wanted now—but Isabel didn't post them, mostly. Anyway, this wasn't a bikini picture. It was just a picture of his beautiful soft gray face.

Her mother was afraid of her, afraid that Isabel would reject her, or that Isabel might be broken forever. The one thing she wouldn't let her do was name the puppy after her brother. So Isabel called him Toby, but in her mind it was short for Hector.

She took another picture that showed Toby's face better. Her father said the wrinkly jowls were for fighting. If another dog grabbed them with his teeth, Toby could still turn his head and bite the dog back. Her father was trying to say something to her, by talking about the dog. But Isabel pretended she didn't understand. She wasn't going to give him an opening like that.

Her parents would never be the same again. They worked and went out and they could hold a conversation, but she saw the permanent sadness in their eyes, even when something made them laugh. Hector had been the great love of their lives—both of them. They'd loved her brother far more than they loved each other.

On the ship, she'd tried to be as nice to the American kids as Hector was, painting their toenails. She'd always measured herself against him, knowing she would come up short. But now Hector was dead, and his bedroom was like a shrine. Her parents actually worshipped him. She would never be able to live up to his example. You couldn't compete with a saint.

She stroked Toby's back, sliding his loose skin, and he wriggled in pleasure in his sleep. He made a funny little noise and she wondered if he was dreaming. The first time she ever picked him up, he lay back in her hands with his belly exposed, waving his paws. Her father said that was a good sign, it meant the dog was submissive and trainable, and would never hurt anyone. She had rubbed the puppy's soft belly and said that this was the one.

The detective had told her, in front of her parents and the social worker, that there would be an inquest and they probably wouldn't prosecute Oscar, so Isabel didn't need to stay as a witness, and could go home. At the time, they were sitting in a room with a window, and the detective's eyes were almost golden, lit from the side. Isabel could feel meaning beaming from them. The detective was not stupid. She was accepting Isabel's account of things, but she was telling Isabel with her eyes that she'd better stick to the story she'd decided to tell.

The social worker had looked concerned and compassionate, understanding nothing. Isabel could have turned to her and said, "*I* did it. Oscar didn't do it. I shouldn't be protected, because I'm *shit*. I let Hector swim away. I went upstairs in that house and I made everything happen. And I killed an innocent man because I was scared."

But she didn't say anything.

Because what was the alternative? Being a murderer. Ending up in some juvenile justice system, but where? Her parents drowning in their sadness. The news cameras camping outside, as they had at the river where the divers pulled up the scrap of Hector's shorts.

Her father and Detective Rivera said it would all be fine, and Isabel believed them. They thought she was worth rescuing, and Isabel held on to that.

Her mother wanted her to see a therapist, but Isabel didn't need one. She had Toby. Talking to a therapist would be too much work, keeping everything straight, telling only the things she was supposed to tell. She understood it all, anyway. Better than a therapist could. She could whisper the truth to Toby, and he would love her anyway. She whispered it now, and kissed his soft, dreaming head.

64.

BENJAMIN WAS CHECKING Sebastian's blood sugar on his phone when Raymond's name came up on the screen, and Benjamin felt a slight dread. He wished they weren't having this uncomfortable dinner, this extended visit from the Ecuadorean strangers, who were right now in the air. He'd dealt with reentry by spending too much time on a new project made of high-tensile aluminum that could not die or wander off. He hadn't kept his vow to stalk the kids at school, but he checked Sebastian's blood sugar more than he really needed to.

He took the call. "Hey."

"Dinner's takeout, right?" Raymond asked.

"It's Zankou Chicken."

"I'll come get you," Raymond said. "We can pick it up."

He turned up at the house in a shiny black Tesla. "So you've decided life is brutish and short, and you might as well spend it all?" Benjamin said.

"It's a safer car," Raymond said. "And no emissions."

"You're just thinking of the polar ice caps and the kids."

"I am!"

Benjamin rubbed a hand over the soft leather seat. He drove a seventeen-year-old Volvo with cracking upholstery and old yogurt spills. Fixing it no longer made financial sense, but he didn't want to be the asshole in the new car. He understood that his was just a different kind of pose, and it was part of Raymond's job to be glamorous. They rode in the eerie electric silence.

"I need to tell you something," Raymond said.

Benjamin felt queasy. "You're getting divorced."

"What?" Raymond said. "No!"

"Oh, thank God." Benjamin was enormously relieved. He wondered what the strength or fragility of Raymond and Nora's marriage indicated about his own. "Sorry. What did you want to say?"

"You know Marcus has been talking to the counselor at school."

"Yeah." Ms. Hong had tactfully released Penny after two sessions. She said maybe they could revisit it later, but Penny really seemed fine.

"Marcus told her it was Isabel," Raymond said. "Who killed that guy."

"Wait, *what*?"

"Cut the guy's throat. Marcus says it was a mistake, that Isabel was scared and thought someone was attacking her."

"But they said it was Oscar."

"I called the detective. She was cagey. I think Oscar took the fall somehow and she knows it."

Benjamin thought about his own teenage arrest, the nolo contendere plea, the detectives showing up at the hotel twenty years later to interrogate him about it. What if the crime had been murder? What if he'd been poor? "What if they prosecute?" he asked.

"She says the inquest is almost over, and they won't."

"Oh, shit," Benjamin said. "Oscar's going to live with that for the rest of his life."

"Imagine the news, though, if it was Isabel," Raymond said. "That bikini picture, with a murder headline?"

"Marcus loves the truth," Benjamin said. He'd never known a kid with such rigorous devotion to facts.

"He also knows what it's like to have photographers waiting for you when you go for pizza. I think he waited for my mother to go home before he said anything. She kept taking him to church, and all the talk about sin was freaking him out."

"Jesus."

"It's not like Isabel will kill again, right?" Raymond said. "She's just a kid."

"I guess." Benjamin felt dazed.

"The detective said it was Oscar who pushed for Noemi to get to New York," Raymond said.

"Wait—what does that mean?"

"She was cagey as hell. But I think Oscar made some kind of deal."

They had pulled up outside Zankou Chicken, and went in to collect the food Liv had ordered, as if everything were normal. They loaded the bags into the Tesla's front trunk, the smooth unnatural compartment where the engine should have been.

"What about June?" Benjamin asked when they were on the freeway. "What does she say?"

"That it was dark. That she didn't see anything."

"You believe her?"

"I think so. But she's been so freaked out. I wonder if she knew it was a lie."

The smell of garlic sauce and roasted meat smothered the smell of new leather. "Should we try to get Oscar some money?" Benjamin asked.

"You want that to come out in the press?"

"Or some legal help?"

"We could talk to Gunther," Raymond said. "The detective said he was already doing that."

They rode in silence, feeling the dread of calling a man who had lost so much.

As they were unloading the bags in the driveway, Nora pulled up, and June tumbled out of the back, braids flying. "Hi, Benjamin!" she shouted, and she tackled his knees.

"Hey, kiddo."

"Did you get hummus?"

"Oh, no, we forgot hummus!"

"You *did*?"

"What do you think?"

She grinned up at him. "No."

Marcus climbed out, too. He'd grown taller and skinnier and his hair was longer, the curls twisted into points.

"Dude," Benjamin said. "Cool hair."

Marcus smiled a noncommittal smile.

"I'm getting a new bunny!" June said.

"Hey, that's great!" Benjamin said.

Liv pulled into the driveway in the minivan, and Penny hopped down from the passenger seat. Noemi, the guest of honor, wore a pink dress and white tights. Her parents were dressed up, too: the mother in a silky blue patterned dress, the father in pressed trousers and dress shoes. They were small and looked shockingly young. Benjamin felt self-conscious in his shorts and T-shirt.

Raymond was wearing, Benjamin noticed now, a button-down shirt. He'd known what to do. He shook Noemi's father's hand. "Welcome to Los Angeles," he said.

"You are the astronaut," Noemi's father said, beaming.

"You don't really want to trust me with your spaceship," Raymond said.

There were introductions all around, in English and halting Spanish. The father's name was Miguel and he admired the Tesla. They carried the food inside. Liv had first considered putting Noemi's family up in a hotel, but all the hotels were so far away, and so expensive. It would be a lot of driving to pick the visitors up and drop them off, and it might seem like they were afraid to have them in their house, where there was plenty of room.

Benjamin took a suitcase to the guest room and saw that Penny had put cut flowers in a glass, and placed stolen hotel soap in paper wrappers by the sink and bath, to make it all properly fancy. He demonstrated the tricky handle on the shower.

Then they showed Noemi to Penny's room, where there was an extra twin bed. "Or you can go with your parents," Liv said.

Noemi sat happily on Penny's spare twin bed, and bounced a little. "Here." She was admirable and unsettling, this child who had traveled across borders and ridden trains and lost her uncle and seemed so untroubled. Benjamin wondered what she remembered, from her fever. He wanted to get some air.

"I'll get the pool cover off."

Raymond joined him. There were still a few hours of light yet, for the kids to play in. *Please, God*, Benjamin thought. *Don't let anyone drown*. They rolled up the insulated tarp, and Marcus came and stood at the edge of the pool deck, looking down through the rippling surface. He took a sleek new phone out of his jeans pocket.

"Oh, wait a minute!" Benjamin said, and he looked to Raymond. "I thought we were waiting!"

"I got it for my birthday," Marcus said.

"Sorry, man, we caved," Raymond said.

"Does Penny know you have it?"

"Not yet," Marcus said.

"Put it away," his father said. "Ringer off."

Marcus slipped the phone back into his pocket. "She's going to notice."

Benjamin shook his head. "Maybe it'll distract her from asking for a puppy."

"Isabel got a puppy," Marcus said. "It's called a blue shar-pei, but it's gray."

It was the first time Benjamin had heard him bring up Isabel, or not change the subject when her name came up. "Yeah, I heard," he said. "So what, you're on Instagram now? Snapchat?" Just saying those words he felt like such a *dad*.

Marcus nodded.

"Does Isabel respond if you comment?"

"Sometimes," Marcus said. Pride and pleasure glowed in the kid's face, at this tiny attention from Isabel. She'd killed a man, and Marcus had covered for her, and she'd done him the great favor of responding—sometimes—online.

But she was just a kid. She was fourteen years old. She'd been raped, and had lost her brother. Was she suffering for the lie? Or just living her wounded, photogenic life? Presumably there would be a price to pay someday, it was just a question of what it would be.

He wondered if this sweet, serious kid had understood how it would play out, if Marcus had known he'd hit on a story that the grown-ups would accept, that would let everyone move on. Or if he'd stumbled on it blindly, desperate to protect Isabel, and had lucked into success. Benjamin wanted to ask what he'd been thinking, but he couldn't. If he was honest, he was a little afraid.

65

NOEMI'S PARENTS HAD prepared her for Penny's parents to be very rich, but it still took her a little while to realize that this was all Penny's house. It wasn't like New York, where the spaces she moved through were connected to each other, stacked on top of each other, communal. She and her parents shared their apartment with two other families, with curtains and plywood dividers in the rooms.

Penny's house stood apart from the other houses around it, on a strangely silent street lined with spreading trees. The stillness was unsettling, and Noemi wasn't sure she liked it. There weren't any other people outside—no one walking by or playing music. Over the houses was sky. The adults each had their own cars, except the American husbands, who arrived together in the shiny black one. She still thought of Marcus and June's father as an astronaut, as someone who'd been to space.

She had been to space, sort of. She had flown in a plane. Her mother had held her hand as they looked out the window at the dizzying world below, at the city and the ocean, and then fields and more cities, all the way across a country that was too big to keep at once in your mind. She wanted to fall into the soft clouds, but her father said they were made of water, you would fall through. Her parents were excited and afraid on the plane, too, but they tried to act like they weren't.

She wished her grandmother could come see all of this. Not having her grandmother felt like a cold, round stone in her heart. Her parents said they were lucky that Noemi had been able to come to them, and anyway her grandmother wouldn't like New York. It would be too much for her. Noemi thought she would just stay in the apartment and argue with the other grandmother who lived there, and use the flush toilet, and cook things when they came home. But it wasn't allowed.

Noemi didn't want to ask, "Is that expensive?" about everything in Penny's room, with the two beds, but she did wonder it. There were books and toys and a silver scooter. A doll with round eyes and silky brown hair, and so many stuffed animals. She remembered Chuy handing her the stuffed pig from the front seat. Her memories of Chuy had been absorbed in the strangeness of her fever and the dislocation of their journey, but she saw his face very clearly for a moment, giving her the Christmas present. She regretted losing the pig. Chuy had carried the baby scorpions outside—or had she imagined that?

"Take off your shoes," Penny said, demonstrating with her own. "We have a really good game."

66.

LIV FINISHED UNPACKING the Zankou Chicken, still trying to sort out what Nora had told her. It was hard enough to try to live a moral life when it was just a question of public or private school. Now it was a question of someone else's child taking the blame for a murder he hadn't committed.

Noemi's parents, Miguel and Lucía, came from the guest room, looking freshly scrubbed. They were so young. Liv knew from booking their tickets that they were both twenty-five. Which meant they'd been seventeen-year-old parents. She tried to put an expression on her face that wouldn't look too ghastly, but she saw their eyes widen at the amount of food, and she winced. She'd been afraid of not having enough.

There was shrieking from Penny's room that Liv should probably attend to, but it sounded like happy shrieking.

"Is this game okay?" Lucía asked, with a worried look.

"I hope so," Liv said. "I'll call them to dinner."

Marcus had appeared from the backyard. "I'll go," he said.

The adults smiled at one another awkwardly. Liv was about to offer drinks, but then the kids came running: Noemi in her candy-pink dress, Sebastian with his hair falling in his eyes, Penny's face shining with the glory of having her very own guests.

June said, "We were playing Sharkies! The floor between the beds is the water! You might fall in!"

Penny whirled on her. "You're not supposed to tell the rules, Junie!"

"Why not?"

"Because they're secret!"

"Well, *you're* not supposed to jump on the beds," Liv said.

"It's okay," Benjamin said.

She raised an eyebrow at him. They were supposed to back each other up. But she couldn't stop an activity that had been generating so much noisy happiness. And that seemed to be about processing deep, elemental fear. How to forbid Sharkies?

"So how does the game work?" Benjamin asked.

Penny stood up straighter. "We can't tell you."

"Ah," Raymond said. "The first rule of Sharkies is you don't talk about Sharkies."

There was a feeling Liv had been having for about a month now that she had not yet articulated to Benjamin, or to her therapist. She had just articulated it to herself, but she felt it very strongly. It was this: Now that she had her kids back, she also had the terror that went along with them, the need to keep them healthy and alive and happy.

She could barely formulate this thought without shame, but in those scorched-earth moments when she'd believed that Penny and Sebastian were dead, there had been a kind of stillness in the primitive parts of her mind. There'd been nothing more to be afraid of, because there'd been nothing more to lose. She had cleaned out the heartbreak account. The worst thing had happened, and nothing else could.

Now she had her joy back, and also her fear. She warily opened her arms to both, in the clear and vivid knowledge that her heart could be ripped out of her chest again. It could happen any day.

Penny was explaining the finer points of Zankou Chicken to the guests. "I like the mutabbal but not the tabbouleh," she was saying to Noemi, who nodded agreeably.

Sebastian was vibrating with excitement from the game. Liv checked his levels and pushed his hair off his face. "Sharkies, huh?"

"It's *so* fun, Mom," he whispered, so Penny wouldn't hear him.

But his sister was busy giving orders on where to sit at the dining room table, like a duchess, arranging everyone by relative importance. She seated Noemi next to her, in the place of honor. Liv was at the far end, in Siberia, but that was fine.

She felt the old vertiginous horror at the thought that she might never have had these children. If the chair hadn't fallen from the fort at brunch, if they hadn't started trying when they did. One wrong step and then the endless drop. It was like that now, the woozy fear of losing them. The floor between the beds is the water. You might fall in.

He just wanted a decent book to read ...

Not too much to ask, is it? It was in 1935 when Allen Lane, Managing Director of Bodley Head Publishers, stood on a platform at Exeter railway station looking for something good to read on his journey back to London. His choice was limited to popular magazines and poor-quality paperbacks – the same choice faced every day by the vast majority of readers, few of whom could afford hardbacks. Lane's disappointment and subsequent anger at the range of books generally available led him to found a company – and change the world.

'We believed in the existence in this country of a vast reading public for intelligent books at a low price, and staked everything on it'
Sir Allen Lane, 1902–1970, founder of Penguin Books

The quality paperback had arrived – and not just in bookshops. Lane was adamant that his Penguins should appear in chain stores and tobacconists, and should cost no more than a packet of cigarettes.

Reading habits (and cigarette prices) have changed since 1935, but Penguin still believes in publishing the best books for everybody to enjoy. We still believe that good design costs no more than bad design, and we still believe that quality books published passionately and responsibly make the world a better place.

So wherever you see the little bird – whether it's on a piece of prize-winning literary fiction or a celebrity autobiography, political tour de force or historical masterpiece, a serial-killer thriller, reference book, world classic or a piece of pure escapism – you can bet that it represents the very best that the genre has to offer.

Whatever you like to read – trust Penguin.